Alchemy's Daughter

MARY A. OSBORNE

Lake Street Press
4044 N. Lincoln Avenue, #402
Chicago, IL 60618
www.lakestreetpress.com
lsp@lakestreetpress.com

Cover photo by Mary Buczek
Cover design by DM Cunningham
Book design by Erin Howarth
Maps illustrated by Rachael McHan

This is a work of fiction. The characters and events are inventions of the author. Actual personages are true to time but have imagined personalities and interactions.

Osborne, Mary A.
  Alchemy's daughter / Mary A. Osborne. -- Chicago, IL : Lake Street Press, c2014.
  pages ; cm.
  ISBN: 978-1-936181-17-9 (print) ; 978-1-936181-22-3 (ebook)
    Summary: In medieval San Gimignano, seventeen-year-old Santina apprentices to Trotula, the village midwife. Some say she is the victim of the midwife's spell, but Santina is determined to follow in Trotula's footsteps even as calamities strike.--Publisher.
  Audience: Young adults.
  Includes bibliographical references.
    1. Midwives--Italy--San Gimignano--14th century--Fiction. 2. Religion and science--Italy--San Gimignano--14th century-- Fiction. 3. Science, Medieval--Italy--San Gimignano--Fiction. 4. Medicine, Medieval--Italy--San Gimignano--Religious aspects-- Catholic Church--Fiction. 5. Plague--Italy--San Gimignano--14th century--Fiction. 6. Alchemy--Italy--San Gimignano--14th century--Fiction. 7. Middle Ages--Italy--San Gimignano--Fiction. 8. Bildungsromans. 9. Young adult fiction. 10. Historical fiction. I. Title.

PS3615.S274 A43 2014   2014958378

813/.6--dc22   1505

Printed in the United States of America

Alchemy's Daughter

MARY A. OSBORNE

LAKE STREET PRESS
CHICAGO, ILLINOIS

Acclaim for *Alchemy's Daughter*

Gold Award 2014 Literary Classics for Young Adult Fiction
Gold Award 2014 Literary Classics for
Young Adult Historical Fiction
Grand Prize Winner 2014 Paris Book Festival

"Author Mary Osborne's adept portrayal of a spirited and intelligent young girl growing up in Italy during the Middle Ages is an alluring tale that provides an intriguing blend of history, romance, and adventure. *Alchemy's Daughter* is a story with timeless appeal which speaks to young readers on many levels pertaining to the choices one must make when embarking upon the threshold of adulthood."

> —Literary Classics International Book Awards &
> Reviews

"Ancient texts, family intrigue, and the perils of the plague flow through *Alchemy's Daughter*. In this coming-of-age novel set in the Middle Ages, young adult readers will identify with Santina's struggles as she learns about choices and their consequences."

> —Sr. M. Paul McCaughey, O.P., Superintendent of
> Archdiocese of Chicago Catholic Schools

"Mary Osborne's *Alchemy's Daughter* is first a simple love story and foremost a nuanced sociological probe. Osborne transports readers, along with her chief character, Santina, to a remote, ancient landscape whose burdens and biases remind us eerily of the here and now. Hard science and faith and witchcraft all inform the beliefs of those who hold sway over Santina's fate, and ultimately we root for a cocktail of enlightenment, luck and love to give her a life she deserves."

> —Don Evans, author of *Good Money After Bad*
> and Executive Director of the Chicago Literary
> Hall of Fame.

"In *Alchemy's Daughter* Osborne has woven a richly textured tapestry of medieval Italy with its mysterious meld of piety, bloodshed and gnostic power, and she has also created characters that one comes to know intimately and care for deeply. Osborne's Santina Pietra is a woman of strength, vulnerability and wisdom whose overarching desire to heal transcends historical forces and class strictures. As spirituality, as esoteria and as history, *Alchemy's Daughter* is a well crafted, engrossing and ultimately moving story."

> —Joseph M. Malham, author of *John Ford: Poet in the Desert*

"Mary A. Osborne's *Alchemy's Daughter* is filled with deeply-researched history, the mysterious world of alchemy, and an in-depth portrayal of midwifery in its early stages."

> —Lois Hoitenga Roelofs, Ph.D., author of *Caring Lessons,* Professor Emerita of Nursing at Trinity Christian College

Acclaim for *Nonna's Book of Mysteries*

"In *Nonna's Book of Mysteries*, Emilia defies what is expected in order to create a life filled with happiness. Readers will enjoy a unique storyline, identify with Emilia's personal struggles to become a good person, and be encouraged to step beyond expectations to pursue their own passions and happiness despite the odds." —Alicia Sondhi, *ForeWord* Reviews

"Nonna's Book of Mysteries is a fascinating and fun read, not to be missed." —*Midwest Book Review*

"This young adult novel set during the Italian Renaissance is a tale of female empowerment." —Theresa Budasi, *Chicago Sun-Times*

"I loved *Nonna's Book of Mysteries*! It's a wonder of a book—exciting, mysterious, and wise... I can't wait for another from Mary Osborne." —Karen Cushman, Newberry Award winner

"Nonna's Book of Mysteries is a young adult novel that will appeal to readers of all ages in its celebration of icon writing, fresco painting, alchemical wisdom, and Renaissance Florence. 'Spunky' doesn't do justice to Emilia, the young heroine, whose fierce determination to make her own way in a man's world grows out of her deep rooted vocation as a painter." — Robert Hellenga, author of *The Fall of a Sparrow* and *The Italian Lover*

In loving memory of my grandmothers:
Ann Bengston Bloom, Grace Lindblade Bloom, and
Mary Frazel Bohaty.

Acknowledgments

Alchemy's Daughter, begun when my son was in preschool and finally completed during his seventeenth year, has come to fruition through the assistance of wise mentors and faithful friends. Deepest thanks to Joseph Malham for his invaluable support, spirited artistic debate, and insight into the Medieval Period. Gratitude to Mary Buczek, Mildred Kemp, Kathleen Haleas Kuziel, Crystal Riley, and Kathryn Rose for their early readings and candid feedback; to Hazel Dawkins, whose skillful editing has been essential to this book and to *Nonna's Book of Mysteries*; to Lauren Franzen, Paula Tongs-Ketteringham, and Annie Ziemba for generously sharing their valuable expertise and experience in the field of midwifery (any inaccuracies in the portrayal of medieval childbirth within this book are due to my own misunderstanding); to book designer Erin Howarth for her craftsmanship and attention to detail; to author Emily Hanlon for her tutelage in the art of fiction writing; to author Susan M. Tiberghien, whose inspirational workshops led me to C.J. Jung's writing on alchemy; to Tam Dillman for her sustaining friendship and encouragement; and to Matthew Osborne for bringing joy, laughter, and reprieve from the writer's desk.

Contents

Timeline of Historical Events

Alchemy's Daughter is a work of fiction, but there just might have been a girl like Santina Pietra somewhere in 14th-century San Gimignano. While I am an artist and not a historian, I have attempted to represent the period as accurately as possible. Below is a list of events that are either relevant to the story or offer a general sense of the time period.

BCE	Thoth, the great sage of Egyptian myth, writes the Emerald Tablet.
977-1010	Abu'l-Qasim Firdawsi, the Persian poet, writes *Shahnama.* The epic poem mentions a Caesarean section and the use of anesthesia during the operation.
1023	The Order of Hospitallers, Knights of St. John, is founded to provide care for poor, sick or injured pilgrims to the Holy Land.
1048	Al-Biruni, one of the greatest scholars of the medieval Islamic era, dies. In one of his manuscripts, Al-Biruni gave three references to the Caesarean section.
11th-12th C.	Trotula of Salerno, a female physician, authors *Diseases of Women* and *Treatments for Women.* The texts serve as a major source of information for women's health in the middle ages.
1309-1378	The Papacy is relocated from Rome to Avignon, France.

1330	Pope John XXII gives funds to his physician to set up a laboratory for "a 'certain secret work,' which is perhaps alchemical in nature."
1333	Novella d'Andrea dies. Novella, who was taught law by her father, was a legal scholar at the University of Bologna. Legend has it that she delivered lectures from behind a curtain so as not to distract the students with her beauty.
1339	Pope Benedict XII orders an investigation into the alchemical activities of some clerics and monks.
1340	A woman is tried for diabolism in Novara, Italy.
1344/46	In Florence, Italy, a widow, a monk, and a rector of a church are interrogated by the Inquisition for using charms.
October 1347	A fleet of ships bound for Genoa stops in Messina, Sicily, after which the plague sweeps through the city.
1348	The plague devastates Europe. Herbed vinegar, also known as "Four thieves vinegar," is thought to be antipestilential
1460	A monk named Leonardo of Pistoia brings a Greek manuscript, which would become the *Corpus Hermeticum*, to Florence. Leonardo was one of the agents sent by Florence's ruler, Cosimo de' Medici, to search Europe's monasteries for forgotten, ancient writings.
15th C.	First mass witch trials begin in Europe.

SAN GIMIGNANO, ITALY

A. Collegiatas Collegiate Church
B. Santima's House
C. Piazza della Cisterna
D. Papa's Shop
E. Fountain
F. Palazzo del Podestà
G. Palazzo del Popolo
H. Church of Sant' Agostino
I. Trotula's Cottage
J. Calandrino's Cottage
K. San Damiano Friary

CERTALDO, ITALY

A. ISABELLA'S HOUSE
B. GIOVANNI BOCCACCIO'S HOUSE
C. PRETORIO PALACE
D. CHURCH OF SAINTS TOMMASO & PROSPERO
E. GIORGIO & NICCOLOSA'S HOUSE
F. PIAZZA DELL ANNUNZIATA

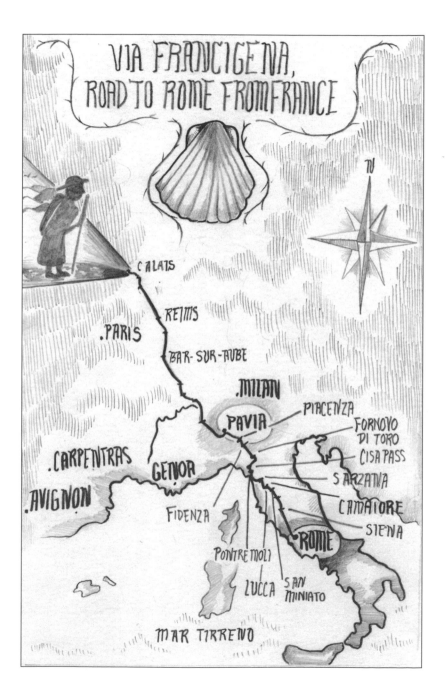

The Tutor

"Too much learning is vanity," Santina's older sister put forth. She threw open the shutters, admitting the early morning light, before covering her hair in a serviceable white wimple. "Mama would not have approved."

Lauretta always seemed to know what Madonna Adalieta, who had been taken by the Lord three years earlier, would have thought. Santina considered her sister's admonition as well as the fact that Lauretta, who was twenty, would soon be married to a portly, balding, and widowed apothecary. After Lauretta moved away from their home on Via San Giovanni, Santina would have more time to hide away undisturbed with her precious books. There was nothing wrong with young women seeking out knowledge. In fact, Madonna Adalieta would surely have approved of her lessons with Calandrino.

Santina's father, Iacopo Pietra, was the first to befriend the young scholar; the two met while hunting wild game in the woods near the friary. Although Papa was fully occupied with the business of importing cloth and overseeing his two stores, he shared Calandrino's interest in the subject of alchemy. Before long the two had taken to working together in the attic room of the Pietras' home, measuring and mixing salts and metals, trying to make gold.

He is the most learned man in San Gimignano, **san jee mee NYAH noh,** Papa always said. He could speak Latin, Arabic, Greek, and French. Calandrino, an orphan, was given to be raised by the good friars of San Damiano, although he was not called to the mendicant life and took no vows. When he was just ten years old he went to Sicily to serve as a page for Sir Ugo, a knight of the Hospitaller Order of St. John. Sir Ugo had been to the Holy Land years before, and he had taught Calandrino wondrous things about alchemy and Arabic medicine.

Calandrino, five years Santina's senior and possessed of many gifts, was unlike the other men in her village, for he encouraged her ambition to improve her mind. No doubt Madonna Adalieta would have done the same. "Mama read Dante. She taught all of us Latin," Santina reminded Lauretta. She pulled a mulberry-colored gown over her head. "She would not begrudge me an education."

"Pay me no heed if you will, but you will never find a husband if you persist in this manner."

"The jeweler from Certaldo might marry Santina," offered Isabella, who was arranging her pretty blonde hair in numerous braids and ribbons, trying to copy the style of a noblewoman she had seen. Santina's youngest sister, who was in love with the blacksmith's son, regretted that she was fourteen and too young for marriage. "I heard him asking Ruberto about you at the store," she said when Santina looked at her skeptically.

"I have no interest in marrying," she mumbled. The mere

mention of the jeweler soured Santina's mood, not because the man was distasteful in any particular respect, but because he was the unexceptional type of man Papa would choose for her. Trying to put the jeweler out of her mind, Santina picked up Aristotle's *De Caelo*, "On the Universe," and started out the bedroom door.

"Not yet," Lauretta called. She held up Mama's illuminated *Book of Hours*, which contained devotions to be read at various times throughout the day. Obediently, Santina paused to pray.

When the hour of *prime* finally neared, Santina gladly left Lauretta and Isabella to the work of candle making and departed for her lesson. Although it was less than an hour's journey by foot to Calandrino's cottage, young ladies did not travel unescorted and Giacomino was made to accompany her. Giacomino was the son of Margherita, who had served as Mama's beloved maidservant and now tended to Mama's daughters. He seemed more like a brother to her than Papa's employee, and he made no secret of his disdain for the task to which he had been assigned.

"I'll be missed at the shop," he complained, as they started out on Via San Giovanni.

"I am grateful to you for taking time away for my sake," she replied. It was the truth, even though she knew full well that Giacomino often wandered off to his favorite food stalls, taverns, and bakeries when he was meant to be delivering cloth.

With Giacomino lagging a few steps behind, Santina hurried along the route she had taken countless times. It was a summer-like May morning; the main road was perfumed with a pungent mix of ripe cheese, fresh-baked bread, butchered meats, horse dung, and human sweat. Santina moved through the thoroughfare that was crowded with merchants selling their wares, housewives carrying baskets, gentlemen in wide-sleeved tunics and assorted hats, ladies in bright-colored dresses, a cleric en route with a holy relic, and barking dogs. She paid little heed to Giacomino's mood or the townsfolk who bid her *buon giorno*, for her thoughts were all of her morning lesson with Calandrino.

Although she tried to reflect upon her assigned reading and prepare a clever discourse, Santina thought mainly of the wonders of the young scholar and the joy of another Wednesday beyond the village wall. Papa paid Calandrino a few *soldi* each week for tutoring Santina, although it was Calandrino who had initially proposed the arrangement. Having taken note of Santina's keen intellectual curiosity—as well as her new ladylike gown, she dared to hope—Calandrino thought to offer lessons in Greek and philosophy. While Papa was not convinced that Santina's imaginative mind required improvement, he knew that the promising young scholar was in need of additional funds.

Calandrino had recently returned to the quietude of his beloved Tuscan countryside following his fourth year at the University of Bologna. Although he had not yet completed his studies, his reputation as a scholar had grown. He had a patron, Master Leolus da Firenze, who was a physician in Bologna. Master Leolus had charged him with the translation of certain writings by the Arab philosopher and physician, Avicenna, concerning the treatment of wounds. Despite his rising stature, Calandrino had not forgotten Papa or his interest in the art of alchemy. Upon his homecoming, the two promptly sequestered themselves in the attic room where they resumed their alchemical experiments. With Calandrino's many commitments in mind, Santina felt honored that he chose to serve as her tutor on Wednesday mornings.

Continuing past Papa's draper's shop en route to the scholar's home, Santina reached the busy city square with the octagonal well in the center, the Piazza della Cisterna. Years ago, when Mama went to the square to do the marketing, Santina used to play with her sisters on the stone steps leading to the well. Sometimes she would gaze off into the distance at the soaring brick towers built by Tuscan nobility long before she was born, and she would imagine the world that existed beyond those towers, beyond the village wall, beyond all of Tuscany.

Now, at seventeen, Santina gladly departed the square and soon passed beneath the Roman arch of the north city gate. She traveled along the Via Francigena, the road that led all the way to France, into the hills of rolling Tuscan countryside, and moved up along rocky terraces planted with vineyards and olive orchards. When at last she came to a wide expanse of grassy meadow, the enormous bell tower of San Damiano came into view. She had been here before with Papa on numerous occasions. It was the place where Calandrino once pointed out the St. John's wort growing wild.

The herb-filled meadow fronted the scholar's one-room cottage—timber frame with stones around the door and windows—on the outskirts of the friary grounds. Santina thought the tiny shelter that belonged to the brothers of San Damiano was quite splendid, but Lauretta thought it peculiar that such a learned and refined young man chose to reside beyond the wall.

Upon arriving there was no need for Santina to knock on Calandrino's door, for she spotted him even before she crossed the meadow. Giacomino, having safely delivered his charge, disappeared into the surrounding wood without a word to Santina, whose eyes were fixed upon the scholar. Bow in one hand, pheasant in the other, there was little about Calandrino's appearance that suggested a life committed to the study of natural science and philosophy.

"*Buon Giorno*, Santina!" the tall, broad-shouldered young

man with a tousled mass of black curly hair called out as she stared at him from across the field. He wore long breeches and a coarsely woven sleeveless tunic, revealing arms grown strong and brown from physical labor out of doors. As he strolled toward her, she was almost certain he would sweep her into his arms and kiss her.

Madonna Adalieta

Santina had perhaps loved Calandrino since she was fourteen, since the day she ran to find him after Mama had gone into labor. She knew that Madonna Adalieta was having some sort of problem, and she thought Calandrino might have a remedy that could help. In her youthful imagination, she somehow hoped he would share with her the alchemist's secret, the philosopher's stone that could restore health and reverse misfortune.

"Thank goodness you're here," she said, out of breath, when she reached the cottage on that dreadful day.

"What's the matter?" he asked, his lighthearted expression turning sober when he saw the look on Santina's face.

"Mama's having the baby, but something's the matter."

"Surely the midwife has been summoned?"

"Trotula can't seem to help her. But I thought…I thought you might be able to," Santina began, "if you could give her the philosopher's stone."

"The philosopher's stone," he repeated. "What do you know of the philosopher's stone, Santina?"

"I know it is not a stone at all, but the elixir of life," she replied. "It is said that those who drink the elixir are granted eternal youth and forever changed, but I think the potion is only a powerful healing draught."

"You have been eavesdropping," he said, smiling just a little.

Too worried about Mama to feel embarrassed by his accusation, Santina merely shrugged. It was true she often spied Papa and Calandrino as they conducted their experiments in the attic room that served as Papa's "bottega," or alchemist's workshop.

Calandrino did not comment further upon the stone and instead began to speak of the Egyptians and the origins of the ancient science. Walking beside the scholar, Santina waited for him to finish his story about Osiris, a beloved pharaoh of Egypt, who was killed by his evil brother, chopped into fourteen parts and thrown into the Nile River. Beautiful Isis, his wife, came to search the water and collect the fragments of the corpse and then magically unite them. In this way Osiris was reborn.

Santina understood, to some degree, that the Egyptian legend of death and rebirth had something to do with alchemy and the mysterious process of turning lead into gold. But at the time, she had little patience for Calandrino's tale. She just wanted him to give her the elixir that would help her mother.

"Those who died and went through the ritual of the resurrection could move freely between life and death. They could appear in any shape, any day," Calandrino waxed *lyrically as he referred to the Egyptians. "The dead could leave their coffins and walk out of the tombs of the pyramids in broad daylight. They could appear as crocodiles and swim in the Nile or turn into birds like the ibis and fly through the sky."*

Calandrino spoke of what was written in the papyri of the Egyptian prayers for the dead, and Santina imagined the ability to transform, to change shape, to be able to walk through closed doors, to defy death. She was not sure what to think of the Egyptian mysteries, but she could envision an eternal kingdom where sickness and death no longer reigned. It was a world where Mama would always be safe.

"Do you have the stone then, Calandrino?" she asked the instant the young man had finished talking. "Can you help my mother?"

As though suddenly remembering Madonna Adalieta's plight, Calandrino looked downcast. "I'm afraid not, Santina," he said. "But I will pray to the One who gives life to all things. You must also."

Then he picked up a red stone flecked with gold and black. Pressing the stone into Santina's hand, he said, "There are many things we might not understand in this world, but the truth of God's love is pure and simple, just like this stone."

As she had that fateful day three years earlier, Santina looked expectantly at Calandrino. Her heart sank when he began talking about a new book he had been loaned by one of the friars at San Damiano. Although she had hoped for an altogether different sort of welcome, she sat beside him beneath the shade of a flowering pear tree and tried to listen attentively.

"*The Book of Thoth,*" he said, handing her a slim volume from a small collection of texts strewn across the grass.

Santina thumbed thoughtfully through the pages, taking time to study the strange images of human figures with animal heads, long-legged birds, and undecipherable characters bearing significance she could not begin to fathom.

"Who is *Thoth?*" she asked, wanting to understand the significance of the text.

"To the Egyptians he is represented by the ibis god, but the Greeks know him as the great sage, Hermes Trismegistus." Indicating the image of a figure with a birdlike head, he said, "Thoth was said to be one of the early kings—the inventor of hieroglyphics, the father of alchemy. His work has inspired all great thought. He's older than Plato. Older than Moses even."

Santina tried to absorb the weight of Calandrino's words. Her mind flooded with images of ancient Egypt, open deserts, palm trees, and tall pyramids. It was as though the text had flown from that faraway place into her hands. "I'd like to read this *Book of Thoth*. It would take me far from San Gimignano, I'm sure."

Calandrino smiled at the thought. "The book speaks of the highest reality and the spiritual path that prepares one to receive the greatest of truths."

"Might the book hold the secret to the philosopher's stone?" she asked. Although Santina no longer envisioned the stone as a healing draught that could restore health to the sick—as she had wanted to believe when Mama was dying—she imagined it to be an elusive bit of knowledge that held the key to the transformation of human suffering as much as the transmutation of the base metal.

"There is surely wisdom to be found within the pages, but the text does not promise to unlock the *Great Secret*. That book has yet to be found."

Santina returned to *The Book of Thoth* and studied the curious images. She wanted to ask him more about this mysterious book from Egypt, but the original lesson plan for the day seemed to dawn upon the young man. In a more measured tone he began to speak of *De Caelo* and the perfect motions of the spheres.

"Is it true?" Santina asked. "Do you believe such perfection exists?"

Calandrino appeared to contemplate her question as he stood and casually plucked a sprig of pear blossom. Sitting beside her again, he playfully tucked the spring flower behind Santina's ear. It was a simple gesture, and yet to an infatuated young woman it was as though he had offered a token of his undying love. Besotted, Santina gazed upon the scholar as though he was the only one who existed for her.

Perhaps aware, for the first time, of the beautiful young woman before him, Calandrino's expression registered surprise and, finally, understanding. As though examining a rare flower, he looked into her soft gray eyes and touched her silky brown hair. "*Si*. Most certainly."

Santina did not look away shyly but dared to return his stare. Calandrino Donati was four years her senior and would eventually return to the university. Regardless, she hoped something more would come of their friendship. Papa thought highly of him and might very well approve the match, never mind that Calandrino was a scholar.

"I do, too," Santina murmured. "I think there is perfection in this world."

Calandrino hesitated before resting his hand on her shoulder. As he drew her close she was startled, but she never thought to resist the young man who was her tutor. Out in the sun his kiss tasted warm and sweet, and Santina thought there could be nothing more she would ever desire. *This must be love,* she thought as Calandrino's arms encircled her. The two tipped over and fell laughing to the ground, intoxicated with the scent of spring and the inspiring words of long dead philosophers.

Recollection of the outside world seemed to dawn upon Calandrino, who pulled himself away, regret in his eyes. He tried to speak of Aristotle, but Santina could not easily pay attention. She could only look at him longingly until Giacomino returned for her. When Calandrino handed her *The Book of Thoth*, Santina was not sure how she would endure the long wait till the following Wednesday.

As she began to make her way home that afternoon, she felt nothing would ever be the same again. God had seen fit to grant her this earthly happiness. She had only walked a few paces down the road when she turned to look at Calandrino once more. He had already returned to his texts. Perhaps it was the work of Avicenna that recaptured his attention.

In the back of her mind Santina was aware of the inherent obstacles to her clandestine romance. She was expected to marry the usual type of man—such as Taddeo da Certaldo—not a poor scholar who popped in and out of San Gimignano on occasion. But Santina had no desire to contemplate an end to something that had only just begun. *Papa can be persuaded*, she told herself as she walked to the village. On that lovely May afternoon, Santina did not pause to consider Calandrino's view of the future or the ways of a dedicated scholar.

When Santina and her sisters were children, Mama had warned them never to visit the public fountain alone. Although the cool water beckoned on hot summer days, one never knew who would be visiting the spring, located just outside the city wall, or what people were up to in the baths. Of course women did their laundry in the basins, and bathing was permitted when Mama or Papa was present. On a scorching hot day in July of 1343, Santina thought to ignore Mama's warning and walk alone along the *Via delle Fonti*, the steep road leading to the fountain.

It was Friday at midday when most everyone in San Gimignano rested, but thoughts of Calandrino kept Santina wide awake. As an excuse to visit the fountain, Santina carried a few handkerchiefs and linen chemises to wash. Continuing along the road, she briefly contemplated *The Book of Thoth* given to her by Calandrino. She tried to cultivate, as the sage advised, the proper orientation of the mind required to see the true face of God. However, her attention soon turned to her new romance, to Calandrino's touch, to the way he smiled and said *mia cara*, my darling, in greeting.

The scholar had come to occupy the center of Santina's thoughts through the hot days and nights of that summer. Neither her father nor sisters were privy to the romance, but Giacomino surely knew what his master's daughter was about. Although Santina recognized the risk of being discovered, she imagined the revelation would only hasten her betrothal to Calandrino, an outcome she perceived as inevitable.

As she imagined her future with the scholar, the heat seemed to rise in waves from the diaphanous hills and the cool water within the stone basins beckoned. Santina, wearing a fine gown sewn of the lightest pink silk and her hair in a heavy braid wound over her head like a crown beneath her veil, imagined the pleasures of the cooling waters.

The road she traveled curved alongside a series of Romanesque arches that enclosed the forbidden springs. Santina rounded the bend and made her way to a stone ledge beneath one of the arches. As she sat on the ledge, she saw a vision as though from a dream: there within the basin stood Calandrino.

He appeared not as his former self, but as a magnificent sculpture of antiquity, half naked in linen breeches as he washed his clothes in the bath. She almost felt as though she ought to apologize for the intrusion or at very least look the other way. But she could only stare, mouth agape, at the sight of his tawny skin and muscles like carved stone flecked with glints of sunlight.

The Fountain

Calandrino made no effort to dress when he saw Santina, for it was not unusual to bathe in the shallow waters of the fountain on a hot summer day. The spring-fed fountain consisted of ten stone arches that opened into the basins. Unabashed, the scholar stood in the center basin and greeted Santina as though they had met at the market. "You ought not to visit the fountain unescorted," he said, although he was clearly pleased to see her.

The young man set aside the garment he was washing and lowered himself into the water. Santina watched as Calandrino dipped beneath the surface. When he did not reappear after more than a minute, she began to feel uneasy.

Finally his head rose up and he emerged laughing, shaking glistening droplets from his curly wet hair. "Cool yourself, Santina."

He means only for us to bathe together, she thought as she kicked off her backless leather slippers with thick leather soles.

She glanced about, making sure they were well alone and then, feeling the lightness of the moment, she hastily loosened the laces of her gown and pulled the garment over her head. Wearing her linen chemise, she moved gingerly from the ledge into the water. Feeling Calandrino's eyes upon her, she slowly entered the bath.

"*Fa freddo*! It's cold!" she said. The shock of it was thrilling, and Santina lowered herself in the water.

Calandrino approached her. Teasingly, he sprinkled drops of water on her head. "Don't be afraid, Santina. You will dry again."

Thinking not to appear overly cautious, she immersed herself. Momentarily forgetting Calandrino, she enjoyed the cooling waters. Gazing out upon the sunlight in the trees, she felt a sense of lightness, as though everything around her was in its proper and perfect place. Perhaps there were troubles, failing banks, hunger, and sickness somewhere in the distance, yet if the suffering existed at all, it was far away. Santina Pietra, the cloth merchant's daughter, concerned herself with matters of love and philosophy. She did not worry over what to eat or how to warm herself when winter came.

"*Molto bella.* You are beautiful, Santina." She turned to look at Calandrino as he spoke. He made no pretense of not staring as he neared her. Although she knew he was her tutor from the prestigious *Studium Generale* in Bologna, he had become much more than this. She remained unmoving as he lowered his head to kiss her cool wet lips. He kissed her reverently at first, then ardently, again and again.

Finally, he paused to take her hand. "Santina, *ti amo,* I love you," he whispered.

Their eyes locked as he held her hands. Against the brilliant blue sky, Calandrino appeared haloed in gold, a vision of holiness and wonder. Santina could little understand why, in the next moment, he rose from the water, grabbed his wet clothes, uttered some excuse, and hurried away. Santina loved him so innocently, with complete trust and adoration. She could see nothing standing between them, only sunlight.

***

After drying in the sun, Santina dressed hurriedly and covered her damp hair with her veil. By the time she made her way back home, her skin had turned pink, and she had been gone far longer than she could easily explain to Lauretta.

She would have to fabricate a tale to explain her whereabouts. Nevertheless, she thought God could not entirely condemn her for loving Calandrino. He was a good man, wrought so beautifully, and they were young and in love. Surely, they would marry one day and her sin would be forgiven.

When she returned home she tried to evade notice, but it was impossible to reach her bedroom without encountering her sisters as they sat practicing their lutes in the central salon. The music stopped abruptly when Lauretta took note of Santina's untimely return.

"Wherever have you been, Santina? It looks as though you've been careless in the sun again."

It was futile to try to explain how her entire world was changing. Santina could only apologize before slipping quietly upstairs. Soon enough her sisters would know that Calandrino loved her.

***

Santina's lessons in Greek and philosophy continued on through the summer. The scholar seemed intent on maintaining his professional demeanor and teaching his pupil all that was promised, and yet the morning inevitably ended with Santina in his arms. While he sometimes cited the obvious reasons why they ought not to continue their romance, he seemed little inclined to stop what was started. While Calandrino urged caution and suggested the lessons might take place at Santina's home rather than the cottage, his actions spoke of love, which was all Santina chose to hear.

In retrospect Santina would see that her idyllic days with Calandrino were not meant to continue on in this manner forever. The turning point came the first of September, when she was asked to mind Papa's store. As it happened, Ruberto, the shopkeeper, was indisposed due to a stomach ailment. Santina, who normally enjoyed helping at the shop, was not at all happy to oblige because Ruberto's illness coincided with her weekly lesson. She had not the heart to ask Lauretta to take her place. Her older sister was soon to be married and thoroughly preoccupied with details concerning her nuptials. Asking Isabella was out of the question because her mind often wandered, and she could not be relied upon to keep an accurate accounting. Papa, who trusted few with his luxury goods or even the cloth at his draper's shop, might have worked at the store himself if he had not been called to the *Palazzo del Popolo*—the governor's palace—for a meeting with the Sienese painter, Lippo Memmi.

With the thought of reminding their fellow citizens of San Gimignano's independence from Florence, Papa's guild had commissioned the great artist to paint a fresco in a meeting room near the palace's reception hall. The hall—known as the *Sala di Dante* in memory of the poet Dante Alighieri's visit on behalf of Florence and the Guelph League thirty years earlier—was already decorated with a fresco by Memmi. The new fresco would not only honor the Virgin but also commemorate the accomplishments of the merchants and the sovereignty of San Gimignano.

Memmi had traveled from neighboring Siena in order to meet with the guild and the *podesta*, the chief magistrate, so Santina could not very well deny Papa's request. Her duty at the shop was to greet Papa's customers and recommend his fine jewelry, saddles, armor, religious vestments, and other such items. Giacomino, who helped at both of Papa's stores, was on hand to lift the heavy merchandise while Santina accepted payment and recorded each sale in Ruberto's book. When there was a lull between customers that morning, Santina perused a collection of newly arrived vestments in the back room. Admiring a silk robe richly embroidered with gold thread, Santina imagined Father Filippus, her parish priest, dressed in such finery as he married her and Calandrino on the steps of *Collegiatas*, the Romanesque church. Her thoughts were all of the much hoped for wedding when she heard the shop door open. Peering out from the back room, she saw the jeweler from neighboring Certaldo standing at the entryway.

Reflexively, Santina darted out of sight. She could hear Giacomino saying something to the visitor.

"Santina!" the young man called out indelicately. "Messer Taddeo da Certaldo is here!"

She peered around a tower of wood crates to observe the visitor standing at the counter. He was tall, near thirty years old, and handsome in a rakish, irregular sort of way with a long straight nose, wide eyes, and shoulder-length hair. She ought to have greeted him, for he came regularly to the store to offer Papa his choice Egyptian emeralds and Indian sapphires, which were displayed on blue velvet in the glass case. Even so, Santina could not countenance the conversation that would take place if she were to step forward. She was afraid Isabella was right in thinking the *gioiellere*, jeweler, had taken a personal interest in her even though she had done nothing at all to encourage him. From her hiding place, she watched as the man scanned the room as though sniffing her out.

"Are you quite sure she is not here?" she heard him saying. *"I thought perhaps I had seen her crossing the piazza this morning."*

When she saw Giacomino approaching the back room, Santina busied herself folding the vestment.

"Didn't you hear me? Messer Taddeo wants to speak with you." Having no choice but to acknowledge the visitor, she left the back room and bid him welcome.

"It's a pleasant surprise to find you here today, Monna Santina." The man eyed her closely.

"Ruberto is indisposed, I'm afraid. Can I help you, Messer Taddeo?"

"I must ask your opinion," he said, opening his velvet-lined box. He turned it toward her so she could see the prized collection of bodkins, rings, and pendants. "Which of these strikes your fancy?"

"They are all beautiful, Messer Taddeo. But you must speak to Ruberto when he returns."

"Yes, but today I am not selling, I am giving away." He picked up a small pendant—amethyst set in silver, surrounded by four tiny pearls—and pressed it into her hand.

Although she could not help but admire the piece, Santina shook her head. "*Grazie,* you are very kind, Messer," she said, "but I cannot accept this."

"Beautiful young women ought to be adorned with jewels," he said, snapping his box closed as she tried in vain to return the necklace. "Please tell Ruberto I will call again in one week," he said, moving to the door.

Left with an uneasy feeling, Santina dismissed Giacomino for his midday meal and hid the necklace away in her silk purse. She was about to lock up and return home herself when the door opened again.

"Calandrino!"

"Hello, *mia cara,*" he said, sweeping her off her feet so that her embroidered slippers fell to the floor. He kissed her on each cheek before pulling away. "There is a matter I must discuss with you," he said with some seriousness as she locked the door behind him.

Santina was little inclined to discuss much of anything with Calandrino. Rather, she imagined all that might transpire between them now that the store was closed. Any thoughts of midday romance were momentarily forgotten as Calandrino removed an old text from his linen sack. "First, I want to show you this," he explained.

The precious leather volume, no bigger than the palm of her hand, had a very old copper binding, a hand-tooled leather cover, and edges of painted gold. The pages were not made of paper but of thin tree bark, and the writing was in an undecipherable language. There were strange diagrams that were completely unintelligible as well. The author, as put forth in Latin on the first page, was Isaac the Jew, priest, adept in Cabala, master of the elixir of life and the *philosopher's stone.* On the second page, Calandrino pointed out, the same hand had written a terrible threat against the life of anyone who looked at the book who was not a priest or a scribe.

"The strange thing is," Calandrino explained, undaunted by these warnings, "I knew about the book before I came upon it."

"How is that possible?" Santina asked.

"I had a dream—I was walking outside the church of St. Augustine, and something on the steps caught my eye. I picked it up and saw it was a book. A very old, very holy book. Then just a few days after I had the dream, I was walking past the bookseller's shop and a peddler who was shabbily dressed approached me and offered to sell a book to me for two florins. '*I have something you might like,*' he told me. It felt quite strange, almost as though I had walked into my dream. I bought the book right away. I didn't even bargain."

Santina moved in close to Calandrino to study the pages. Noting an illustration of a pyramid decorated with odd symbols, she recalled what Calandrino had said the day in the meadow several years ago when Mama went into labor. He had spoken of the Egyptians' ability to transform, to walk through walls. Was it possible that the Egyptians truly possessed secret knowledge? Studying the image of the pyramid, she wondered if this little book held the key to the philosopher's stone so coveted by the alchemists.

"You'll be able to translate it, won't you?" Santina asked. She could not make out a word of what was written, but the characters were so exotic and fancifully drawn that she was sure Calandrino had discovered a rare treasure. Whoever studied the rich contents of this book might very well learn the alchemists' secret.

"I'll have to find someone who is familiar with the Cabala," he said, referring to mystic rabbinical teachings of the remote past. "A learned Jew I suppose—much of it seems to be written in a form of ancient Hebrew."

Santina did not foresee any difficulty in finding a Jew who could provide the translation. In her young mind she supposed that Calandrino would be able to read what was written in the book before long. Her confidence in the scholar was such that she imagined there was nothing he could not easily accomplish.

Calandrino handed the precious text to Santina and went to inspect a leather saddle decorated with bone inlay and images of St. George and the dragon. Book in hand, Santina walked in stocking feet to the back of the store where she sat at Ruberto's desk and lost herself in a world of sacred antiquity. Although she could not read the foreign script, it was as if the book spoke to her in a language beyond words and beckoned her into a world of mysteries. *Whoever discovers this book shall discover the secrets of the eternal* it seemed to say.

In her mind's eye Mama appeared, looking young and beautiful, and began to read over Santina's shoulder. *It is a wonder of a book. You must keep it with you, Santina.*

But it's not mine—and Santina realized she had spoken her thought. She looked up and wondered if Calandrino had heard. The scholar, however, had moved to the opposite side of the store and was peering into the jewelry case. As she returned to the book, she had a sense that Mama was with her and that the Egyptians were right about spirits being able to walk out of their tombs.

She was still pondering the matter of Egypt when Calandrino stood over her and tenderly kissed her head. "Perhaps I have erred in offering you too much knowledge. You are more interested in the book than your tutor," he said in jest.

She set the book aside and stood to face him. "It is you I think of, Calandrino. Nearly always."

When he held her face in his hands and gazed into her eyes, she was sure they would remain in love for the rest of their days. After Calandrino, there could be no other.

As the scholar softly kissed her, Santina dared to hope he had come to talk of their shared future together. There would be no interruptions, for the shop door was locked and all of San Gimignano slept. Hopefully, she waited for him to speak.

"*Mia cara*, there is something I must tell you," he said softly. From the tone of his voice she sensed the subject he wished to discuss held a degree of gravity. "If only you knew how much you mean to me."

He loved her; she could feel this. As long as he loved her, no harm could ever befall her. With Calandrino, life took on the glint of the precious metal, and there could be no returning to the dreary, pointless routine she had once known. Santina gladly anticipated the day when she could spend every waking moment with him. Perhaps that time was drawing near.

When he started to speak once more, she was startled to hear a faint sound at the front door, as though someone was trying to break in or open the lock. Santina froze in fear of the unseen intruder. Calandrino reached out quickly to grab her by the waist and pushed so hard to the back room that she nearly fell to floor.

"Who's there?" Calandrino said, challenging whoever had come to rob Iacopo's store in broad daylight.

"I should ask the same," a man, who was now inside the shop, replied.

Santina knew the voice. It was Ruberto, apparently recovered from his ailment. She edged close to the doorway, peered out cautiously, and saw Ruberto brandishing one of Papa's heavy jeweled swords. In response Calandrino reached for his dagger and pulled it from his scabbard.

"You are the scholar," surmised the shopkeeper, no doubt surprised by the sight of Calandrino, the absence of Giacomino, and perhaps Santina's slippers strewn about the floor.

"Do I know you?" asked Calandrino, still gripping the dagger as though ready to pounce.

Ruberto, moving closer, pointed the sword at Calandrino's chest. Santina, hidden in the other room, feared the shopkeeper would strike if she did nothing. Then Ruberto lowered his weapon to point at one of Santina's slippers on the floor.

"We met some time ago at the home of my employer," he said, glancing about the room. "I must wonder if you have taken liberties."

Calandrino returned his weapon to its sheath. "I have taken no one's honor," he replied in all honesty.

"Where is she?"

Clearly, Ruberto would not leave while he feared for Santina's safety. Emerging from the back room, she said quietly, "Calandrino only came to show me a book. He is my tutor, after all." She picked up the alchemical manual from the desk and held it up for him to see.

"Perhaps I am mistaken, but I doubt that your father intended for your lesson to take place here, unchaperoned."

"Giacomino only just left," she said.

"And I was about to leave myself," Calandrino added.

"It is poor payment to one who entrusted you with his daughter," Ruberto said, clearly sensing that Santina and Calandrino were bound by more than books and learning. "I don't wish to see you here again, Calandrino. Neither would Messer Iacopo, I am quite certain."

After Calandrino left the shop, Santina retreated to the back room to hide her tears. She wept because Papa would surely learn of Calandrino's visit, because her honor would be questioned, because she was no longer certain that her father would allow her to marry the man she loved.

Our only sin was to fall in love, she thought. Still, she was afraid Papa would never forgive her, let alone Calandrino. In the midst of the calamity brought upon by Ruberto's arrival, Santina forgot all about whatever it was the scholar had come to tell her. She considered, instead, how she might explain herself to her father.

Abelard

"It's true that I love Calandrino," Santina confessed to her father. Ruberto had told Papa about the irregular goings-on at the shop, and Margherita was now charged with keeping close watch over the young woman. While Santina insisted that Calandrino had only come to show her a book, she found it impossible to deny her feelings for the scholar when Papa asked.

"He has dishonored you; he has dishonored the *famiglia*, the family. If he so much as comes near you again, he'll suffer the same as Abelard."

Santina had never seen Papa so angry with her. She feared for Calandrino, and she felt the anguish of Heloise, Abelard's student and lover. Surely, her father would not have Calandrino castrated, as Heloise's father had done to the famous scholar two hundred years earlier in Paris, would he? Her life was in ruins, and she blamed Ruberto. At the same time, she knew Ruberto had little choice but to share what he had witnessed.

"But we did nothing wrong," she maintained.

"Under the pretense of study, he took advantage of you, Santina. He was my friend, a guest in my home. He was treated like a member of my family, and this is how he repays me." Papa paced the room, too angry to look at her. "You were his student. I was paying him to teach you. And I was paying Giacomino to keep an eye on you."

"Calandrino is an honorable man. And he is teaching me well, despite what you think," she tried.

"It's over, *finito*. You are not to see him again."

"Will you not speak to him of a marriage contract?"

"*Marriage contract?*" Papa scoffed. "Calandrino is probably halfway to Bologna by now. His life is devoted to his books, Santina. He is as likely to marry as a monk. You have been duped."

She was taken aback by Papa's words. Was he speaking the truth? Had Calandrino only meant to toy with her affection before returning to his solitary life in Bologna? She could not easily believe that he had intentionally misled her. Calandrino loved her. Didn't he? Or had it all been a lie, a figment of her imagination, like the alchemist's elixir of life?

There was only one way to find out: she had to confront him directly. Leaving the house would prove a challenge, for Margherita was keeping watch. Furtively, she began to plot her escape. It would not be the first time she had stolen away from the house and slipped out unseen through the city gate.

She feigned illness the following morning. It was easy enough to do, for she was truly heartsick, despondent over her separation from the scholar. She wondered why he sent no missive, no gentle, reassuring words to comfort her. Or perhaps he had, but the letter was intercepted by Papa.

She took to her to bed, refusing her favorite spiced pears offered by Margherita. The maidservant eventually left Santina alone to nurse her grief. Very quietly, Santina dressed and tiptoed down the stairs to the front hall. Just as she was about to pull the handle of the massive paneled door, she saw Isabella out of the corner of her eye.

Her younger sister approached knowingly but said nothing. Imploringly, Santina whispered, "*Per favore*, please."

Isabella smiled, and Santina kissed her cheek. "Bless you, Isabella," she said before disappearing out the door. *May you find true love one day.*

She rode Lauretta's old mare, long brown hair flying behind her in the wind, to the north gate, the *Porta San Matteo*. It was possible that Calandrino had already departed, fearing for his life, to Bologna, although Santina was loath to think he would have left with matters unsettled as they were between them. *He cannot so easily forget me, can he?*

When she arrived, heart racing, at Calandrino's cottage, she knocked, praying he was still there. "It's Santina," she said, not waiting for a response and pushing the door open.

He was at the table, a reassuring pot of soup simmering over the fire. But as soon as she looked about the room and saw there were no books, papers, or clothes lying about, she understood he had made up his mind to go.

"You can't leave," she blurted.

He stared at her as though transfixed, but her presence seemed to bring him little joy on this occasion. "It's for the best," he said, setting aside his pen and paper.

"For whose best?"

"Your father has made it clear that I am no longer welcome here."

"My father is not the *podestà*, though he might sometimes act as though he is. You are entitled to live in the place where you were born," she said. "Why let him drive you away after all that has come between us, Calandrino?"

Slumped at the table as though resigned to his misfortune, Calandrino sighed. "I cannot give you the life you deserve, Santina. Your father has reminded me of this fact."

"You would have my father dictate our future?"

"No, Santina. It is my choice to return to Bologna."

Hearing this, Santina broke into angry tears. "You are too cruel, Calandrino. Have the past months have meant nothing to you? Nothing to you at all?"

He held her in his arms and kissed her head, trying to still her mournful sobs. "Being with you has meant everything to me, Santina. If I am fortunate enough to grow old, I should look back upon my life many years from now and count this time as the best of all days."

His words only filled her with greater sadness. "If you have to leave, why not take me with you to Bologna? I have no wish to remain here in San Gimignano without you."

Calandrino sighed, saying nothing at first. Then he replied, "I'm expected to resume my studies. And I'm making plans to travel to Toledo. It's not a journey you would much enjoy, Santina. It would not be the life to which you are accustomed."

"Toledo?" she echoed. "Why do you have to go to Spain?"

"Because of the school for translators—it served to attract Jewish scholars. I think Toledo might be the place to find someone who can translate the book of Isaac the Jew."

"So it's the text that matters to you more than anything."

"No Santina, the text is not what matters to me most. But it's my calling. I cannot ignore what God has asked me to do."

"Did God also call you to take what you could from me and then leave?" she said, bitter in her heart.

Calandrino released her and slumped again on his bench at the table. He appeared exhausted, dark crescents beneath his large eyes, and he looked almost gaunt beneath his loose fitting tunic. She only wondered why she had not noticed the change in him before.

"Perhaps you're right. I have been selfish. Terribly selfish. But I do love you, Santina. I will always love you."

She sat beside him, trying to take in what he had said. None of it made sense. He had never loved her if he would take his leave so easily. Yet deep in her heart she felt his affection for her. It was just as real as when they had kissed at the fountain.

She turned to look at him, to try to comprehend his unrest. No matter what she said, he would leave her, leave the hilltop town and continue his knightly quest to the foreign city of Muslims, Jews, and Christians in Spain. For the second time in Santina's life, her heart was breaking. As when Mama died, she wished for the philosopher's stone, for the knowledge that would transform her suffering soul into a haven of peace. But there was no stone; her hands were empty.

"Will I see you again?" she asked Calandrino.

"I don't know when or how," he replied. "But somehow I am certain we will see one another again."

Calandrino drew her close and kissed her as though he would never stop. Sun streamed through the open door, and Calandrino's woodsy scent enfolded her. For a brief moment all was well. She almost thought he had changed his mind about leaving. But then he released her, and the sadness in his eyes revealed the end had come. Santina could not bear the pain as she walked to the door and looked at him for the last time.

"*Ti amo,* I love you, Santina," he called out when she hurried away in a flight of despair.

Riding back to the village, Santina mourned for herself and mourned for what might have been that was not. Soon Calandrino would take his precious books, recite St. Julian's *Paternoster*, and pick up his life as a scholar where he had left off. Santina would remain behind in San Gimignano, contained by walls of brick.

***

Following Calandrino's departure from San Gimignano, Santina could not bring herself to return to the attic room where he and Papa had tried to precipitate gold. When she was a young girl, the philosopher's stone had seemed close enough to touch. But now Santina began to suspect that no one had ever completed the transformation and that the *Great Work* of alchemy was all just an inglorious lie.

Whether Calandrino had been misguided about alchemy mattered little to her; it was being abandoned that cut most deeply. It was as though she was trapped in her own *nigredo*, the first stage of the experiment, in which the ingredients—lead, mercury, and sulfur among them—were melted down into a dark putrid mass. She felt as lost as a novice alchemist, as though she would never find gold, her heart's true desire. Hopelessly, Santina wandered the village through the biting wind that autumn, reliving her memories of Calandrino, reciting the many things he had said as though they were passages of the Gospel. She cried endless tears and wrote him long letters never to be delivered. Santina could see no future for herself. Anything beautiful she once imagined had slipped beyond her grasp, lost like the fragments of a dream upon waking.

Her village, as well, seemed to have taken on a starker reality. The faces she saw in passing seemed tinged with hopelessness. Loud, crude, devilish voices that disparaged the lawyers, politicians, and clergy poured out from the taverns and every corner seemed to spawn leering men, haggard women, children in tattered, filthy clothing, beggars, the blind, the deformed. There was nothing lovely here. There were only those who would laugh at the folly of pursuing the philosopher's stone and think Santina a stupid, naïve girl for nurturing an absurd infatuation with a wayward scholar.

Santina began to wonder why she had ever imagined her life would be different from anyone else's in San Gimignano. All were asked to carry the cross; she was no exception. She went to confession, asking forgiveness for her selfish and worldly desires. Upon leaving the church, she dropped a coin in the outstretched hand of a blind woman and tried to remember she still had much for which to be grateful.

Lauretta's wedding day arrived the first of November, nearly two months after Calandrino's departure from San Gimignano. Santina, putting her sorrows aside for the time being, did her best to convey lightheartedness. She would not have her older sister's happiness clouded by her own foul mood. Although she had once complained of Lauretta's frequent admonishments, Santina knew the house would be all too quiet without her.

She was still reeling from the loss of Calandrino and adjusting to the daily routine without Lauretta when Isabella took up with Bruno Ansaldo, the nephew of Papa's sister, Aunt Benedetta. The young saddler from Certaldo was slight in stature, but he was unquestionably handsome and carried himself proudly in a fine mantle lined with saffron silk and a plumed hat over his well-groomed hair. Aunt Benedetta thought him a good and pious man, for he had taken the pilgrim's tour to the shrine of Saint James in Santiago, and he had told her of many miracles attributed to the saint.

Although Bruno traveled often to Florence, Siena, and Pisa to sell his saddles, the dazzling young man sent many letters written in his beautiful, flourishing hand to Isabella that winter. He professed his love, told her he would return to San Gimignano when the last of his saddles were sold. Santina could only dream of receiving such a letter. Enviously, she watched as fifteen-year-old Isabella held her latest missive to her heart and dropped to her bed with a faraway look on her face.

The winter of 1344 passed slowly. Santina practiced her Greek, read Dante, and attended Mass. Her loneliness felt like a wound that would never go away completely. She wondered if she would have to live with the pain forever, just as she had learned to live with the pain of losing Mama. There was a form of solace in imagining herself a reclusive alchemist, working her way from the *nigredo* to the *albedo,* the second phase of the *Great Work.* In the *albedo,* the dark lump of material at the bottom of the cauldron was distilled in order to remove the heavier, impure substances. Papa's *Codex Pankratios* said that the process might seem to go on endlessly, but eventually the purification would stick and all traces of blackness would be gone. *The white stone is achieved at the darkest hour, at the time of dawning light,* she had read. If this was true, perhaps her suffering had only begun.

While Santina considered the phases of alchemy and the phases of her life, Papa purchased a number of leather saddles for what he considered a trifling, and the refined saddler requested Isabella's hand in marriage. To celebrate the marriage contract,

Rosa prepared a special dinner of apples and pears with pine nuts and honey, roast pork, and cheese *torta*. After dinner Isabella entertained them with a number of beautiful songs on her lute. Sitting beside Papa, Bruno Ansaldo appeared spellbound as he listened to the sweet music.

It occurred to Santina that she might become a forgotten old woman and die in the same house in which she was born. Perhaps she was letting life pass her by as Isabella prepared for her bright new future with Bruno. While Calandrino was traveling the world, unraveling ancient secrets and meeting with foreign scholars, she was relegated to the mundane tasks of baking, spinning, and weaving. She could continue living with Papa, keep the pantry stocked, and manage the servants as Lauretta used to do. Or she could become the wife of someone she cared little for. Santina could not easily countenance either choice.

"You should find someone else," said Isabella the following morning, as though sensing Santina's melancholy. "You must forget Calandrino."

"I suppose you're right, Isabella. But it's not an easy thing for me to do."

"Come now, Santina. You can't stay home and do nothing but embroider pillows," Isabella admonished. "I think you might see Master Traverseri."

"Master Traverseri? What can he possibly do to help me?"

"Or Trotula, perhaps."

"I don't know," Santina replied. She doubted that Papa would approve of her seeing the midwife who lived in a hilltop cottage outside the wall of the village, especially after what happened to Mama.

Of course, Trotula was not to blame for the loss of Pietro and Madonna Adalieta; the dangers of childbirth could simply not be avoided at times. While mention of the midwife would surely bring back painful memories to Papa, it seemed that nearly everyone else in San Gimignano viewed Trotula favorably. She was a wise woman who was skilled with herbs, and she was known to attend Mass regularly. It might be true that she knew the old ways of the grandmothers, the *nonnas*, but everyone understood she used her skills to heal, not to harm.

Having considered Trotula's talents, Santina decided that Isabella's idea was not entirely out of the question after all. Then she began to wonder if the midwife could offer her a love charm, *fattura,* which would persuade Calandrino to return to her. She had nothing to lose, for the one she loved was already far away.

Beyond the
Village Wall

Santina traveled to the midwife's cottage in secret, for she hoped Trotula would give her a charm that would return Calandrino to San Gimignano. She knew that Mama had trusted Trotula and in fact preferred the midwife's old ways to the scientific knowledge of the learned Master Traverseri, who had studied at the prestigious medical school at the University of Salerno. However, Santina had not seen the midwife since the day Mama died three years before, and she could not help but feel apprehensive at the thought of facing Trotula again. Santina had no reason to fear the midwife, but as she neared the cottage, her memories of that disastrous day rose up from the past like a specter before her.

"God help me!" came Mama's muffled cry through the closed bedroom door.

Santina's mother had gone into labor at daybreak, and Trotula had just arrived with her basket of herbs and fragrant ointments. When the midwife was ushered into Mama's room, Santina tried to follow her.

"You can't go in there," said Lauretta, who stood blocking the door, daring Santina to defy her.

"Why not?" fourteen-year-old Santina wanted to know. The groans from the bedroom were frightening her, and she wanted to make sure Mama was all right.

Trotula, who carried herself like a great lady even though she was a woman of modest means, paused to look kindly at Santina. She was the niece of old Ninetta, who had delivered babies in San Gimignano as long ago as anyone could remember. Unlike all the other women Santina knew, Trotula had never married or become a nun.

"I'll take good care of your mama," she said. "I'll let you know how she's coming along."

The heavy wood door banged shut, separating Santina from Mama and the mystery of whatever Trotula would do to bring the new baby into the world. Santina slid to the floor and might have stayed there all day if Margherita had not led her away.

Santina sat in the kitchen, adjacent to the central room on the second floor, with Isabella, her younger sister, and the two watched as Rosa, who helped with the cooking, went to work making the day's bread. Santina listened to the voices and footsteps coming from Mama's room and watched the maidservant, who was alternately wringing her hands, pacing back and forth, and praying to remove "malocchio," the evil eye—an attack of magic caused by *envy. Whenever trouble of any sort occurred, Margherita seemed to think this was the cause.*

"Your poor Mama. She's beautiful and the house is so fine, and especially now with the new baby other women are terribly jealous," she lamented. "I don't know how much longer she can go on like this."

"Madonna Adalieta's done it three times already, Margherita. She'll be fine with the fourth," said Rosa, brushing flour from her hands. She set some soft cheese and figs on the table, but Santina was not tempted.

Again she heard the cry, "Dio mi salvi—God help me."

Santina rose from the table, darted toward the bedroom, and before Margherita could catch her, burst through the door. Trotula and Aunt Benedetta both turned to look at her but said nothing. Then Santina saw Mama, dewy with sweat, her long black hair strewn across the pillow. She had never seen Mama look so pale and weak. Sensing that something was the matter, something more than the usual pains of labor, Santina threw her thin arms around Mama's shoulders.

"Please be all right, Mama," she murmured.

Mama kissed Santina's cheek. "I love you, cara," she whispered before Margherita pried Santina away and closed the door behind her once again.

Tears streaming down her cheeks, Santina ran out the back door, away from Lauretta, Isabella, and Papa— wherever he was. She had gone to find Calandrino.

Santina tried to put aside thoughts of that fateful day as she knocked on the little door of the single-story cottage with smoke billowing from the chimney. The next moment, the door was open, and Trotula stood silently before her. Feeling the heat of the midwife's gaze, Santina wondered if she had made a mistake in coming.

"What the devil has happened to you?" Trotula demanded, her dark, penetrating eyes focused on her unexpected visitor. "You look like a shadow of yourself, Santina."

She sat on a bench at the roughhewn oak table near the fire and rubbed her hands together, trying to warm herself that cold February morning. "I've not been well," she admitted to Trotula.

The midwife appeared not a day older than she did when she came to the house to see Mama, though her hair glinted with silver. Wearing but a plain work dress of brown wool, Trotula carried herself in such a way that she might have been wearing a garment of fine velvet instead. She was fair-skinned, but her cheeks were flushed pink from her work. The same delicate fragrance of sweet herbs that blew out from her chimney into the surrounding air was light on her clothing and skin.

Clearly trying to understand something more about her, Trotula continued to scrutinize Santina. "I knew you when you were a little girl, remember. You were such a feisty little thing. Your mother had me come see you once—you had a terrible cough and a high fever. But you wouldn't stay still. Not for a minute," Trotula recalled.

Santina vaguely recollected the time Trotula had come to see her when she was a child of seven or eight. That was before Papa insisted that Mama put her faith in the learned Master Traverseri. As Santina sat at the midwife's table, the cottage itself began to seem more familiar. She noticed the broom at the front door —to protect the threshold, the *nonnas* believed. She wondered if she had been here before with Mama some years back.

"I'll bring you a bowl of nettle tea. It will give you strength. A woman has to take care of herself, Santina," Trotula was saying as she walked past the brazier, where a fragrant brew was bubbling over the hob.

As Trotula prepared the tea, Santina took in the unexpected elegance of the midwife's little home. Over the stone fireplace was a colorful fresco depicting the baptism of St. Peter, and Trotula's chair, she noticed, was upholstered in rich scarlet. Most stunning of all was a stained glass window depicting Christ. The window was simple in design but vivid with colors of blue, red, and gold that sent a brilliant cascade of light throughout the room.

"Your home is not what I thought it would be," Santina said, candidly.

"I take my payments in kind more often than not."

Beyond the main living area there appeared to be a workroom, where bundles of herbs—yarrow, sage, and lavender—hung from the beams overhead. Breathing in the sweet scents of the cottage, Santina recalled the herbs that used to hang in Mama's kitchen.

Trotula brought a ceramic pitcher to the table, took a seat, and poured two small bowls of the pale green brew. "So tell me, Santina, what have you been doing with yourself?"

She took a sip of the hot infusion. She was no longer sure she wanted to confess her troubles to the midwife. Never mind she had known Mama, Trotula was nearly a stranger to Santina. The idea of telling the midwife about her relationship with Calandrino began to seem ill-conceived.

"Sometimes I help my father at his shop," she said. "Mostly I've been keeping to myself."

"Have you now?" Trotula said. "I only wonder how keeping to yourself has helped you work out whatever it is that's been bothering you."

Santina was not sure how to respond, nor could she understand how it was that Trotula, whom she had only seen in passing over the past few years, seemed to act with uncommon familiarity toward her. Once again she had the sense of having been to the cottage before. "Did Mama ever bring me here, Trotula?" she asked. "I almost feel as though I remember it."

"Ah, do you?" Trotula said, nodding her head. "You're right, Santina. Your mother used to visit me here, and you came along with her once or twice. We were friends, she and I. Just like you and I will become friends, I have a suspicion." Trotula looked at Santina as though searching somewhere deep inside her.

The midwife's stare made Santina shift in her seat, but she still wanted to know more about Mama's visits to the cottage. "Did Papa know?" she asked. "About you and Mama, I mean."

"To tell you the truth, your Papa didn't like it at all. He was afraid for her, is what it was," Trotula said. "Your mother sometimes accompanied me when I tended to people. She'd always bring something along—some bread or meat or a chicken. Kept a peasant family from starving more than once, I daresay. And she knew something about birthing babies herself, you know."

"She did?"

"Your mother delivered her maidservant's last child. The boy. I forget his name."

"Giacomino? Margherita's son?"

"That's the one," Trotula said. "She would have had a bad time of it if your mother hadn't been there. The labor came on very suddenly and there was a powerful storm, so no one could make it out to summon me.

"Your father didn't want it known what Madonna Adalieta had done for them. He didn't think it was proper. But your mother, she never listened to him," Trotula told an astonished Santina. "A seeker, Adalieta was."

"A seeker?" Santina asked.

"She was looking for ways to be herself," Trotula answered. "She had more ideas than San Gimignano would allow for."

Wondering what Trotula meant by this, Santina looked up to the image of Christ baptizing St. Peter. The saint was nearly submerged in water, on the verge of sinking into the waves if not for the outstretched hand of Christ. It was near death and then rebirth. A baptism in which one would nearly die and then be resurrected and discover eternity. Santina briefly closed her eyes and saw herself immersed in the water. Then she felt a warm, strong hand resting on her own.

"She wanted *freedom*," Trotula told her, releasing her hand. "It's something your father didn't always understand."

Santina nodded, acknowledging the secret divulged by the midwife. "Freedom," Santina repeated quietly. "I suppose that's something I don't understand very well either. I've never been free to do what I've wanted. Not really."

"You have to know what it is you want before you're free to have it, Santina. That's the first thing you have to learn."

"I did know what I wanted," Santina insisted.

"And what was that?" the midwife demanded.

"I loved a man, Trotula," she replied. "His name was Calandrino. He's a scholar at the University in Bologna," she admitted at last.

Trotula went silent for a moment. "A fair young man," she said.

"You know him?"

"His cottage is not far from here. We've spoken mainly of remedies," Trotula said abruptly. "He learned a great deal from a knight who traveled to the Holy Land."

"He left San Gimignano. He's returned to the university."

"Are you carrying his child?" Trotula asked with little ado.

"*Dio,* no!" she exclaimed. "Calandrino is entirely honorable. The truth is that I came to ask if you might help return him to me."

"You mean a love charm?"

"*Sì.*"

"You need no *fattura,* spell, Santina. You must look to yourself for strength," she said firmly. "Calandrino has gone off on another crusade. He's in search of his next battle. I'm afraid he is not someone to give your heart to."

Perceiving that Trotula had quickly dismissed her feelings and that she presumed to know Calandrino so well, Santina was taken aback. "It's not easy when people leave. It's hard when you've loved them."

"Of course it's difficult when people leave. Yet you cannot continue to fret about what you don't have. If you want contentment, true contentment, then you must come to know yourself first. Do you really believe a man will make you happy? Much less a wandering scholar?"

"We *were* happy together. Or at least I thought so."

Trotula rose from the table to fill the pitcher with more of the brew. "He's *gone,* Santina. He's not coming back for some time, if at all, and he's not worth wasting any more breath on. You need to get on with your life and do something useful. You're a young woman for heaven's sake," she told her visitor. "You have to find what it is God intends for you."

"It's not an easy thing to find," Santina said darkly.

Trotula stood with her hands on her hips. "You have to search for it instead of sitting there feeling sorry for yourself. You might take a look around and see plenty of folk who are a lot worse off than you are. I see them every day, Santina. You should be thanking God that you're someone who can help them and that you're not one of them."

Stunned by Trotula's remarks, Santina thought to leave. She had not come to the midwife's cottage to suffer insults. She rose from the table, thinking to put on her cloak and walk away. Santina could allow that there was some truth to what the midwife was saying, but she also knew that she was more than a self-pitying, tiresome young woman who thought only of herself. She did want to do something more with her life, but she wasn't sure how to go about it. While Santina decided whether she should defend herself to Trotula or simply depart, the midwife spoke again.

"You know a little about alchemy, don't you Santina?"

Shocked once more by the midwife's words, Santina said, "Why do you say that?"

"Your scholar told me about the cooking upstairs in your father's house," the midwife said wryly.

"I used to think there were miracles in that art," Santina said, wondering what else he had revealed to Trotula. "Calandrino and my father tried to make gold. They have books that explain how it's done, only the recipes didn't work."

Trotula nodded her head. "The experiments are well and good, Santina. But you won't find the secret to the transformation just by reading about it in books."

Santina was surprised that the midwife could speak of the *Great Work*. "Do you believe it's even possible to make gold, Trotula?"

Trotula smiled at this. "You can find the secret, Santina. But you have to search for it outside your father's workshop. You have to let go of the small, petty ideas you have for your life and let God's plan work through you. The divine order is much more than what you can dream up all by yourself," she said. Returning to the table with the pitcher of tea, she looked into Santina's eyes. "How big do you want your life to be?"

Santina sat down again. Considering all that Trotula said, she began to see the challenge set before her. Perhaps it was true that whatever she was looking for lay beyond the workshop, beyond the texts, beyond Calandrino even. For a long while she had been asking God to grant her small, human wish. But she had not felt compelled to ask God to guide her or to use her in the manner He thought best.

She thought about Mama accompanying Trotula to the homes of the sick and the poor. Had Mama thought she was doing the work God intended her to do? Mama worked with Trotula despite Papa's objections. She must have felt determined to do so, or she would not have disobeyed Papa.

"Trotula," Santina said, "I'm glad you told me about you and Mama."

"It's good for you to know who your mother was, Santina."

She tried to imagine her mother tending to expectant women at their bedsides. How strange that no one had ever mentioned this detail about Mama before.

"I wonder what it was like for Mama when she went with you," Santina began. "Do you think—do you think I might do the same one time? Go with you, I mean?"

"Do you have the courage for it?"

"I think I do," Santina replied. "I know I do."

"Very well," Trotula consented. "It can be arranged."

"When?"

"Tomorrow, if you like." A smile broke through Trotula's hardened expression, and she laughed to reveal straight, white teeth. "Maybe you're the one."

Mystified by this remark, Santina waited for Trotula to explain. "I'll bring you with me to see Isotta. We'll see how well you can handle it."

"I won't be fainthearted, Trotula," Santina said, though in truth she felt a little afraid of what she would see. But if Mama had done it, then so could she.

She only wondered how to explain her intentions to her father. He would not easily accept her plans to follow along with the village midwife who had caused Mama to defy him.

Isotta

antina made her way once again to Trotula's cottage, which seemed to her as though under some form of enchantment. But if Trotula practiced magic of any sort, it was surely white magic. Mama had trusted her, after all.

She kept these thoughts to herself as she continued on from the cottage with the midwife, who led the way at a brisk pace to a neighboring farmhouse. Walking silently across the grassy hillside, Santina was not entirely sure why she felt compelled to follow alongside the woman who was once her mother's friend. She had the sense, nonetheless, that the experience would lead somewhere.

Entering the home of a woman named Isotta, Santina felt uneasy. Trotula, on the other hand, appeared in her manner completely calm and knowing. Isotta had given birth three days earlier, although the baby had not been expected for several more weeks. The young woman had tried to ignore her pains, especially when her mother-in-law said it could not possibly be time yet. Consequently, poor Isotta was left with no one to help her through the delivery but an assortment of neighbor women who meant well but hadn't the skills to handle the abrupt birth. When Isotta tore badly as a result, Trotula was finally summoned to come repair the damage.

"She's still keeping to bed," Isotta's sister-in-law complained as she greeted Trotula at the door. "My husband's none too happy I'm still here with her." Two small children raced into the room and stood giggling behind their aunt's full skirt.

"*Bene,* she must do as I have advised if she would be well." Trotula moved to the bedside, followed by the beleaguered aunt. "*Per favore*, please, Madonna," she said, turning around. "Keep the children occupied while I tend to your sister-in-law."

When the door closed Trotula greeted the new mother warmly. "*Come sta?* How are you, Isotta?" she said as she sprinkled the corners of the room with salt in order to rid the house of harmful spirits.

"*Sto meglio.* I'm better," she said, eying Santina. "Who do you have there with you, Trotula?"

"This is Santina, my assistant today," said the midwife, offering no further explanation as she knelt beside the tiny infant who wore a tiny packet of herbs—rue and lavender—around his neck for protection.

Isotta eyed Santina's fine dress. "Such a lady coming to see me," she observed.

Having ascertained the baby was well, Trotula focused her attention on Isotta. "Is your sister-in-law brewing the chamomile I left for you?" she asked. "It will keep down the fever."

"I can't ask Cecca to do anything more than she already is. My husband is none too pleased with me, either. He doesn't think much of me staying in bed like a queen."

"Enough of that talk, Isotta," Trotula replied. "If Giovanni would have you get better, he must do what he can to help you in-stead of complaining. He's not the one who did the work birthing the baby, I might add."

Before Isotta could protest, Trotula instructed Santina to bring a bowl of water.

"She reminds me of someone," Isotta remarked, as Santina left the room.

"She is Adalieta's daughter," Santina heard Trotula say.

When Santina returned with the water, Trotula washed her hands, pulled up the blankets, and pushed Isotta's knees apart. Then she motioned for Santina to move closer.

"You need to see," she encouraged her.

Santina's first inclination was to turn her head away, but she realized this was no time to appear squeamish; Isotta was the one she needed to be thinking about. Santina edged close to the bed-side and watched as Trotula removed the poultice and took a close look at the flesh she had sewn together by candlelight after the baby tore through without any strong, expert hands to guide him.

"This is why you have to oil the opening before the baby comes, Santina. You have to make it soft so the baby can slide through. The skin is thin, like paper—it can tear to pieces."

Trotula prepared a clean, fresh poultice and applied it to Isotta's wounded skin. "It's healing nicely," she said. "You should rest an-other day, Isotta. You have to give your body time to mend itself."

"I have the animals to tend to. And a husband and children to feed."

"Giovanni and Cecca can manage for another day," Trotula insisted. She bent to pick up the baby, who had started to wail. Putting the infant to Isotta's breast, Trotula advised, "Just worry about yourself and the little one for now. Think of the joy he'll bring you."

"My mother-in-law doesn't think I should allow myself to get so attached to my babies," Isotta said.

"Yes, some would withhold their affection till they're sure the babes won't die, but that is not the way to help them live," Trotula said. "Keep the dark thoughts away, Isotta. As with the mind, so with the body."

When all that could be done for Isotta was accomplished, Santina helped Trotula gather her supplies. Inside Trotula's box of herbs, she noticed several stones and an amulet—a miniature horn wrought of bone that was attached to a leather string. Margherita had one like it—the maidservant brought it out whenever she suspected *malocchio,* the evil eye. Santina wondered if Trotula had carried the charm with her to Mama's delivery. *If so, it had done little good*, she thought as she closed the box.

By the time Santina had fastened her cloak, the midwife was already whisking through the house, past the sister-in-law, past the children. Santina quickened her pace as she followed Trotula out the door to the road toward home. Her mind was filled with questions. She wanted to know how Trotula had sewn the wound and made the poultice, and she wondered about Trotula's thoughts on caring for infants. Santina was fascinated by everything she had seen that day and by the way the midwife had rendered her care.

"I can understand why my mother wanted to go with you," she said.

"Yes, but it's not always this easy, Santina. Some days things don't go the way one plans."

Santina recalled her mother's tragic delivery. Master Traverseri, dressed in his scarlet robe trimmed with fur, had stood speaking to Papa in hushed tones outside her mother's room. Santina could still picture Margherita standing down the hall in the shadows, listening, wringing her hands.

Four years later, Santina wondered why Papa had called Master Traverseri to help Trotula. She knew something out of the ordinary had happened.

"What went wrong when Mama died?" she dared to ask Trotula, just as they were about to part ways. "Why did Papa call Master Traverseri to our house?"

Trotula nodded her head sadly, acknowledging the tragedy of that day. "There will be time for questions. But later."

Santina hoped that this meant she would be allowed to accompany the midwife once more. "May I join you again?"

"You have your mama's touch, Santina. If you had the inclination, I think you would make a fine midwife."

"Do you mean I might work with you?"

Trotula smiled. "Why the sudden interest in midwifery, Santina?"

"I'm not sure," the young woman answered truthfully. "I admire what you do, the way you tended to Isotta. And the freedom you have."

Trotula appeared to consider this before asking, "What will you tell your father?"

"I'm not sure I can tell him everything just yet."

Trotula nodded then started up the hill. "Come one week from today, after daybreak. We'll have some distance to travel."

Santina watched Trotula continue down the dirt road, and she glimpsed a new future before her. Perhaps it was possible that the *albedo*, the white phase, was coming into view. Although the *nigredo* had passed, there were still shadows and uncertainties ahead. Calandrino said the *albedo* was when Hermes, the god of tricksters and thieves, was at play. The alchemist was advised to remain on guard, for it was still possible to fall back into darkness once again.

When she disappeared beyond the wall throughout the spring and into the summer, Santina offered any number of excuses: she was going to church to pray; walking to market; visiting the poor widow—Madonna Puccio; or giving Lauretta's old mare some exercise. Isabella, however, began to see through her sister's guise.

Upon returning from the midwife's cottage on one occasion, Santina found her sister sitting alone, halfheartedly plucking her lute before the empty hearth. Cheeks flushed pink from the sun, she offered the bride-to-be a cheery greeting.

"Your *hair,*" Isabella observed.

"I was riding," Santina said, trying to smooth her windblown locks into place.

"You ought not to ride unaccompanied," Isabella reminded her. Santina thought it was not so much concern for her safety as being left alone that bothered her sister.

"Giacomino was with me," she lied.

"What is the secret you would keep? You're meeting someone. If you won't tell me, I might just go to Papa," Isabella said, knowing her sister all too well.

"And tell him what?" Santina said sharply.

Her sister would indeed be surprised to know it was not a man but the midwife with whom Santina passed the time. A forbidden meeting with a man would be simpler to explain. She could not easily share her desire to discover the mysterious knowledge held by Trotula, for Isabella thought only of marriage and romance.

Santina reflected upon the young men she might marry. There was Dioneo, who was always waiting for her outside the Duomo. He never knew what to say after she greeted him, but he had written a song for her. Papa had once encouraged both her and Lauretta to consider Ruberto, but he was nearly forty, set in his ways, and apparently disinclined to marry anyone. She considered the jeweler from Certaldo. Taddeo was handsome enough, but there was something unsettling in the way he looked at her when he came to Papa's store. Neither Taddeo nor the others could compare to Calandrino. But Calandrino would not have her. He had not sent a single letter since his departure. Or if he had written, Papa made sure the letter did not reach her hands.

"I care for none but Calandrino," Santina said truthfully.

"Are you seeing him?"

"He's in Bologna," she reminded Isabella.

"You're up to something."

How could she explain that she was trying to find whatever it was God intended for her, now that she had lost the one who mattered most? "I'm only trying to understand what my life is meant to be."

Isabella shrugged. "People are beginning to talk, you know."

Hurt by the remark, Santina asked, "What is it they say?"

"They say you keep to yourself too much. That you'll end up an old maid if you don't change your ways."

Even if they were right, Santina could not easily ignore the voices that were calling her, compelling her to follow the village midwife as Mama had done. Was she truly heading in a direction that would lead to nowhere but loneliness? More than this, she wondered how long she could keep her secret life from Papa. If Isabella made her disappearances known, her father could easily discover what she was about. After her previous disgrace with Calandrino, he would be none too pleased to learn that she was once again venturing beyond the wall.

Mercury

"Where is it you go when you ride?" Iacopo Pietra demanded. It was just before the feast day of Saint Michael in September. Papa, in his tasseled cap, sat at his wide mahogany desk scattered with account ledgers.

Santina had, by this time, accompanied Trotula to a number of births, and she had helped the midwife tend to the wound of a farmer named Caravaggio. The man's calf had been pierced by sheep shears and though the barber surgeon thought to saw off the leg, Trotula had been able to save it. But rather than tell this to Papa, she kept silent.

"Your sister says you often disappear," he continued. "She thinks you're hiding something."

Santina avoided his gaze as she obeyed his command to sit across from him. No matter what she said to her father, it would only be a matter of time before he discovered that she had taken up with the village midwife. She supposed she was fortunate to have carried on unnoticed for as long as she had. The time had come to explain.

"I've been with Trotula, the midwife," she said. "She's teaching me."

"Trotula?" His eyes narrowed. "What could she possibly be teaching you?"

"Practical things. Like how to use healing plants," Santina said quietly, as though to lessen the shock. "And deliver babies."

Rising slowly from his chair, Papa towered over her. "For what unholy purpose is she teaching you these things, Santina?"

"She thinks I have skill. She has allowed me to work with her."

"You mean to say Trotula believes it is possible for you to work as a midwife?"

"_Si_," she said, almost inaudibly. She knew well enough the response her confession would elicit. Silently, she asked Mama for a way to explain things to Papa so that he might understand.

Her father's face bloomed scarlet. "Has the devil got into you, Santina?"

"I want to be useful, Papa. I can think of nothing that should prevent me from becoming a midwife except for what people might say about it. That hardly seems like a reason not to do it," Santina managed to say. "Trotula needs someone to help her. Many rely on her work. You know that."

Papa tapped his fingers on his book before looking to the ceiling as though seeking an answer from above. "Just because Trotula can't find a suitable apprentice does not mean the job is yours for the asking."

"You let Mama work with her." Somehow, Santina hoped that Papa might decide to allow her the same freedom he had reluctantly granted Madonna Adalieta. "Mama helped deliver Giacomino. Trotula told me about it. I know what Mama used to do."

When Papa closed his eyes and was silent, Santina feared she had made a mistake by revealing what she knew. Trotula had said that her friendship with Mama was something Papa never understood, so perhaps mention of this past disagreement only served to provoke him further.

"*Figlia mia.* My daughter. What your mama did was out of necessity. It was an emergency, she had no choice," Papa said slowly, as though trying to keep himself from exploding again. "If you want to know the truth of it, Trotula took advantage of your mama's good will. She put ideas in Mama's head. Now she's doing the same with you. I want you to stay away from her," he commanded. "Her ways are strange. Do you understand me, Santina?"

"It's not possible," she murmured.

As Papa moved closer, she edged back, afraid he was going to hit her. When he grabbed hold of her arm, Santina fought back tears.

"I *forbid* you to see that woman again."

Caught in his unforgiving grip, Santina looked away, defeated. Perhaps she had been foolish to think she could persuade him. In her mind's eye Mama appeared, looking young and beautiful. *He would have kept me in my place, too, Santina. There are times when a woman must be more like a man. You must hold fast to your dreams.*

When he finally released his hold on her, Santina stepped back. She understood there was nothing she could say that would convince him to accept her apprenticeship. Santina had given long, hard thought to the idea of becoming a midwife. If she could not be with Calandrino, then working with Trotula was all that was left. She had no choice but to disobey her father.

"I'm very sorry, Papa," she said as she dared to look into his eyes. "But it has already been decided."

Papa's expression hardened. He was furious with her, and Santina matched his anger with her own. She could not yet understand it was fear that was causing him to oppose her in this way. It would take some time before she understood Papa was afraid for her future, for his own reputation in their village, for her safety, and of the things Trotula knew.

"You are my daughter, Santina. You forget your place."

Her place? She had already left her place by falling in love with Calandrino. Before that, she had left her place by helping Papa in his workshop. She recalled the strange and wonderful discussions about alchemy that Papa and Calandrino had in the *bottega*. The two men had traveled a curious path of their own while searching for gold and the philosopher's stone—that elusive elixir that could bring wellness and immortality to all. She thought to remind him of this.

"Are you no longer a believer in the sacred art, Papa?" she asked. "Haven't you been looking for the Great Secret?"

"What does this have to do with your disobedience, Santina?"

"You've been cooking your metals up in the attic, although few know of it. You and Calandrino didn't avoid the experiments in spite of what others might think. You followed your own ways. Don't I have the right to do that as well?"

"It's not the same. It's not the same at all."

As Papa spoke, Santina knew all too well that virtually everyone in San Gimignano would agree with him. Faithful daughters were not to choose unsuitable professions, let alone disregard their fathers' wishes. Despite this awareness, she tried to plead her case. "You've practiced alchemy for years, but you won't allow me the freedom to find what's important to me."

"This is absurd," her father replied. "You can't truly believe that running about the hillside with Trotula is of such vital importance."

"But it *is*," she said, even though she knew the argument had become futile. "If you would keep me from midwifery, then I cannot remain here."

"You have nowhere else to go," Papa reminded her. He appeared calmer upon saying it, as if this fact would settle the matter.

Santina felt herself weaken again, for Papa was right about this. Where else could she go? She could not leave the safety of her childhood home and live on the street like a pauper. Perhaps there was one other choice, though. There was an option she had not considered until that moment.

Her voice quivered as she spoke. "I will live with Trotula, then."

In that instant Santina committed herself to an action that would bear no small consequence, even though she had never planned for this to happen. She had been angry with Papa and eager to prove her point. While she had known Papa would resist her plan to work with Trotula, she had not considered how far she would go in order to pursue her ambition.

Now that it was done, she would not turn back. She left the room with only the vague notion that she would go and gather up her things. The polished brick floor beneath her feet no longer felt hard, but soft and uncertain. She did not want to disobey her father, and yet she saw no other way but to follow up on the threat she had impulsively made.

As she dashed up the stairs, Papa called after her. "Come back here, Santina! You cannot be serious about this."

"But I am, Papa," she replied, turning to see him at the foot of the stairs, looking incredulous that he could not contain her. When their eyes met, Santina refused to look away. She thought her father might very well lock her in her room in one last desperate effort to keep her from leaving.

"You are no longer my daughter." Papa stood at the door of her room as she packed the *cassone*, wood chest, which had once belonged to Mama.

Although Papa would not make Santina a prisoner in her home, he made it clear that she would pay for her disobedience. He turned and left. Tears streamed down Santina's cheeks as she tended to her packing. In her saddlebag she placed a chemise, wool hose, a handkerchief, a comb, and an embroidered purse. Her eyes moved to the delicate glass vial that stood on her washstand. She picked up the vial, recalling a happier day when Calandrino had given her the precious gift.

Bringing his hand from behind his back, Calandrino presented her with a small silk pouch. Opening the pouch, Santina discovered a round glass vial with an unusual silver image welded on its surface.

"Mercurius," Calandrino said in Latin, pointing to the silver image of a man. "The god Mercury, called Hermes in Greek."

"He's wearing the sandals with wings."

"The god of travelers and thieves," the scholar said.

Mercury was, as well, another name for quicksilver, which she had seen in her father's workshop. It was the mysterious, glittery substance that would adhere only to precious metals. It was both liquid and metallic at the same time. Papa said that quicksilver had the ability to dissolve gold.

While mercury was an ingredient in the experiment, it was also a symbol of the Great Work, Santina understood. She listened, spellbound, as Calandrino spun the tale of the god who moved between Olympus and Earth, between Earth and the underworld. He was the escort of souls, accompa-

nying the dead as they crossed over. When Persephone was abducted and raped by Hades, it was Mercury who rescued her and returned her to her mother, Demeter.

Santina imagined Mercury, the god of travelers and thieves, in his messenger hat with wings, his golden sandals and cape that concealed magic tricks. As she held the vial in her hand, she wished Mercury would whisk her and Calandrino somewhere far away.

She closed her eyes and the scholar's arms encircled her in a heady, forbidden embrace....

Margherita appeared at the doorway. Tucking the vial into her bag, Santina asked the maidservant to have Giacomino deliver her *cassone* to Trotula's cottage the next morning.

"Maybe you should wait until morning." Margherita fingered her *corno*, horned amulet, as she watched Madonna Adalieta's middle daughter prepare for a hasty departure. "You've upset your Papa so much," she said. "But I suppose this is something your mama would have understood."

Santina nodded. "I know Mama delivered Giacomino. Trotula told me."

Margherita looked to the floor. "I don't know what I would have done if your mama hadn't been there. A lot of people loved her for the kindnesses she showed them, Santina. She didn't always see eye to eye with your papa, but they loved each other so much. They always forgave one another."

Santina studied the face of the faithful woman. It seemed impossible to imagine day-to-day life without her. Willing herself to continue with her plan, Santina handed Margherita a letter sealed with wax. "Please give this to Isabella when she returns." She kissed the maidservant good-bye before hurrying away to hide her tears.

Feeling eyes upon her as she began her journey along Via San Giovanni, she sat tall on Lauretta's old mare but was plagued by uncertainty. Puffy gray clouds glowed orange in the open sky to the west. When she had been arguing with Papa, she had felt quite sure of herself. Now that she had gone and followed through on her threat, she was less convinced of her plan. She turned around to look once more at her house where she was born. Was her father right? Perhaps she was mad to forsake home and those who loved her for some vague and improbable dream. Too late it occurred to Santina that Trotula might refuse her. If the midwife sent her away, where would she go?

Trotula di Ruggierio

ven as she feared being refused by Trotula, an unseen
current kept Santina moving forward, past the Piazza
della Cisterna, up Via San Matteo, and out the north
city gate. It was as though one part of her life was over
and another was beginning. She could not return to the home of
her childhood any more than she could return to childhood itself.
Knowing this, Santina traveled with both a longing to turn back
and an awareness that her future lay beyond the village wall.

When she approached the cottage, Santina saw that Trotula was
out in her garden clearing away fallen brush. The midwife waved in
greeting, but the gesture gave Santina no assurance that she would
be allowed to stay. She tied her horse to an almond tree and started
when a large orange and black cat mewed loudly in welcome.

"My father's forbidden me to work with you. I've left home
because of it," Santina said, her face somber as she approached
Trotula.

The midwife appeared none too pleased with this turn of events. When Trotula said nothing at first, Santina fought back tears. Finally the midwife remarked, "We both knew your Papa wouldn't like what you were doing. I suppose it was only a matter of time before the cauldron came to a boil."

Disheartened, Santina said, "Do you think I've done the wrong thing, then?"

"You did what you thought was right. You faced the consequences," Trotula replied, matter-of-factly. "Let's go inside and get you settled."

Santina welcomed Trotula's firm and knowing guidance even as she wondered what would become of her now that she had gone against Papa's will. She was also afraid of being a burden to Trotula, who surely had not counted on another mouth to feed. "I mean to cause you no trouble," she said. "I'll help however I can."

"Oh, you'll earn your keep, Santina. You said you wanted to learn how to be a midwife, so now that's just what you'll do." She showed Santina to a snug little room beside the kitchen. "I used to sleep here when my aunt Ninetta was alive."

After she and Trotula cleared the room of blankets, assorted baskets of herbs, and the birthing chair, Santina thought she would be comfortable enough in the tiny space. The room had a low bed covered with embroidered pillows, a little altar with an image of the Blessed Mother, and a small washstand and basin beneath the shuttered window.

"It's not much, but it will do," Trotula said, unapologetically.

Santina was still not sure if Trotula welcomed her arrival, but at least she had been accepted without hesitation. She knew she should be grateful for a roof over her head, and she was truly relieved that Trotula had not turned her away. As she sat in the unfamiliar room, Santina told herself she had done the right thing. Papa had given her no choice but to leave home, after all. At the same time, there was a part of her that doubted her decision. She intended to become a midwife, but what if her apprenticeship proved unsuccessful? She could not be sure that Papa would accept her back.

"After you've rested a bit, we'll have some soup. Tomorrow we'll go see Cristoforo," Trotula was saying, speaking of a little boy who had broken his arm. "He seems to be healing just fine, thanks be to God and the Holy Mother."

Too dazed by the events of the day to give much thought to tomorrow, Santina nodded her head in agreement and sat on the edge of the little bed.

Trotula studied Santina silently before sitting beside her. "You followed your heart today. That's not always an easy thing to do." The midwife began to speak of her own childhood. Trotula revealed that she had been brought to the cottage when she was just a child, after both her parents died.

"I was eight years old at the time and I had no wish to live here with Ninetta—she was a widow with no children of her own. I wouldn't speak to her for days. I wanted to be with my two brothers, but they were sent to live with our uncle."

"Wasn't Ninetta kind to you?"

"She was kind enough. It didn't matter. My family was gone, and I was a scared little child. But eventually there came a point when I was so busy helping Ninetta that I forgot to be scared."

"I can hardly imagine you being anything other than a midwife," Santina remarked. It never occurred to her that there might have been a time when Trotula thought to do something other than deliver babies.

"The first years with Ninetta were very hard, but by the time I was twelve I thought no more of leaving. I came to accept God's plan."

Santina began to see that Trotula was setting another challenge before her. She did not have to look far to see her own resemblance to the scared child that Trotula once was. Despite her pangs of homesickness, Santina sensed that all the events in her life had led up to this day. She was picking up where Mama had left off with Trotula. For better or worse, she had made her decision.

Trotula left the room, and Santina was alone with her thoughts. Closing her eyes, she wished that some day she would be as strong and assured as this formidable woman who could work magic with herbs and seemed to need no one.

In her little back room, Santina wrote letters to Papa and tried to explain that although she loved him dearly and had no wish to disappoint him, it would have been a form of death not to continue on with Trotula. She explained the many skills the midwife was teaching her, she told him of the births she had witnessed, the healing of young Cristoforo's arm, and the unfortunate loss of a carpenter named Manuel who had suffered long with consumption, despite Trotula's supplications to the Virgin. Many times she asked for Papa's forgiveness.

Most reverend Lord Father, Santina, unworthy daughter, greets you well.

In the most lowly manner, I recommend me unto your good will, beseeching of your fatherly blessing and desiring to hear of your welfare.

For the sake of your health, I pray that the unfortunate manner of my departure will soon cease to vex you. It

greatly troubles my heart that I have caused you cruel
suffering, and yet I believe God has commanded me to do
this work, as Mama once did, to assist those whose needs
are greater than my own. You were able to forgive dear
Mama, and so perhaps in time you will be able to forgive
my absence as well.

> *Written on this 9 of October, 1344*
> *Your humble daughter,*
> *Santina*

Despite her efforts to communicate with Papa, no reply was
forthcoming from the village. Papa, like Calandrino, had abandoned her. The losses cut deeply. Though she could not very well
write to Calandrino, whom she had not heard from at all since his
departure the year before, she continued sending conciliatory letters to her father. When two months had gone by in this manner,
the midwife spoke out at last.

"It's not for you to decide how others ought to feel, Santina.
If your father chooses to deny you, there's nothing more to be
done. It's a shame he has the notion you shouldn't be here," she
said. "But unless you'd return home and be married off like your
sisters, you'll have to live with the situation as it is."

"If he comes to see that I'm learning something useful, then
he might be able to understand. Don't you think, Trotula? He *is*
my father. Despite everything."

"You must set it aside for now," the midwife advised. "He
does love you, Santina. You can be sure of that. I suspect in time
he'll grow tired of his anger."

Santina prayed that Papa would forgive her. The sorrow of
missing him only added to her pain of losing Calandrino. She
wondered if the scholar remembered her at all. Perhaps she was
destined to live a lonely life in the cottage, for it seemed that

everyone had forgotten her. Even Isabella and Lauretta wrote in-
frequently. Removed from those she loved, there was little she
could do but turn her attention to the tasks at hand. The work she
did with Trotula was often tiring, and there were times when she
had to awake in the middle of the night to attend a birth. There was
the usual housework to be done as well, for there were no servants
at the cottage, no cook to prepare the meals, only a washerwoman
who came on occasion. Despite everything, Santina felt little desire to return to Papa's house, for her will to learn about midwifery
was stronger than her pangs of homesickness.

When granted permission, Santina read Trotula's old text-
books. There was the beautifully illustrated *Theatrum Sanitatis* of
medical knowledge written by an Arab physician and translated
into Latin. She was intrigued to discover a practice of medicine
based upon observation rather than superstitions and the old ways.
She read of the importance of hygiene and climate, food, drink,
sleep, and happiness. In Trotula's Greek text, *De plantis*, she read
about the classification of plants. Most interesting of all was *De
Passionibus Mulierum Curandorum,* an exhaustive text on matters of women's health by the famous female doctor who studied
at the school of Salerno in the eleventh century.

"You have the same name," Santina observed when she first
came upon the text.

"Ah, it's only because Ninetta took to calling me Trotula when
I read the book so often and would talk of nothing else. I was born
Agnesa."

"You were?" Santina said in surprise.

"Yes, but I am so long Trotula that no one knows me by my
former name."

"Trotula suits you," Santina observed.

"Trotula di Ruggiero was one to follow, that is certain."

"How did Ninetta come upon these books?" Santina wanted to know. These were precious texts, not typically owned by a midwife, she surmised.

"Only *De Passionibus* was Ninetta's. The others are mine."

Santina waited for further explanation but none was offered. She could not help but wonder where Trotula had acquired the books and if the midwife would have wished to study at the famous school like her namesake. Trotula had done well with Ninetta's teaching and the knowledge she had acquired, but perhaps she might have become a physician, like Master Traverseri, had she been given the chance. For whatever reason, she had remained alone in her small cottage, a spinster tending to those in need.

⁂

As autumn passed and the chilly days of Santina's first winter at the cottage began, she dwelled less often upon Calandrino. While she did not cease to long for her beloved, there seemed to be little hope of hearing from him. After all, the scholar had no way of knowing she now lived with Trotula and any letter sent to Papa's house would not likely find its way to the cottage. She often wondered if there were letters waiting for her, opened or unopened, inside Papa's desk drawer. The thought sometimes troubled her at night, but she was too exhausted after the day's work to stay awake worrying for long.

During the following months of bitter cold, Santina saw a fair amount of sickness and seven more births. Trotula praised Santina for her demeanor at the bedside, for her ability to discern the appropriate uses of certain remedies, and for the careful way in which she set the broken leg of a little boy who fell from a barn roof. Trotula's confidence in her was surely growing, a feeling that was reinforced when spring arrived and Santina was asked to attend the delivery of the carpenter's wife on her own. The occasion arose just after Easter when Trotula was called to see her friend Sister Maria, who suffered the excruciating agony of a kidney stone at the same time Adriano's wife began her labor.

"I can't go alone," Santina protested as Adriano waited outside. "What if something goes wrong and I don't know what to do?"

"Send for me at once if you need me, but Monna Lisa's already had three children without any trouble," Trotula reassured her as she filled a small box with forbidden herbs—the tinctures that Santina was not yet allowed to administer on her own—to take to the monastery. "I've taught you what to do when a good number of things do go wrong, so make a point of remembering what I've told you, Santina. Keep your wits about you, pray to the Holy Mother, put the *corno* around Lisa's neck, and all will be well. A woman's body knows what to do. Your job is to help nature take its course."

With that, Trotula headed off to the Monastery of San Girolamo in the village, leaving Santina with little choice but to do as she was told. She carried the birthing chair out from the cottage and felt uneasy when the orange and black cat followed alongside. Hopping into the cart, she reminded herself of the wisdom of the Arab physicians and the senselessness of the *streghe's* feline omens. She hoped Trotula's confidence in her would be justified.

As she followed behind Adriano though a grove of olive trees, Santina tried to remember everything she had been taught, but she began to think that whatever she knew was not nearly enough. Soon she was unable to recall much of anything about birthing babies. Trying to calm herself, Santina looked up to the blue sky and prayed for guidance. *Don't let me fail, Sancta Maria. Let me do what I have been asked to do.*

In her mind's eye she saw Madonna Adalieta smiling down upon her. She could almost hear Mama speaking. *You wanted to find the elixir of life, Santina. Remember? If it is your wish to assist those who suffer, you must have courage. Trust your own good efforts as well as guidance from above.*

She scanned the trees along the side of the road. Mama was not there, and yet Santina no longer felt so alone. Realizing that she had not run away from home just to live in the dim shadow of doubt, she snapped the reins and hurried to catch up to Adriano.

At the home of the carpenter, a tiny barefoot girl with enormous brown eyes led Santina through the house. All the cabinets and drawers had already been opened to free up the womb. In the darkened bedroom, warmed by fire and strewn with fresh rushes, half a dozen women fluttered about. As Santina stood at the door, all eyes turned to her in surprise. The silence was brief.

"Where is Trotula?" the laboring woman asked.

Putting Trotula's trusted amulet around the woman's neck, Santina replied, "She is indisposed at the moment, Monna Lisa. But rest assured, Trotula has taught me well."

She commenced by rolling up her sleeves and pushing back the coverlet so she could feel for the position of the baby. Once she was satisfied that the baby was set to come out the way it was supposed to, she went about preparing a brew that would ease the pain of the delivery and another one that would tighten the womb after the baby was born. Santina's palms were sweaty by the time the child's head began to crown an hour later. She wanted desperately to succeed at the task Trotula had sent her to do. *Let the baby arrive safely,* she prayed.

Monna Lisa

"*B*ene, you're doing well," Santina said to Monna Lisa. "Now, you must *push*."

The carpenter's wife was clearly spent. Nevertheless, she found the strength within her to do as Santina advised as well as to talk and laugh now and then with the other women in the room. It appeared that Trotula would be proven right about the delivery. Lisa, having given birth three times without difficulty, needed little more than reassurance from a midwife.

"Now breathe," Santina said, not wanting the baby to emerge too quickly, for that could cause Lisa to tear. Very gently, she put her hand to the infant's head. Santina would not give Trotula cause to come sew the woman up, as she had needed to do for Isotta.

A minute later, a dainty baby girl with red ringlets of hair emerged from watery darkness and cried out her greeting. Exultant, Santina tied off and cut the cord and bathed the child. As advised in *De Passionibus*, she took care to wash the infant's tongue with hot water so that she would speak properly. After placing a *brevi*—a small packet of rue and lavender for protection—around the baby's neck and wrapping her in swaddling clothes, Santina presented her to the open arms of her mother, who would call her Agnola.

"*Sia lodato Iddio*, praise be to God," murmured Santina. Having shared in this miracle, she began to believe that she might truly be able to follow in Trotula's footsteps one day.

Santina left Lisa's house with ten silver soldi and heartfelt thanks from Adriano. As she started home, her first impulse was to find her sister, for she wanted to tell Isabella everything that had happened. In the next breath she recalled her state of exile. At least a warm welcome awaited her at the cottage, where Trotula would be heartened by the news of an uncomplicated birth and Adriano's payment.

Her good spirits continued through the next day, even as she was charged with cleaning the barn and feeding the tired old horses. Pleased with the progress she was making as Trotula's apprentice, Santina hummed a tune from her girlhood days, Francesco Landini's *Behold the Springtime*, as she worked. Looking up from her task, she saw Trotula standing at the door.

"You have a letter," her mentor announced with little enthusiasm. She handed Santina the sealed, cream-colored parchment and turned to leave.

"*Grazie,* Trotula," Santina called after her. She dared to hope it was an invitation to Isabella's wedding banquet, for the June date was soon approaching. But the letter was not from Isabella. It was from *Calandrino*.

To my well beloved Santina be this letter delivered. I, Calandrino, send greetings in the Lord.

I pray you are in good health and still desiring to hear of my welfare. Whilst I wrote several letters previously, I fear none were delivered for no response from you was forthcoming. I recently learned that you have taken up residence with Trotula, the midwife. I confess this news came as quite a surprise, and yet I happen to know through my acquaintance with this worthy woman that she is highly skilled in the healing arts.

Truly, I regret the abrupt manner of my departure from San Gimignano last year, and I pray you will find it in your heart to forgive me for the suffering I have caused you. I was wrong to think only of my desires and to have betrayed your father's trust as I did. I pray daily for your health and happiness.

I am writing also to inform you that I will soon be leaving Bologna, the translation of Avicenna and another year of studies having nearly been completed. In a few weeks' time, I will begin the journey to Spain, taking with me the alchemical manual, which you will remember from our time together. I go by way of the pilgrim's route, the way of Saint James to the shrine in Santiago, before continuing on to Toledo. Please pray for me as I undertake this journey and the translation of the text.

May Almighty God have you in keeping. Farwell, sweet and amiable Santina, and think upon me as I think upon you.

Written at Bologna, 9 April 1345
Calandrino

Reading the letter over and over again, Santina wept. She lamented the letters that were not delivered, the loss of the man she could sense but not touch. Calandrino still loved her. And yet he would move still farther away, to distant Spain. He promised her nothing, he did not ask her to join him, and yet he made known his enduring affection. She felt the same torment she had experienced the day he said goodbye to her in his cottage. As the painful memories returned, Santina thought she would have been better off never hearing from him again. Vowing never to write the scholar, Santina slipped the letter into her apron pocket and tried to resume her work. She kept wondering how Calandrino had discovered she was living with Trotula. Had Isabella written to him at the University? Or had Giacomino perhaps informed him? With matters concerning the scholar unsettled once again, it would not be easy to pretend all was well when she sat across from Trotula at the dinner table.

Facing the doors of the *Collegiatas,* the Collegiate Church that was once a cathedral, on the twelfth of June in 1345, Isabella and Bruno stood side by side and recited their vows. Santina observed the ceremony from the back of the small crowd, amid the distant relations and unknown townspeople. From her ignoble position she finally spotted Lauretta, but her older sister seemed to take no notice of her. She saw Papa as well, but he kept his gaze fixed on the steps. *So that is the way it will be*, Santina thought. Still, she did not regret coming, for Isabella had asked her to be there.

After the nuptial Mass, Santina tried to hurry away from church, for she thought to avoid a scene with Papa. She was taken by surprise when seven-year-old Francesco, Aunt Benedetta's grandson, caught up with her. "Is it true you ran away from home?"

The daughter of Rosana, Madonna Adalieta's youngest sister, was now beside her as well. "Is it true you live with the midwife in that strange cottage near the friary?"

"There's nothing strange about it," Santina said, laughing at the notion. "Many folk would be sorely lacking if Trotula were not here to help birth babies and dispense her fine herbs and specifics."

Lauretta, who now approached, caught the remark in passing. "I can only wonder at a woman who condones a daughter's willful disobedience," she said, drawing Santina aside. "Our poor father, Santina. His heart is gravely wounded," Lauretta admonished.

"Surely you realize it was never my intention to hurt Papa," Santina replied, feeling a familiar defensiveness arise in her older sister's presence.

"Do you truly fancy yourself a midwife, Santina?" Lauretta demanded. "What can you be thinking, leaving Papa to manage on his own?"

"You left home as well," Santina countered. "I wonder why I'm the one who is expected to stay behind."

Lauretta gasped. "Wherever have you learned such selfish ways, Santina? It was the will of God that I marry Sandro and take care of those poor children who needed a mother. You cannot compare my marriage or even Isabella's to what you have done so impulsively."

Santina began to see that Lauretta would not be persuaded about the matter. She had not seen her sister for many months and thought not to spoil their reunion with a bitter argument. "I'm sorry, Lauretta, truly sorry. It grieves me to cause Papa such distress," she tried. "You should not be troubling yourself over my affairs, especially in your condition."

Lauretta's hand moved reflexively to her stomach. "You can tell?" she said, a smile breaking through. "Does it show already?"

"Only to one who pays close attention to such matters. And to your own sister." Reaching for Lauretta's hand, Santina suggested the two of them speak no more of their differences.

"You're right. I must not become sorrowful over your mistakes. It would not serve the health of the infant."

After saying her goodbyes, Santina prepared to leave and tried to forget the splendid wedding banquet she would miss the following day. She would not enjoy the feast of wild game, fowl, delicate sauces, pies, delicious sweetmeats, and barrels of wine. She would not hear the musicians or dance with her cousins. There would be no witnessing the ceremonial act of placing the youngest child in the bride's arms and a gold florin in her pretty silk shoe to ensure riches and fertility. Santina was to be banished from the celebration, for Papa had not yet forgiven her.

She could almost hear Mama's voice speaking to her from above. *Pazienza, patience. Do not allow Papa's stubborn nature to fool you, Santina. Of course he still loves you. He behaves this way because he is fearful for you. Just as he used to be fearful for me.*

The thought of Mama brought a smile to her face. The next moment she ran into Ruberto. Feeling uncomfortable under his gaze, she mumbled *buon giorno*. She could not help but think of the time when he had discovered her with Calandrino at Papa's shop.

"Watch yourself out there beyond the wall," he warned.

"*Grazie,* I will be fine. The Lord protects me."

He nodded then hesitated before speaking. "People can speak unkind words."

She guessed at once that he was referring to her work with Trotula. With a sigh she asked, "What is it people are saying, Ruberto?"

"They say Trotula would have you do work that is unfit for the daughter of the cloth merchant."

"As you surely know, Trotula is a good and honest woman. Her ministrations have helped many."

"That may well be, Santina. I only thought you would want to know," he said in all sincerity. "Some say she has used *attaccatura*, attachment, to have her way."

"She uses no magic," Santina replied impatiently. "I remain at the cottage of my own accord."

"Forgive me," he said politely.

As they parted Santina fumed silently over the false accusations. Trotula deserved to be appreciated, not judged, for the assistance she rendered to those in need. It was absurd to think she had worked a spell. *If they think this of Trotula, will they think the same of me someday?* she wondered.

Monna Dianora

When Santina returned to the cottage after Isabella's wedding, Trotula was not at home. Walking into the main room, she noticed an unopened letter on the table. The script, she could tell, was Calandrino's.

I am arrived in Toledo, the scholar wrote, and he went on and on about the wonders of the Spanish city. At the end he added a personal note. *If it pleases you, send word of your welfare. I can take little comfort in the Spanish sun lest I know of the continuance of your honorable favor toward me and the establishment of your happiness.*

If he were truly concerned with my welfare, he might not have run off to Spain, Santina said to herself. While she could not deny that she was glad to know he still thought of her, little good could come of a correspondence. Although he might love her, he offered her nothing.

Wishing she could manage to forget Calandrino once and for all, Santina went early to bed and was lulled to sleep by the sound of pouring rain. She did not see Trotula until the next morning, when the midwife returned after having attended the birth of a set of twins. Clearly exhausted, Trotula was about to retire to her room when the blacksmith's young son arrived, rain dripping off his broad-brimmed cap, to say that his mother had gone into labor.

"I can go by myself," Santina offered.

Trotula considered this before replying, "Send word at once if you should need me."

Having delivered Lisa's child, Santina felt less fearful of being sent off on her own. She filled the wooden box with packets of herbs according to Trotula's specifications. There was chamomile, John's wort, shepherd's purse, and raspberry leaf as well as the forbidden herbs, which included a tincture of poppy with henbane and mandrake. Santina was not to touch the tincture, which could slow a woman's labor, unless it was clear the pain could not be borne.

Riding along by cart with the blacksmith's son through the lingering rain, Santina wore her woolen hood over her head. While she had grown more confident in her abilities, she was also aware of the inherent risks of childbirth. Still, most of the deliveries she attended with Trotula had been blessedly uncomplicated thus far. Throughout the course of a year there had been one stillbirth and two babies that did not make it past one week, but every mother had survived. As she exercised the skills she had been taught, she felt the risk of failure diminish with each successive birth.

Trotula often attributed their success to the intercession of the blessed mothers: the Virgin Mary; Elizabeth, the mother of John the Baptist; Anne, the mother of Mary. The older midwife also put stock in the charms worn by many of the laboring women—birth girdles fashioned of parchment inscribed with scriptural texts, charms, and prayer. While Santina did not doubt the influence of the saints, she was more doubtful of the countrywomen's magic.

Approaching her destination, Santina spied Tedaldo pacing back and forth outside the shop. "My wife is in terrible pain," the tall, wiry man wasted no time in saying.

"I'll do what I can to help her," she assured him as he lifted the birthing chair from the cart. Santina followed him up a dark narrow staircase to their living quarters above the shop.

"It's not like it was with the others," he said as they reached the bedroom.

"Every birth is different," Santina replied before closing the door on the man.

Upon entering the dark room, Santina sensed little hopeful anticipation in the faces of the women gathered there.

"So much blood," lamented a neighbor woman, who was sweeping up a pile of red-streaked straw.

It certainly appeared to be more than the usual bloody show that often preceded a birth. Santina drew a deep breath before seeing the woman through a painful contraction.

Recalling what Trotula had taught her about maintaining a calm and capable demeanor so as not to alarm the patient, she tried to reassure Dianora while at the same time she hoped her confidence would not prove false. "You need to drink, Dianora. You have to restore yourself to regain your strength. Bring some broth. And more hot water," she said to Dianora's sister, imitating Trotula's firm voice. She placed the *corno* around the woman's neck. "She must have shepherd's purse."

Feeling the woman's swollen belly, she wondered if the child's head was not facing down as it ought to have been. Noting the frown on Santina's face, the woman asked, "Is something the matter?"

"Your baby might be a breech. I know what to do, Dianora."

Not two weeks earlier she had watched Trotula position a

woman with her hips up high in order to induce a baby to turn. However, when the birth was imminent there was no choice but to birth the baby back end first.

Santina reminded herself that she had seen a breech delivery twice before. In her mind she heard Trotula's voice telling her exactly how to deal with the situation. *You get the mother down on all fours. You let the baby come out on its own. Don't try to pull it down. You remember how it's done. Now take hold of yourself.*

Santina also knew that the show of blood meant the child could be in danger and should be birthed as soon as possible. But when Santina examined Dianora, she found her passage not fully open and the bag of water still intact. In this case, she had to act quickly and decisively in order to hasten the delivery. It was as though Trotula was whispering into her ear, telling her that she could not afford the leisure of allowing the child to come in its own time. Using her fingers, Santina broke through the delicate tissue.

"I broke your waters," she explained.

"Will she be all right?" asked her worried sister.

The troublesome bleeding seemed to have stopped. "God willing," Santina replied.

Feeling as though the situation was now in hand, Santina prepared chamomile tea to relax the womb. There was nothing to do but wait, see Dianora through the pain, and pray.

"It's been too long," said the neighbor.

"*Si*, Madonna, we must pray to the Virgin that the baby will make haste."

The three women soothed Dianora through her contractions, in between offering her bites of bread soaked in the broth. All the while they continued their appeals to *Sancta Maria.*

"You're doing well, Dianora," Santina said, for Trotula had taught her the importance of offering reassuring words. It was typical for a woman to feel as though the pain would kill her and she would fail in her attempt to give birth.

As Santina hoped, Dianora's labor began to progress after the breaking of the water. After several more hours of painful contractions, she thought the child was about ready to make the final journey through the pelvis. Santina recognized this difficult point in the delivery where the wails grew louder and the pleas to the Holy Mother became more fervent. This was the hardest stage, right before the pushing could start.

"I can't do it!" Dianora screamed. *"Che Dio mi salvi!* God help me, I cannot!"

Santina wiped the woman's forehead with a cool cloth scented with rosemary while the neighbor woman who knew the old ways thought to make sure the stoppers were out of every bottle and jar in the house. Although Dianora was in terrible pain, Santina was afraid to give the poppy lest she slow the birth. In the end she decided to give just a small dose of the tincture.

In another hour Dianora's passage was fully open and she was more comfortable, but Santina was shocked to see a foot rather than a hind end descending through the birth canal. She thought to call for Trotula, but she quickly reminded herself of what she already knew. Besides, there was no time to send for help; Dianora had to begin the active work of pushing the baby out.

Although her confidence wavered, Santina was determined to appear calm. "The worst is over. The child is ready to be born. You have to start pushing with everything you have."

Dianora assented as they moved her from the chair to the floor. Surely the woman would find the strength within her to do it. Santina helped her to her hands and knees. Trying to speak with authority, she instructed the neighbor to support Dianora's shoulders and the sister to sit at her feet.

"*Bene,*" Santina said. "You can do it, Dianora."

As they continued on for more than half an hour, Santina felt sure the baby was indeed descending. She continued to praise Dianora's efforts, yet the woman's confidence continued to fade as time went on and there was still no baby. Santina allowed her to rest for a moment while her sister positioned the clean cloth that would catch the child. It was then when Santina noticed more blood. The quantity of the stream and the timing of it made her heart quicken. Once again she feared for the lives of the mother and child.

"Go to Tedaldo," she said to the neighbor. "Tell him to ride to Trotula's. Tell him I need her here at once."

Without waiting for further explanation, the woman ran to Dianora's husband. The following minutes seemed to stretch out into eternity. Santina returned Dianora to bed in hopes of ceasing any further progression until Trotula arrived. She forced the woman to drink more of the shepherd's purse, but neither herbs nor prayers would stop the bleeding. After a quarter hour, a tiny leg began to descend on its own as the wet sticky blood still flowed.

The three women returned Dianora to her hands and knees. As the infant's trunk was delivered, Santina supported the baby's body on her hand and forearm. Dianora might manage to do it after all. Hooking her fingers on either side of the fragile neck, she gently pulled down on the shoulders until the baby's head appeared. *Quickly now,* she prayed. *Don't let the head be trapped.*

"That's it, Dianora," she cried. "The baby's almost here. It's very close now."

Santina gently lifted the baby's body to deliver the mouth, nose, the brow, and finally the crown of the head.

The baby appeared blue when finally free. Santina's heart sank when she saw the little body, a boy, struggling to breathe, but she knew he still might live. She moved without thinking, tying the cord, clearing the baby's mouth. She rubbed him briskly with the cloth and waited for sounds of life to come from his mouth. But the infant would not cry even as Santina laid him on the table and rubbed his small chest. In her weak voice Dianora was asking to see him, to know if he was all right.

"Breathe, child, breathe," Santina whispered, even as she knew this child would not.

Suddenly the bedroom door swung open. In flew Trotula like a great silver bird.

"My baby, help my baby," Dianora cried when Trotula rushed to her side.

Scooping up the infant, Trotula dipped him into the basin of water, baptizing the child as the bishop had authorized her to do in such cases. The brief ceremony completed, Trotula began to blow into his small mouth and rub his chest, trying to revive him. The minutes passed and the baby turned darker and darker, and it became all too obvious that he was not coming into this world after all. He had lived for nine months within the darkness of his mother's body only to leave the moment he came into the light of day.

The older midwife shook her head, signaling that there was nothing more they could do. Santina watched sadly as Trotula gathered up the exquisitely formed child and placed him gently in Dianora's arms. "He's a beautiful boy, Dianora. The Lord saw fit to keep him. It was no one's fault. This one didn't come to stay."

The mother touched his tiny fingers and kissed his cheek. Her eyes filled with tears as Tedaldo, finally admitted to the room, knelt at her side to gaze at his perfect little son who had not lived.

Santina and Trotula moved through the fragile silence, gathered up the bloodied linens, prepared Dianora some raspberry leaf tea, and washed her. When they could do no more, they left the couple alone with their sorrow.

Outside the birth room Santina was afraid to look her teacher in the eye. No doubt Trotula would berate her for waiting so long to call for help. She had every reason to fear that Trotula would send her home after making such a grave mistake.

When they returned to the cottage, Trotula settled into her chair with a bowl of nettle tea and commanded Santina to tell her everything that had happened, from start to finish, at Dianora's house.

"She was bleeding before I arrived," Santina began, thinking to withhold nothing from Trotula, whose gaze was fixed upon the image of Christ baptizing St. Peter. She explained how she had given the shepherd's purse, broken the bag of waters, and allowed Dianora to rest. Tearfully, she described Dianora's suffering, the presentation of the foot, and the recurring bleeding that had caused Santina to send for help at last. When all had been told, Santina waited fearfully to hear what her mentor would say.

A sharp scolding would have been easier to accept than Trotula's show of utter disappointment. "You might have known to call for help at once, Santina," she said finally. "You waited far too long. And to try to deliver a breech on your own?"

"We delivered several breech babies before easily enough."

"Not a footling breech. Furthermore, she was bleeding. That's when you ought to have sent for me," Trotula said sharply. "These skills take years to acquire, Santina. You're still an apprentice, and you will be one for some time. *Pazienza.* You must have patience."

"What should I have done differently? Is it my fault the baby died?"

Trotula sipped her tea. "I'm not sure you did anything wrong at all, Santina," she admitted finally. "Sometimes it can't be helped."

Although Santina understood this to be true, she wanted to believe that with her care, every mother and baby would be safe. She had become a midwife to bring forth life, to discover the alchemist's secret elixir that would allow all under her care to avert death. But she had not found the elixir. She had encountered the limits of her very human hands.

Santina retreated to her small room and took to bed. That night she dreamed of vermilion red blood, wet, sticky, and flowing over Dianora. Then the figure was no longer Dianora, but Mama. Lined up in a row on the floor of the room were ten or twelve dead babies—she had not arrived in time to save them. She saw that her brother, Pietro, was among them. She was on her knees, washing the babies and wrapping them in clean, dry clothes. Dianora stood over her, accusingly, with dark, sunken, unforgiving eyes. Santina ran fleeing from the room of her dream.

It was well past daybreak when Santina awoke to the sound of Trotula's clattering at the stone sink. She washed and dressed but had little appetite for the warm bread sitting on the table. Her thoughts were only of her painful failure, the baby's death.

"You cannot blame yourself every time a life is lost," Trotula said, watching her. "There will always be mothers and babies who die despite our best efforts. You must accept this. You must also know when to ask for help."

Santina was well aware of her mistake. She also knew that mothers and babies died even under Trotula's watch. Her own mother counted among Trotula's losses. "Mama couldn't be saved," she remarked. "It couldn't have been easy for you."

Santina had pressed Trotula about the events of that day on

more than one occasion, but Trotula response always drifted to vagueness.

"No. It was not."

"What went wrong that day, Trotula?" Santina asked. "Why couldn't you save my mother and Pietro?"

Trotula sat down across from her at the table. The look of sadness on the midwife's face almost made Santina wish she hadn't asked again. This time, however, her question would be answered. The young woman fell silent and prepared to hear what Trotula had to say.

Al-Biruni

"Your mama had some bleeding during the months before her labor. I tried to convince her to rest, for I feared she would lose the child. She made it to the end of her term, though, and all seemed well enough. But she was laboring with a face-up baby and having quite a bit of pain. And then midway through she started losing blood again, just like Dianora," Trotula began.

Santina had wanted to know the exact reason why Mama had died, and yet it was painful for her to hear of Madonna Adalieta's fearsome suffering. "I did everything I could to hasten the birth when I saw the danger she was in," Trotula said. "You see, the placenta was in the wrong place—down too low, near the opening to the birth canal—and it began to tear as the opening widened."

"So Mama bled to death because the placenta was in the wrong place?" Santina inferred.

Trotula appeared to choose her words carefully. "The situation was complicated by the fact that Pietro was a very large baby with a very large head, wedged tightly into the womb," she explained.

"When it was clear we lost Pietro, Master Traverseri thought it best if the surgeon try to save your mama."

"Surgeon? You mean a surgeon cut the baby out of Mama?" Santina began to envision a horrific scene of Pietro's skull being cut apart with knives so he could be removed from Mama.

"Your father put a lot of faith in the doctor's opinion. And it's likely enough that I could have done no better," Trotula said. "This was your mama's fourth child, and her labor had gone on for hours—and so the womb was very thin. She was bound to rupture as she did. Adalieta bled to death, and Pietro never breathed."

"So nothing could have saved Mama and the baby?" Santina said.

Trotula did not answer at once. "A Caesarean operation might have been attempted, but Master Traverseri was afraid of it, naturally," she finally replied.

Santina recalled the image of Master Traverseri, dressed in his scarlet robe trimmed in fur, talking with Papa before Mama died. The details of that day, imprinted upon her memory, flashed before her as Trotula paused again in her story.

Santina had just returned from Calandrino's cottage. Still holding the red stone the scholar had given her, she cracked open the door of her mother's room. In horror she watched as Master Traverseri plucked four slimy, black leeches from a glass jar and placed them, one by one, on Mama's delicate white ankle. Santina knew that bloodletting was considered a beneficial therapy for many ailments, yet seeing the worms grow fat with Mama's blood turned her stomach.

She disappeared into the dark recesses of the hallway and slipped to the floor. Eventually Master Traverseri emerged from the room and was joined by Papa. In hushed tones the doctor spoke of Mama's humors—the four bodily fluids that influenced her health. She understood little of what he said, but she knew he had tried to help Mama. Margherita, who was surely listening in as well, hovered in the staircase as she sprinkled more salt to deter the evil spirits that were troubling Mama.

"It's the baby's size and position, Iacopo," Master Traverseri was explaining. "And Adalieta is losing blood."

"Surely there must be a way to help her, Maestro," Papa said, his voice desperate, running one hand nervously through his silver hair. "Why is it so difficult?"

"Trotula has her own ways. But it's time to do what is necessary."

Santina panicked, sensing Mama was in serious danger. Barging in on Papa and Master Traverseri, she cried, "Why is Mama having so much trouble? Why doesn't anyone know what to do?"

"It's in God's hands," Papa told Santina. He stroked her head, trying to comfort her, but she could see the torment on his face.

Another worrisome moan, more sad and quiet now, followed Santina as she retreated down the hall and joined her sisters in their bedroom. Lauretta tried to smile in greeting, but Santina could tell that she was afraid, too. Isabella crawled into their shared bed and hid beneath the soft wool blankets while Santina tried to hide her tears.

"Did Papa tell you anything?" Lauretta whispered to Santina.

"I heard him talking to Master Traverseri," Santina admitted. "The baby is trapped, and Mama is bleeding."

Isabella poked her head out from beneath the covers.

"Is the baby never coming out?"

Lauretta scooped up the youngest one in her arms. *"It's just taking a very long time."*

Santina huddled close with her sisters. Except for an occasional whimpering, like the sound of a trapped, wounded animal coming through the thin walls, the house was quiet.

"She's going to be all right," Lauretta said, convincing no one. *"It is not an easy thing to have a baby. It was very hard when you were born as well, Isabella. It took nearly two days before you finally came."*

"It wasn't like this," Santina said.

"You can't possibly remember, you were too young," Lauretta replied. *"We should pray for Mama and the baby now. Soon our new brother or sister will be here."*

Prayers nervously mumbled, Santina and her sisters waited in the uneasy calm, pierced here and there by the sound of men's voices and footsteps, comings and goings from the lying-in room, the scratching of a branch of the apricot tree against the shutters. Lauretta lit a candle to keep away any darkness that had fallen upon them, in case Margherita was right about evil spirits. Mama's bedroom door opened and closed once more. Santina heard someone walking down the stairs. Then there was nothing, just a long, uninterrupted silence within the gloaming.

The silence stretched on and on. Santina sensed that something had happened. Had the baby brother or sister finally arrived? She did not hear the cries of a newborn infant or relieved, happy voices. Aware of the eerie stillness of the house, Santina stood upright. She did not want to know what she already sensed in her heart.

Eyes brimming with tears, she looked over to Lauretta and Isabella, who seemed unaware. Still, she prayed that she was wrong. Don't let her be dead. Don't let Mama be dead.

She felt something waft through the room. Was it a soft breeze? She turned to the window but the shutters had been tightly closed to protect the baby. Then she saw a misty, silver film, almost like smoke, suspended at the foot of the bed.

"It's Mama," Santina whispered. "Mama's gone," she said to her sisters, who seemed lost in their own thoughts and uncomprehending. "Do you see it?"

"See what, Santina?"

"It's not there anymore," she said, for the spirit had already faded away. "It was Mama. I'm sure it was Mama."

"Did she have the baby?" Isabella asked.

Lauretta, then Isabella, jumped out of bed and ran toward Mama's room, but Santina knew what they would discover. Following slowly behind, Santina saw her two sisters standing before Papa, whose eyes revealed everything.

He stretched out his arms, encircling his three daughters. "Mama died," he said. "Your brother too. They're with our Father in Heaven now."

Santina stood sobbing with Papa and her sisters until the priest walked out of Mama's room, followed by Margherita and Master Traverseri. The doctor nodded solemnly as he departed. Lastly, Trotula emerged, teary-eyed.

"I am deeply sorry." Trotula looked at each of them in silent, sincere apology before proceeding soundlessly along the hall.

Papa hardly took any notice of the doctor or Trotula. Wordlessly, he left his daughters and continued down the stairs while Santina followed behind.

"Why did she die, Papa?" she called after him, though he did not answer. "Why?" She hurried across the hall, trying to catch up, but Lauretta held her back.

"He needs to be alone now," Lauretta said, wiping her cheek and guiding her younger sister back upstairs.

They both started nervously when the back door of solid oak slammed shut and shook the house. Later that night, when she tried to sleep, Santina could hear Papa crying out. She tore open the wooden shutters and looked to the courtyard below. Papa stood there, a shadow in the pale light of the moon, before Mama's herb garden.

"This cannot be! Dio mio! How can this be?" Papa wailed into the darkness. Then he was crying out for Mama. "Adalieta! Adalieta!" Santina watched and listened as Papa went on and on, cursing the loss of Mama and the baby.

Frozen at the window, Santina was unable to move, unable to call out to him. She thought of Calandrino's alchemy. She recalled what he said about the alchemist's ability to transform, to change shape, to be able to walk through closed doors. She wondered if Mama could do this now and if she would be able to come and go from Heaven. If what Calandrino said was true, then Mama might find a way to return to them. At this very moment, she might be right here, standing beside Papa, telling him she would be back soon.

Yet Santina could not see Mama. She longed for someone, anyone, to come hold her, to tell her everything would be all right again. It seemed impossible that Mama was gone. Who would take care of her and her sisters?

*Her mother was dead, and yet Santina could some-
how feel her. Before drifting off to a fitful sleep, she told
herself she had to find the philosopher's stone. She had to
discover the Egyptian secret of eternal youth and victory
over death.*

Santina could still envision Mama lying in her bed, pale and
unmoving, after Master Traverseri and Trotula left the room that
day years ago. Papa never spoke of what happened. Now she wondered if Papa had put his confidence in the wrong person. What if
Trotula could have saved Mama?

While Papa would not easily admit he made a mistake in call-
ing for Master Traverseri and allowing the surgeon to work on
Mama, it now appeared to Santina that Trotula might have saved
Mama if the doctor had not interfered.

"Have you cut through a womb before?" Santina asked.

"Old Ninetta taught me. Sometimes you have to take a baby
that way. But only when the mother is gone. When the mother's
death is certain, then you can do the Caesarean. The problem is,
the baby's chance of surviving isn't good by that time," Trotula
explained. Under her breath she added, "In a very rare case it's
done earlier."

"Have you ever seen both mother and baby survive it?"
Santina asked, astonished.

"Enough questions," Trotula snapped.

Santina had already heard what she wanted to know. If Trotula
had been allowed to exercise her skills, two lives might have been
saved.

"They might have lived," she said, struggling to keep her
voice even. "It was Master Traverseri's fault. He wouldn't let you
do the operation."

"No, that's not what I said," Trotula chided her. "You can't second guess what might have been done after the fact. Master Traverseri gave the advice he thought best. He wanted to help your mother. Believe me. He took the loss very hard."

Santina was not satisfied. It was now apparent that Mama's death was the result of something more than bad luck. "Why did Papa listen to Master Traverseri instead of you, Trotula? You could have saved them."

Trotula went silent for a moment. When she finally spoke, her voice was unyielding as she went about setting Santina straight. "I want you to understand one thing: It's never been up to me to decide who lives and who dies. And it will never be your responsibility either. That's entirely up to God," she insisted. "Anyone who imagines she possesses this authority thinks too much of herself. It might appear otherwise, but you and I are not the ones who bring about the cures."

Santina tried to bite her tongue, but she could not entirely agree. She believed they could, in fact, save lives. There were a number of instances when it seemed as though Trotula had succeeded in altering fate. "But you have brought about cures," she countered. "Like when you healed Caravaggio's leg. And the twins might not have lived if you weren't there to deliver them."

"There are miracles all right," Trotula replied. "I've seen a few of them. But they don't come from you or me," she maintained. "You must not confuse your own actions with the power of God." Trotula stood before the stained glass window that scattered a rainbow of colors across the room. "This window was made by a man who is long dead. It's not the glass that makes the light dance like jewels. It's the sun," she explained. "You and I are the windows. We are not the sun."

Rising from the table, Trotula announced her plan to visit her friend, Sister Anna, at San Girolamo in the village. Left alone, Santina was still not convinced by Trotula's argument. With her own eyes she had witnessed the power of Trotula's medicine. The midwife worked with brews and poultices the way a sculptor worked with the chisel. As the slip of the chisel cracked the marble, so would an error in judgment hurt the patient. Santina could not shake the notion that Mama and Pietro might be alive if it were not for Master Traverseri's refusal to allow the operation.

She tried to turn her attention to the tasks she had been assigned. She watered and weeded the garden, pulled the vegetables for the day's meal, started the soup, and swept the floor, yet she felt no easiness with this routine. When she could find no more excuses to delay her departure, she gathered the salve made with Our Lady's mantle for the old grandmother afflicted with bedsores. Standing before Trotula's window of colored glass, Santina paused briefly to gaze upon Christ, haloed in gold. She wondered where His divine presence had been when Dianora's son and Mama and Pietro were in need.

Heavy rains continued through the summer of 1345. By September it was clear the farmers' crops were ruined. While many would go hungry that winter, Trotula had thought to set aside plenty of meal, rice, and beans, and the kitchen garden had not fared too poorly. Santina, however, gave less thought to famine than the idea of cutting a baby from a womb. Not on a dead woman, on a live one. If she could master this skill, then scarcely a mother or baby would be lost under her watch. She would possess the alchemist's secret—the philosopher's stone, the key to immortality.

"Will you tell me how it's done, Trotula?" Santina asked.

"Perhaps in time."

"What if it has to be done to save the mother?"

"The procedure poses great risk. It's unheard of for a woman to survive it," Trotula reminded her. "We are only permitted to do it when the mother's death is certain."

Yet Trotula had already admitted that such operations had been done, in rare cases, on live patients as well as dead ones. She wanted to push Trotula further on the subject but did not dare. Instead, she pored over Trotula's treasured copy of Galen's *Opera Omnia,* trying to understand the hidden mysteries of the female form. Stashed away in Trotula's wardrobe, she discovered two more Islamic texts. She read, with rapt attention, the illustrated work by Abu al-Qasim al-Zahrawi, which had been translated into Latin. The book discussed many wondrous procedures, unknown surgical instruments, powerful anesthetics, and the precautions in cleanliness that must be taken.

Most astonishing of all was the text by Al-Biruni, *Al-Athar al-Baqiyah `an al-Qurun al-Khaliyah*. The book offered a description as well as twenty-four illustrations of the Caesarean operation. After Santina felt she grasped what she had read, she wanted to broach the subject with Trotula once again. However, she could not easily admit she had read the books that were hidden in the midwife's wardrobe.

"You said that both the mother and child can survive the procedure if the surgeon doesn't wait too long," Santina commented one evening. "I know it's very dangerous, Trotula, but it has been done. Will you teach me someday?"

Trotula did not bother to look up from *The Elegy of Lady Fiammetta* by Giovanni Boccaccio, which she was reading by candlelight. "If the time comes, Santina. It can't be planned."

She and Trotula had traveled some distance that September day. The journey had clearly tired the older midwife, leaving her in no mood to discuss the topic. Trotula would never admit it, but she no longer possessed the stamina of a young woman. Santina also suspected her mentor was developing a degree of complacency. This aspect of Trotula could very well prevent Santina from learning everything she needed to learn—in particular, the surgery that might have saved Mama and Pietro.

After Trotula dragged herself off to bed, Santina considered the possibility of finding a surgeon who could teach her what she wanted to know. Surely there were techniques to be learned and followed. The secrets of nature and the ways of God were being revealed more and more each day through wondrous human inventions and the advancement of science. She knew that the learned men from the University in Salerno were able to perform a great number of remarkable procedures. She had heard of a doctor in Florence who could remove cataracts with a silver needle and mend a battle-torn face with a graft of skin from the arm. For every ailment, there was the possibility of a new and wondrous solution.

With so much scientific knowledge to be had, it seemed unreasonable that she could give a woman dying in childbirth nothing more than herbs and prayers. There was only one person with whom she could discuss this matter: Calandrino. She had vowed not to write him, but this was a matter of science rather than love. She could only hope that he was still in Toledo and that the letter would reach him.

To Calandrino Donati, Santina Pietra sends her most kind greeting in the Lord.

Because you especially desire to hear of my welfare, I will tell you I am well pleased to be apprenticed to Trotula and

*to assist this good woman as she provides for the health
and well being of expectant mothers and many others who
reside among us here in the countryside....*

Santina went on, with no mention of what had previously occurred between them, about her desire to advance her understanding of the treatments of disease and the care of expectant mothers.
In a rather matter-of-fact way she explained what she knew about
cutting through a womb, and she asked Calandrino if he had any
knowledge of the procedure. It occurred to her that he might be
rather shocked to hear her thoughts on the subject of childbirth.
On the other hand, he was a scholar who had dabbled in alchemy
and knew a few things about Arabic medicine. If Trotula would
have her remain in ignorance, perhaps Calandrino might offer
some learned advice.

Confessione

The surrounding woods colored over in shades of dark green, yellow, and brown as Santina waited for a reply from Calandrino. She was beginning to think her letter had never been delivered when finally, just before Christmas, the anticipated response arrived.

To Santina Pietra be this letter delivered. I, Calandrino, send greetings in the Lord.

With the utmost of interest I read your letter dated 16 September 1345. It is most heartening to learn of your worthy endeavor to expand your knowledge of the treatment of suffering women. You would do well to continue reading Trotula's texts, for the old Arabs' grasp of medicine and surgery exceeds that which is known by any physician in San Gimignano. In regards to the procedure discussed in your letter, Sir Ugo, who learned much from an Arab physician named Faraj, said that the operation was known to have been successfully performed on living women.

Throughout antiquity the Arabs pursued a disciplined approach to the treatment of disease and the development of surgical techniques. In order to further their understanding of anatomy, Muslim physicians were known to dissect apes. This is, of course, not an alternative you might pursue. But the possibility of utilizing new methods in order to acquire knowledge must be kept in mind. Surely, there are many good and useful discoveries of which we have not yet dreamt.

You must nurture your curious mind, Santina. Also, you must make careful notes of your observations. Only then can you begin to formulate a scientific theory whereby you might affect a useful cure. Trotula has been practicing her art for many years. You will do well to follow her closely.

Here in Toledo I think of you often. Regrettably, I have not located a translator able to decipher the alchemical text. At the present time my patron requests that I turn my attention to a newly discovered work of Avicenna. Upon completion of the assignment in Bologna, I hope to travel to the South of France, for there are Jewish scholars residing in Carpentras who might be up to the task. If I am fortunate, I will find a learned Jew willing to assist me.

Almighty God have you in his blessed keeping. I think of you often.

Calandrino

Written at Toledo 14 November 1345

I think of you often, too, she thought, folding the parchment and tucking it inside her *cassone*. She thought not to reveal the nature of her correspondence to Trotula, although the midwife may have guessed the author of the letter. While it did Santina little good to pine away for the scholar, it was heartening to know that he did not think she was beyond her realm in contemplating matters of science. Having received this bit of encouragement, Santina felt a measure of pride. Perhaps in due time she would find a way to accomplish that which she envisioned.

The cold weather and Santina's second winter without Calandrino was now upon her. She had helped Trotula stock the workroom shelves with jars of herbed vinegar—old Ninetta's recipe, brewed with sage, rosemary, thyme, lemon balm, hyssop, mint, and garlic—believed to ward off any number of diseases. She and Trotula had filled sacks of dried herbs and bottles and vials with specifics for colds, aching joints, wheezing lungs, and chapped, red skin. Santina knew how to make useful remedies from most of the herbs harvested from the physic garden, where the healing plants grew, near the back of the property.

A few special plants grew hidden behind the thicket hen-bane, monkshood, and mandrake. Medicines crafted from these herbs, along with those made from the seedpods of the poppy plants, were to be prepared solely by the mistress. While these forbidden plants had been used for years and years by any number of midwives, Trotula feared that some might misconstrue their ministrations as dark magic rather than the wisdom of the *nonnas* who had been healing with herbs for generations in Italy.

Santina and Trotula were well prepared to treat all matter of ailments in the winter of 1346, but the season progressed uneventfully with nothing more than the usual array of coughs and rheumy noses. Then in February one baby was strangled by the birthcord and a breech baby nearly didn't make it. After these losses, Santina was reminded of what she still did not know and what Trotula refused to teach her.

Every so often the older midwife had a mind to disappear into the village alone, leaving Santina with the dreary routine of her chores. Trotula would explain that she planned to visit Sister Anna at San Girolamo or go to market, yet Santina sometimes imagined the real reason she was left behind was because Trotula wanted to withhold secret knowledge.

Haunted by the loss of Dianora's child, Santina wished the older midwife would teach her something more. While Santina's experience grew, she feared coming upon another situation where she could do nothing at all to save the mother or baby. She continued on with a foreboding sense about what might happen in the future even though the predictable routine of her days suggested such fears were unfounded.

A chilly day in early March offered Santina the opportunity to assist with an altogether different type of delivery. She was drawing water from the well after Trotula had left. Pulling up on the rope, Santina noticed the orange and black cat—which she had not seen for some time—pacing nervously near the barn. As Santina approached, the cat mewed loudly. When the animal stopped to sit and wash herself, an enormous round stomach came into view. It was apparent that the cat would soon give birth.

After carrying the bucket inside, Santina filled a small bowl with almond milk. She brought the bowl and a box lined with brown wool out to the barn and made a comfortable nest for the mother-to-be. Knowing Trotula expected her to check on Filomena and her infant down the road, Santina reluctantly departed from the cottage. Her concern for the cat was soon forgotten, for she knew cats birthed their kittens easily enough on their own.

The instant she returned to the barn later that afternoon, Santina knew that something was terribly wrong with the cat. The animal lay unmoving in a small pool of blood and there were no kittens to be seen. When Santina nudged her, the cat growled but barely stirred. She saw that a kitten had started to emerge, backside first, from the bloody birth canal.

Santina tried to ease the tiny creature out, but it was obviously trapped. Racing back to the cottage, she snatched up the necessary supplies as well as a sponge that had been steeped with soporific herbs and then dried. Trotula kept several of them on hand for emergencies. She soaked the sponge in water and returned to the barn where she held the sponge over the cat's nose and mouth. The thirsty cat eagerly chewed on the sponge and was soon put to sleep. Santina then placed the cat on the workbench and positioned her on her back. Praying that the animal would not suffer and hoping that her motive somehow justified her madness, she prepared to make an incision into the soft furry belly. *In order to further their knowledge of anatomy, Arab physicians were known to dissect apes*, Calandrino had written.

Hardly daring to breathe, she drew a long, shallow slice down the animal's center. Feeling faint as the cat flinched and blood oozed onto the table, Santina lowered her head. Forcing herself to continue, she cut all the way through to the wall of muscle. Tentatively, she pressed the knife down through the resistant muscle, through what had to be the round, red womb. With trembling hands, she pierced the sac and stood motionless, wishing she had never started.

Gathering her wits, she pushed aside the tissue and reached in with her hand to find the tiny wet creatures enclosed in their protective coverings. One by one she extracted the kittens—four including the one that was trapped—and set them on a square of soft linen. Quickly, she worked to remove the placenta from their faces and mouths. Rubbing them briskly with the cloth, she begged each one to wake up. Nearly lifeless at first, they gradually began to breathe and open their sleepy eyes.

Returning her attention to the mother, her heart sank. The victim of her unskilled hands, the mother cat lay helpless, blood seeping into her matted fur. Santina could only imagine what Trotula would do if she saw this hasty butchering.

It was obviously too late to save her, nevertheless Santina began to sew the cat together. The cut had been imprecise, jagged, and the procedure had taken too long. Yet the kittens had been birthed and three of them were still alive. Maybe she had not failed completely, though the sight of the dead cat filled her with remorse for what she had done.

The kittens' eyes were tightly closed. They were so weak, so helpless, and there was no mother to lick them clean of the yellow sac or nurse them. Santina knew what she could do to help the kittens live: almond milk strengthened with oil was needed. She would cover them with straw and keep them warm in the shed. She would tell Trotula they were orphaned.

Later that day, Santina wrapped the dead mother cat in the bloodstained wool and buried her well beyond the cottage. Teary eyed, Santina laid dried rose petals on her grave. She could only hope that her impulsive actions would not be discovered.

Repentant, Santina nurtured the kittens with as many tiny feedings as she could manage. Only the largest—the orange male—managed to survive. After six weeks, Santina brought him his first meal of finely chopped pieces of meat mixed with almond milk. His survival was something of a miracle, leading her to wonder if God completely condemned her efforts. Whatever the judgment, she thought not to write Calandrino about what she had done. As she was entering the barn to retrieve her work gloves, Trotula came upon Santina and the newly adopted pet.

"Where did you happen about this creature?" she asked. "You ought beware of cats, not take them in, Santina."

Recalling her sinful deed, Santina's face grew warm with shame. The mother cat and her other kittens were dead and buried in the woods, but Trotula had no way of knowing what Santina had done.

"It looks like the cat that used to sit in the garden," Trotula continued as Santina's face flushed deeper. Sure that Trotula could read the guilt on her face, Santina winced. "She must have been the mother," her mentor surmised.

Santina's eyes filled with tears, her sin no longer contained. "The mother was near death, Trotula," she blurted out. "I cut through her womb to deliver the kittens."

Trotula's eyes became slits as she took in this confession. Santina knew at once there would be penance to pay. Her fool-hardy actions had caused the death of innocent living creatures. Santina desperately wished she had never touched the cat, but it was too late to take back what she had done. All she could do now was apologize for her sin and hope that Trotula would not send her back to Papa's.

"So you decided to take matters into your own hands then?" Trotula finally asked, gazing in the direction of the village.

"The first kitten was trapped, Trotula. It was a breech. I tried to ease it out, but it was no use."

"Was the mother cat dead or were you hell-bent on doing the operation?" Trotula demanded.

"No. I mean *Si!* The cat was near lifeless. It's the truth, Trotula," Santina stammered, doubting the sincerity of her own words. "It's true I wanted to learn how to do the operation," she admitted through her tears. "I didn't plan for it to happen like this." There was little she could say to defend herself.

"Santina, I don't have to tell you what an impulsive thing you did," Trotula said. "No good can come to us from harming a cat. Furthermore, you're far from ready to take your education into your own hands. I've been practicing midwifery for the better part of my life. Do you suppose I learned everything there is to know in one year? Or two? For heaven's sake, *pazienza*! You must have patience, Santina. You can't learn everything overnight.

"You have to acquire more than skills in order to be a good midwife. You have to acquire sound judgment, Santina. You have to know when to act and when not to act."

"I'm sorry, Trotula," Santina said, owning that she had done more than inflict a traumatic death on a feline. She had disregarded Trotula's guidance and failed to trust her teacher. She had committed a grave deception. Despite all this, Santina could not let go of her ideas about the Caesarean.

"I need to know what to do when a woman isn't able to deliver," she began, though she knew Trotula was unlikely to change her mind. "We're midwives, Trotula. We should always know what to do. It's our business to know, isn't it?"

"You know well enough what to do, Santina. When the time comes and an operation is called for, I'll show you how it's done."

Because she was afraid the time would come and Trotula would not be there, the answer did not satisfy Santina. At the risk of infuriating her mentor further, she asked, "Couldn't we try to deliver a lamb this way?"

"Have you heard nothing I've said, Santina?" the midwife replied, clearly exasperated with the young woman. "You're getting too far ahead of yourself. It will get you into trouble if you're not careful."

"But people want us to help them, Trotula. They depend on us."

Santina was distracted when the kitten mewed and scampered away. "There's a limit to what people will stand for in San Gimignano, and it's high time you learn where the line is," Trotula went on. "For the most part, people are indifferent to cunning folk. But they also know that our work can harm as well as heal. If they come to think we use our knowledge to purposely harm someone, we'll be demonized in no time.

"When I was a young girl, Ninetta delivered a set of twins that was fused together at the midsection. They were stillborn. People starting saying that the mother had done something to insult Ninetta before the birth and Ninetta had cast *malocchio* on her. Everyone looked at Ninetta as though she'd caused the misfortune, and no one would call on her. We had little to eat that year," Trotula told Santina, who did not dare interrupt.

"What do you think would happen if anyone learned what you did to that cat? Or if you operated on one of Caravaggio's sheep? You'd be an accused *strega*, witch, in no time," she said. "Tell no one, Santina. *Nessuno*. I mean *no one*."

Her mentor went about purifying the barn with salt and uttering prayers to counteract the evil that had been done. Santina took Trotula's point to heart. The thought of being burned at the stake as a witch made her reconsider her quest for knowledge and the elixir of life. While she would not necessarily concede that there was nothing to be done to alter the painful path of tragedy, she could not help but shudder at Trotula's warning.

Filippa

Near midsummer there was a lull in the midwives' work, during which no babies were due for some time. Santina was returning to the cottage with a basket of lettuce, picked fresh from the garden, when she saw a brown palfrey with a fine saddle tied to a tree. Although it resembled her father's horse, she did not dare to hope Papa had come to visit. Hesitating outside the door, Santina stood listening to the conversation within. Indeed, it was Papa.

"It's time for her to come home, you must see that," her father was saying.

"Just what, exactly, did you hear?" Trotula asked.

"They say she's not herself anymore. The truth is, they say you are both *streghe*."

"Like me, Santina uses herbs to heal, not to harm."

"They can't make sense of why my daughter would give up her comfortable life."

Hearing this, Santina burst into the room. "This is old gossip, Papa. Ruberto said much the same to me at Isabella's wedding."

"Gossip spreads," Papa said, taking in the sight of his daughter in a worn work dress and wimple askew. "People begin to believe what they hear again and again."

"Those who say such things forget there are many who rely upon our help."

"This has gone on long enough, Santina," her father said, although the fight seemed to have left him.

"I can't give up my work, Papa."

"You're still not too old, though no one in San Gimignano will have you. But the reason I'm here is to tell you about Taddeo da Certaldo. He's returned from the East a rich man, and he's seeking a wife in earnest. Something might be arranged."

While Santina thought little of Papa's news, she understood that he had come to the cottage out of concern for her well-being. He still loved her, despite her disobedience.

"Thank you, Papa," she said. "But I cannot marry Messer Taddeo."

A frown flitted across Papa's face before he drank down the last of the wine offered by Trotula. Santina studied his hands—fragile skin stretched across gnarled bone. Her father was growing old. When he rose to leave, he allowed Santina to kiss him goodbye. Having been forgiven at long last, she began to wonder if she was being selfish in choosing to remain at the cottage rather than return with him. Santina watched her father ride away and Trotula, as though sensing her doubt, came to her side.

The wind had picked up and blew the hems of their gowns. "Help me gather the roses before we lose the petals in the storm, Santina."

She plucked the richly perfumed, heavy red blossoms that were already drooping on their slender stems. Her basket was nearly full when she felt the first raindrop. She thought of Papa riding down the road. He would be caught in the downpour; his clothes would be soaked by the time he reached the house. Hopefully, Margherita would see that he put on dry clothes and Rosa would serve him a warm supper. Would he sit in his chair afterward and sip his wine and remember all those who had left him?

Thunder rolled as she and Trotula stood side by side in the workroom pulling apart the petals and spreading them out on long wooden trays to dry. "Do you want to return home, Santina?" Trotula asked.

Santina shook her head. "No, but I do not wish to be called *strega*. People don't understand the work we do."

"There are many things that people in San Gimignano don't understand," Trotula added. "I have learned to pay it no heed."

Santina resolved that she would ignore the gossip and live exactly as she saw fit, just as Trotula had always done. Even so, she could not quell the fear that such unpleasant talk would lead to further acts of unkindness.

Although Papa tried no more to persuade her to leave the mid-wife's cottage, Santina returned home to celebrate feast days and Twelfth Night with her family. When she began her third winter with Trotula in 1347, Santina was almost twenty-one years of age. She had seen babies come into the world and grow into toddlers, and she had seen other babies live only weeks or days before departing in soft whispers. The losses were never easy to take, but Santina persevered while trying to content herself with the knowledge that her work was useful and pleasing to God.

She wanted for nothing material at this time, and yet a vague longing lingered in her heart. Despite all that was right, an awareness of Calandrino's absence stayed with her. The letters they wrote to one another were chaste, composed of the details of their work and the curiosities of the day. Santina learned that Calandrino, having completed the translation of Avicenna for his patron, was safely arrived in Carpentras. She did not know if it was an ambition to translate the alchemical text or a yearning to visit foreign lands that kept the scholar from completing his advanced studies in Bologna or returning home to San Gimignano. She reminded herself that she had not seen him in three years, and there was no point in loving a man who could not be troubled to make the journey to San Gimignano. At this point the bond was friendship, not love, she told herself.

In February, Santina's musings about Calandrino and the usual routine at the cottage were interrupted by a rapid pounding at the front door. It was a woman by the name of Filippa. She was clearly distressed.

"*Per favore.* Please, my sister needs help," cried Filippa, who appeared nearly at the end of her rope herself. "She's been in labor since yesterday morning. A doctor was called, but he said the baby could not be delivered and he left us. I'm afraid she'll die."

Santina, puzzled by the story, was not sure how to answer. She wondered why a doctor had been summoned, why he had left, and what circumstances were preventing the baby from being delivered. Seeing that Filippa, was thoroughly distraught, Santina was inclined to go to her at once. There were questions yet to be answered, but time was of the essence; the woman needed to be seen.

Trotula, who sat at the table with her morning tea, did not stir. "*Un momento,* wait a moment. Tell me what this is all about, Madonna," she said calmly. "Why was a doctor summoned? And why did he leave your sister?"

Santina could see that Filippa was reluctant to answer.

Supposing these questions might be answered at a later time, Santina began to gather the supplies, but Trotula raised her hand as though to stop her.

"This is no time to keep secrets," Trotula chided. It was apparent she would not budge until she knew the entire story. "You must keep nothing from me if you want my help. Who is your sister?"

"Her name is Caterina."

"Who is her husband?"

"She is a widow," Filippa told Trotula. "The widow of Andreuccio Torello, the cobbler."

"So this is Andreuccio's child?" Trotula asked her.

Santina turned in surprise to look at Trotula. Surely Trotula knew as well as Santina that Andreuccio had been dead for some time and could not be the father of the widow's baby.

"Yes, of course," Filippa agreed.

"Andreuccio is long in his grave," Trotula fumed. "If you want me to help you, don't tell me lies, woman."

Santina did not dare move as she waited for Filippa to explain herself.

"Very well. You leave me no choice. The father of the child is Nastagio Palmerini."

Santina's eyes darted to Trotula. Caterina had no ordinary lover; Nastagio Palmerini was the son of the wealthiest man in San Gimignano.

"Ferondo Palmerini's son," Trotula exclaimed. "*Dio mio.*"

"Please, Trotula. Caterina needs help," Filippa begged.

Santina understood that Trotula would not rise from her chair until she knew everything. The scandalous nature of Caterina's situation was now obvious. She was the paramour of Nastagio Palmerini, Ferondo Palmerini's son and sole heir. While Santina knew little of Nastagio, she had heard Papa speak of his father on occasion. Ferondo Palmerini was often despised for his practice of offering noblemen loans with interest so they would not lose their precious properties. He was known to be ruthless.

"Who sent the doctor?" Trotula demanded.

"The doctor is Florentine, a friend of the family," she confessed. "He came as a personal favor to Messer Ferondo. I've delivered a number of babies myself, but nothing I do seems to help."

"You ought to have sent for me in the first place," Trotula reprimanded.

"Yes, forgive me. But we thought the doctor could help Caterina. He was with us through most of the night. Then this morning when the baby still hadn't come, he went to speak with Messer Palmerini. When he returned, he told us it was hopeless, and he left."

Santina was stunned as she came to comprehend that Caterina was left to die. "Who would do such a thing?" she gasped. "We need to go to her at once." At this point Trotula had surely been convinced to offer her assistance.

Trotula held up her hand. "Why is Ferondo Palmerini helping your sister?" she demanded. "Why should a child born out of wedlock be of concern to him?"

Santina did not know the answer. It was true that Ferondo had gone out of his way to show an interest in a child whom he might have viewed as inconvenient at best. He was not a man easily given to charity.

Filippa nodded, as though realizing she had no choice but to answer. "Nastagio is betrothed to Count Bertrand's daughter," she admitted. "But he loves Caterina. He doesn't want to marry the Count's daughter."

"Of course. Caterina and the baby threaten the arrangement," Trotula concluded.

"Then why would he send the family physician?" Santina wondered.

"I would not be surprised if the so-called physician was sent by Ferondo to ensure that the child would not live in the first place."

"No," Santina said. "It can't be." She found Trotula's conjecture hard to believe. Was this man, Ferondo Palmerini, some sort of a monster? "We have to go to her, Trotula. We can't leave her to die."

If Trotula felt similar outrage, she kept it concealed. Having gained a clearer understanding of what she faced, the midwife finally conceded. "I'll see what I can do to help your sister," she said, rising in no hurry from her chair.

Filippa waited outside while Santina and Trotula gathered what they needed. Just before leaving the cottage, Trotula paused before the image of the Virgin on the wall. When Trotula turned to look at Santina, the older woman opened her mouth as though to speak. Sensing Trotula's thought to leave her behind at the cottage, Santina pushed ahead through the door.

Once they were well on their way to the village, Santina stopped to consider the power of Ferondo Palmerini. She began to feel uneasy about the situation awaiting them at the cobbler's shop.

Caterina

Santina and Trotula arrived at the cobbler's shop to find
Caterina beyond exhaustion, her large eyes wide with fear,
her hair an unruly mess. She was a widow, and yet she
appeared none older than Santina. Despite her suffering,
the beauty that had captivated Nastagio Palmerini was apparent.

Trotula held Caterina's delicate white hand within her strong
sturdy grip. "I've delivered hundreds of babies, Caterina. I'll do
everything I can to help you."

As the elder midwife examined Caterina, Santina stood alongside. She noted that the young woman's hips were narrow as a
girl's and the lower curve of her spine was exaggerated. When
Trotula frowned, Santina already suspected why the labor had
ceased to progress and why the doctor had determined that nothing more could be done.

When Trotula was through, she ordered Filippa and the maidservant out of the room. "Your passage is fully open, Caterina,"
she said after she and Santina were alone with the woman. "I suspect it has been for some time. But the baby hasn't descended into
position so that you can push him out."

Caterina grimaced in pain as she endured another contraction. "*Che Santa Maria me salvi.* Please help me!" she pleaded. "I can't go on any longer."

"You see, the baby is large and your bones lie close together," Trotula continued as Santina already surmised the only possible alternative. "That's why the baby hasn't been able to turn or move through the passage."

"Is there nothing you can do to save my baby? Nothing at all?"

When Trotula did not respond to Caterina's desperate plea, she wondered if the woman would be left to die after all. Breaking the silence, Santina spoke up. "We can cut through your womb to take the baby, Caterina."

Trotula threw her a scathing glance but said nothing to contradict her.

In a weak voice Caterina asked, "Is it the only way?"

"I know it sounds frightening," Santina replied, "but Trotula knows how it's done."

"It's not a simple thing," Trotula interrupted. "And we would have to obtain permission—"

"There's no time," Santina said. "She's waited too long already. You said yourself Ferondo Palmerini would not have this child live."

"Please, do whatever you can," Caterina begged.

"You might not survive," Trotula told her.

"Will she survive if we do nothing?" Santina countered.

Caterina and Santina waited for Trotula's answer. Without speaking the midwife went to her box of herbs for the horned amulet. She placed the charm around Caterina's neck then prayed in earnest to San Giuseppe, St. Joseph, that mother and child would be protected from all evil. Finally, she told Santina to prepare the soporific sponge.

Relieved that Trotula was finally moving to action, Santina did as she was told and soaked the sponge that had been infused with the forbidden herbs—henbane, mandrake, and poppy—in hot water. Santina held the sponge over Caterina's nose and instructed her to breathe in the vapors and chew on the sponge as well. While waiting for the sleep-inducing effect to take hold, Trotula whispered in Santina's ear.

"You'll do the cutting, Santina. I will guide you."

How Santina's heart raced at the mere thought. "What if I make a mistake?"

"I will guide you," Trotula repeated firmly.

It was the opportunity Santina had long awaited. If she wanted to learn, then she had to step forward. Besides, Trotula was telling her, not asking.

Caterina grew heavy with sleep, and Santina washed her hands in medicinal waters while silently cursing the physician who abandoned the pregnant woman in such a dire state. The long hours of neglect had weakened the woman, diminishing her and the baby's chances of survival. Santina's indignation served to steady her trembling hand as she accepted the sharp knife from Trotula.

"*Dio lo benedica,* may God bless it," Trotula said before signaling Santina to proceed. "There. Cut right there," she whispered.

Hands shaking, Santina lowered the blade to pierce through smooth, white skin and slice through glistening layers of fat. Caterina's body flinched and streams of blood rolled down her white hips.

"*Push harder, Santina. You're not there yet.*" Hearing Trotula's voice somewhere in the background, Santina applied more force to cut through the layers of muscle. As she passed through the resistance, more blood spurted out, splashing her sleeves. At last she reached the hidden womb.

"*Stop now! Don't go any farther.*" In plain view was the secret crucible of life—red, round, and smooth. It was where the baby lay, trapped inside a dark, watery world. *"Don't be afraid, Santina. Feel where the baby lies."* Santina maintained her focus and uttered a silent prayer. She ran her fingertips over the surface of the womb and understood where the baby was positioned within.

"Be careful now," Trotula was telling her. "Just prick it with the tip of the knife. Very gently. Make sure you're far enough away from the baby."

The membranes had ruptured hours ago, so no fluid sprayed out when Santina made the first tiny cut. She placed two fingers inside and held them there before she began to make the opening. *"Very gently now. Very slowly so you don't injure the baby, Santina."*

The tissue broke with surprising ease even though Santina's hands were still shaky. Trotula wiped Santina's brow with a cool cloth and quietly reassured her. *"You're doing fine, Santina."*

She and the older midwife peered down into the woman's depths. "You've opened her up enough now," Trotula said. "Reach down with your hand. Feel where the feet are. Grab hold of them."

Trotula held the outer flesh apart as Santina plunged her bare hand into the womb. She felt the baby's skull, shoulders, back, and a soft, chubby thigh before running her hand down the limb and taking hold of one ankle and then another. When both were in her grasp, she lifted the infant up into the light.

She held the small, slippery, wet miracle—a boy—in her arms. He did not breathe. He appeared blue and silent. Santina stared in terror. It felt like an unbearably long time but was a mere second before Trotula took hold of the child and began to clean his mouth.

He soon let out a gasp. Trotula continued to rub him, and he began to breathe. Finally, there was a blessed cry.

"He's a sleepy one," Trotula said, a smile escaping as she examined the perfect baby boy. "He's had a dose of the poppy, too."

When she looked at the living, breathing child in Trotula's arms, Santina murmured, "*Grazie a Dio*, thank God."

Santina turned from the baby to Caterina, whose body still lay open and exposed. The woman appeared half dead. Taking in the quantity of blood that had soaked through the linens and mattress, Santina feared again for Caterina's survival.

"Get to work quickly," Trotula said, pressing the catgut—prepared according to the instructions of the Arab physician al-Zahrawi—into Santina's hand. "Sew the womb carefully. Make the stitches close."

Santina began the slow, tedious process of closing Caterina's flesh. The woman's skin was ghostly pale, and yet she still breathed.

"She's steady, Santina," Trotula said reassuringly as she felt for Caterina's heartbeat. "I believe she won't leave us."

"So much blood was lost." Santina silently implored God that two lives would be spared that day. If Caterina lived, then she and Trotula had done the impossible. They would have succeeded at something even the best surgeons and most learned physicians of Salerno had not attempted.

"The body can afford to lose more blood than you think, but she'll be weak," Trotula maintained. "She needs a rich broth. I'll tell Filippa to prepare it now, for Caterina will soon wake."

When Santina finished stitching, she covered the wound with a clean poultice of yarrow and ground ivy. With Trotula's help, she secured the dressing around Caterina's abdomen with lengths of linen. The wound would heal, though Caterina would require weeks of rest in bed and close watching for signs of fever. But at that moment, Santina dared to hope both mother and child would survive.

"You did well today, Santina," Trotula told her.

Immersing her bloody hands in a bowl of clear water, Santina realized the day would have been entirely different if Trotula had not been there to teach her and if Ninetta had not been there to teach Trotula before that. Santina thought of Mama and the countless other women who had died in childbirth. She knew without doubt that what Trotula taught her was good and correct.

"They would have died if we weren't here," Santina said, her voice low.

"We were here, Santina," Trotula said. "Because we were, I fear there will be consequences to bear."

"No one needs to know how the baby was born."

"Unless Filippa would have us burned alive, she'll keep silent."

"Even so, Ferondo will eventually discover that Caterina and the baby live," Santina thought aloud. Trotula seemed certain that Nastagio's father would not take their interference lightly. Although Santina believed that a man who would leave a woman to die was not worth thinking about, she suspected she would be forced to answer to him in some way.

"We'll wait until the time comes," Trotula said as she gathered the soiled cloths. Stepping close to Santina, she said in a whisper, "If anyone does discover what we've done, we will say that I performed the operation."

Santina did not think to avoid responsibility for her own actions, but she let Trotula's comment go for the moment. She was too amazed by what had just occurred to think overmuch of Ferondo Palmerini's accusations or Trotula's motherly concerns.

She looked at the tiny baby, wrapped warmly and already asleep in his cradle. Whether Ferondo Palmerini knew it or not, Caterina and Nastagio's child was a gift from God. The baby lived, death had been defeated, and the elixir of life had been tasted. Their victory was surely a sign of what astounding discoveries the future might hold. She tried to think of this rather than the wrath of Ferondo Palmerini.

The Palmerini

The birth of an illegitimate grandson did not in itself pose a threat to Ferondo Palmerini, for it was not the child that prevented Nastagio's marriage to the count's daughter. The problem lay in Nastagio's unshakable devotion to the child's mother, Trotula put forth. Seated in comfort near the warmth of the fire, Santina paused to consider what Ferondo might do when he discovered that his scheme to dispose of Caterina had been thwarted. Perhaps he would seek another way to be rid of the inconvenience.

Trotula was of the opinion that it was only a matter of time before the trail from the cobbler's shop led to the cottage door. Santina began to imagine how Ferondo might punish her and Trotula for saving Caterina and the baby. She reasoned, on the other hand, that he would only draw attention to his ill deed if he chose to condemn them for the service they had rendered. If he had any sense at all, he would leave them alone.

"Surely Ferondo doesn't want people to know he left her to die," Santina said, although she was afraid Trotula might be right.

"There are many who will believe whatever Ferondo Palmerini tells them to believe," Trotula retorted. "He could turn the facts around to make it appear that we meddled where we ought not to have. The doctor would support Ferondo's claims, of course. And he could easily say that he tried to return to Caterina's but was refused."

As long as Ferondo did not discover the manner in which his grandson was born, there was little he could do to turn the village against them, Santina wanted to think. Worry as she might about Ferondo, it was his son, Nastagio, who came to call upon the midwives.

He was a tall, lanky, fair-skinned man. He was dressed in fine but unadorned clothing, and there was no air of grandeur about him whatsoever. He stood politely at the front door, asking if he might have a word with Trotula. After some hesitation, Trotula told Santina to admit him.

"Filippa confided in me," he said, sitting with the women at the table. "I can't tell you how grateful I am. If I'd lost Caterina—I don't know what I would have done."

Before Santina could say a word in reply, Trotula spoke in a manner that made it clear to Nastagio she had acted as no personal favor to him.

"I am a midwife, Nastagio. I could either deliver the child or watch Caterina die. The doctor from Florence abandoned her. I suspect he was obeying orders from your father rather than his oath."

Nastagio colored at the mention of his father. "My father gave me his word that he would send the best physician in Florence if I did his bidding in Siena. He's lied to me too many times."

"It was heartless of the doctor to leave her," Santina agreed, "but in truth there was little he could have done."

"My father thinks only of his fortune," Nastagio said. "Success has made him greedy. He doesn't care how Caterina suffered."

Santina could not help but admire Nastagio's devotion to the woman he loved. "What do you suppose your father will do now?" she asked. "Caterina and your son make things inconvenient for him."

Nastagio nodded. "He's given Count Bertrand a loan without interest for his castle, and he fully intends to collect his form of repayment—a title for our family. He went to Caterina yesterday and offered her a tidy sum if she would take Ioseph and leave San Gimignano," he said. "His bribe won't keep us apart. I will have Caterina and my son—the count can keep his daughter."

No doubt Nastagio faced a difficult battle if he refused his father's command. While Trotula seemed unsympathetic, Santina understood Nastagio's determination. Given the chance, she would have defied Papa in order to be with Calandrino. Santina had dared to dream of love, and the scholar had spoken of love, but the heartbreaking truth was that scholars shunned marriage to any but their books. Calandrino chose not to fight for her, but if he had Papa might have come around. Perhaps Ferondo Palmerini, despite his ruthlessness, could be persuaded to accept Nastagio's choice of bride.

"If you marry Caterina, perhaps your father will forgive you in time," Santina said.

Trotula stood with her arms folded across her chest. "And perhaps he will not."

Santina shifted uncomfortably under the older woman's stare. She remained silent, yet she thought Trotula was being too practical, too cautious. Trotula did not understand that love bears all things.

Nastagio seemed to agree with Santina. "I won't give up Caterina and Ioseph. My father cannot keep me from them."

"Your notion of love is well and good, Nastagio, and I don't condone your father's tactics," the older midwife told him. "But you have to realize the position your father will be in if you refuse to marry the Count's daughter. He won't take it lying down."

"The situation is his own doing," Nastagio said. "I can't help him. Caterina and I are planning to leave San Gimignano very soon. She has a sister in Naples."

"*What?*" Trotula uttered. "Are you mad?"

Santina's eyes widened as she took in the boldness of the plan. Such a journey would be dangerous, perhaps impossible. But since Ferondo Palmerini was wrong to keep the couple apart, Santina sided with Nastagio. Perhaps there was also a part of Santina that wanted to voice her own convictions rather than remain in the older woman's shadow.

"It's the only way," Nastagio said.

"The plan cannot succeed," Trotula insisted.

"They deserve to be together," Santina dared to say. "It's not for Ferondo to keep them apart."

Trotula snapped, "This is none of your concern, Santina."

She had been summarily dismissed. It was clear that Trotula still considered her to be an inexperienced apprentice, her opinions worthless. Yet Santina was the one who had performed the operation. This fact, she believed, gave her every right to express her thoughts concerning Caterina and the baby.

"Ferondo has no right to keep them apart," she repeated, standing her ground. "If he had his way last week, both Caterina and Ioseph would be dead."

As far as she was concerned, Ferondo deserved to pay his penance. Surely God would punish the man's misdeeds. In the meantime she feared Trotula's insistence on caution would keep the couple from winning the freedom they deserved.

"God is on your side, Nastagio," she said, and Trotula looked at her sharply.

"You realize, of course, Caterina isn't ready to travel yet," said Trotula. "She's very weak. She needs to rest. The ride would be unbearable."

"I know. I need your advice on this matter," he said. "When do you think it will be possible for her to leave? I'll have a comfortable wagon for her and the baby, of course."

"She cannot travel for some time yet, Nastagio," Trotula told him. "It would be imprudent. Much too painful for Caterina."

"My father is making things impossible. He insists on setting the date for this preposterous wedding. If we don't leave soon, he'll drag me to church with a sword at my neck."

Santina saw that his future was in jeopardy. If he remained in San Gimignano, he would lose the ones he loved the most. Trotula would let the would-be murderer win. It was an injustice Santina could not abide. "We can give her poppy, Trotula. She can endure the ride if she takes it for the pain."

Nastagio's face brightened. "Yes, if you could give her something for the pain," he said hopefully. "Then we could leave before my father goes too far."

"The risk is too great," Trotula warned him. "Your father is watching you, Nastagio. And Caterina. He'll go to great lengths to keep you apart. Your hopes are too high."

"I know my father well enough."

"Listen, Caterina is extremely lucky just to be alive. She very nearly wasn't. That in itself is something to be thankful for."

"God wanted her to live. That is why he granted this miracle. Caterina and I are meant to be together, I know this with all my heart."

"You're too young to know what you're meant to be," Trotula scoffed. The midwife began to lecture him about the senselessness of his scheme, and Santina bit her tongue. She had come to her teacher as a grateful student, and for the most part she had been an obedient apprentice. But she was no longer a young girl who knew nothing; she imagined herself to be a midwife in her own right. Deciding once and for all to take matters into her own hands, she slipped away to the workroom.

Taking the bottle from its hiding place, she carefully poured off a small quantity of the tincture of poppy for Caterina. Undoubtedly, there would be consequences to face. Perhaps Trotula would forbid her to work for a time. Whatever the penalty, Santina felt compelled to follow her own judgment on this occasion.

She put a stopper in the bottle and returned to the main room as Trotula continued on about the dangers of travel. When she had Nastagio's eye, Santina pressed the vial of green glass into his hand. She waited for Trotula to say something, but apparently the action had gone unnoticed.

"Just three drops, no more than four times a day. Remember this exactly," she said quietly when Trotula paused.

When she finally became aware of what Santina was doing, Trotula looked aghast. Santina told herself that she had acted with sound judgment. After all, the couple desperately needed her help.

The full heat of Trotula's searing gaze was upon her. For a moment she thought Trotula would reach out and snatch the medicine from Nastagio. When Nastagio slipped the vial inside his purse, nothing more could be done.

"More than this will bring on a long sleep and harm the baby as well," Santina continued, turning away from Trotula. "Listen well, Nastagio—let her take only a few drops."

Nastagio thanked Santina with an embrace while Trotula shook her head as though they were both hopeless fools. Turning to the older woman, Nastagio bowed. "I am in your debt, Trotula."

"I tell you, Nastagio, it's imprudent to leave now," Trotula repeated, though she had lost the argument. "Caterina is not ready."

Nastagio only shook his head and muttered another *grazie* before turning to leave. Still surprised by the boldness of her own actions, Santina watched him disappear out the door. She tried to prepare herself for the inevitable remonstrations that would follow. She had openly disobeyed her mentor. Trotula would not let this pass. However, for the moment Trotula remained quiet. Waiting nervously, Santina considered all that had just occurred.

Now that the poppy was in his possession, Nastagio would soon escape with Caterina from San Gimignano. Even with the medicine, the trip would be difficult for Caterina and the baby. At least they would have a head start on Ferondo. Surely they would succeed. But what if they did not? Santina had been so very sure of herself just a moment ago. As she imagined the little family traveling rough, dangerous roads, she felt the strength of her convictions begin to falter.

"Nastagio's father will never know about the poppy," Santina said, trying to soften the thing she had done. "And they would run away with or without it, Trotula. I've only eased Caterina's suffering."

"*I've* eased it, Santina," Trotula corrected her. "You know nothing about Nastagio's visit. Nothing at all," she said, disappearing to her room.

Santina remained where she was, acutely aware of Trotula's displeasure. For a long while she sat alone at the table, thinking. She had only wanted to help Nastagio. The poor man was willing to risk everything for Caterina and his son. Surely it was a love that deserved to be. For better or worse, a series of events had been put into motion. Time would tell whether she or Trotula was right.

That evening Santina waited for more of Trotula's reprisals, but nothing was said. Finally, before retiring to bed, Trotula approached Santina.

"I have thought to send you back to your father's house."

"Please don't, Trotula," she answered quickly, full of apology. "I'm sorry I gave Nastagio the poppy. I know I disobeyed you, and perhaps it was foolhardy—"

Trotula held up her hand. "It's not for this reason, Santina," she tried to explain. "It's because I'm afraid you're no longer safe here. I don't know what Ferondo Palmerini might do."

Forced to consider the seriousness of the situation, Santina lowered her head. By abetting Nastagio's escape, had she unwittingly put Trotula in danger?

"You should not face this alone, Trotula," she said quietly. "If Ferondo Palmerini wants to punish someone, it should be me, not you."

Trotula shook her head. "You're still my apprentice, Santina. In this respect I must remain in command: the responsibility for dealing with Ferondo is mine."

Santina did not want to be shielded. She wanted to accept the consequences of her actions. The thought of leaving Trotula to face Ferondo Palmerini alone while she withdrew to the privileged protection of her father was unthinkable. "I won't leave you, Trotula. I have to face whatever comes."

Trotula sighed wearily before replying in no uncertain terms, "You are to deny any involvement with Caterina and Nastagio. Either that or I will have no choice but to go to your father, Santina. He would do well to send you to Isabella's in Certaldo for a time."

After Trotula retired to bed, Santina remained before the dwindling fire and shuddered at the sound of a wolf howling in the distance. She found herself wishing Calandrino could be there to protect her, but he was far away in Carpentras. She recalled, with some resentment, the way he had abandoned her after they were discovered by Ruberto. If he had chosen to remain with her in San Gimignano, she would never have become a midwife, of course. Either way, she longed for him that lonely night. She thought he would somehow know what to do in face of the Palmerini. Sitting at the table with pen and paper, she began to write him. Even as she did, she supposed the letter would arrive too late.

> *...I regret bringing this situation to bear upon Trotula. One can only imagine what Ferondo will do when he learns that I have abetted his son in fleeing with Caterina. While I do not wish to burden you, I confess that I fear for our very lives.*
>
> *More than that, if the manner in which the babe was born becomes known, many will condemn us. There would be little understanding of the teachings of Al-Biruni here in San Gimignano....*

She sealed the letter with wax, knowing he was thoroughly occupied with other matters. Even if Calandrino were inclined to help her, it would take him some time to make the journey from the South of France. She could not rely on the scholar and neither could she bring herself to ask Papa for help. For the first time she was not at all sure if she was safe at the cottage.

Christophano

Santina would not be persuaded to return to Papa's house, though neither did she venture from the cottage after Nastagio's visit. When a week passed and there was still no news concerning the Palmerini, she began to hope that nothing more would come of the matter. Still her heart would jump at the sight of a stranger coming down the road or the washerwoman's knock on the door. It wasn't until the ninth day after Nastagio's visit that she learned her trouble with the Palmerini was far from over.

Trotula had returned from the village where she had gone— wearing her hood low on her head—to see about Caterina. "Filippa was there alone. Caterina and Nastagio took off during the night," she said. "Ferondo will have learned of it by now."

It was the news she should have expected, still Santina was shaken. She pictured fragile Caterina and the crying infant in the wagon, bumping along treacherous roads as they fled for their lives. It was a mad scheme, and it no longer struck her as romantic. She could only pray they would make it safely to Naples.

Santina shifted uneasily. "I wonder if Ferondo has gone after them," she said, knowing well enough that Ferondo would not take Nastagio's departure lightly.

"I imagine they're being hunted like wild game at this moment. Hopefully, Nastagio had a good head start," Trotula replied.

"Do you think they'll make it?" Santina asked. She sought reassurance even though she knew none could be given.

Trotula's face revealed nothing. "We can certainly pray for this."

Santina uttered silent prayers throughout the evening, wishing all the while that she had never encouraged Nastagio to leave San Gimignano. It was too late to change what she had done. All she could do was wait and wonder, minute by minute, whether or not Nastagio and Caterina would make it to safety.

From where she sat at the table, Santina watched Trotula reading by torchlight. The older woman fingered the bone amulet around her neck. She had always seemed as strong as a force of nature, yet now there was a vulnerability about her. Half-hidden in shadow, her countenance was etched with worry. A cool gust pushed through the closed shutters, blowing the candles, casting shadows across the room. As night moved in on the cottage, unseen forces were somewhere at work. Santina could feel the approach of an incoming storm.

Santina awoke to the sound of heavy rain. Her first thought was of Nastagio, Caterina, and the baby making their way along wet, muddy roads. She hoped that they had found lodging and that the baby was taking enough milk. She opened the front door and watched the rain pounding the little seedlings that had begun to sprout. In the distance she saw a figure on horseback. Her heart raced, thinking it was someone coming to accuse her or Trotula. As the figure approached she soon realized it was only Papa, *grazie a Dio*. When he stood unsmiling at the door, water dripping down his hat and cloak, she gathered that he brought no good tidings.

"Have you heard?" he asked without so much as a greeting.

"Have I heard what, Papa?" she replied too cheerfully.

"Ferondo Palmerini's son disappeared. He's supposed to be married tomorrow. The guards are out looking for him now. People ran out of their houses this morning, wondering what all the hard riding was about," he said, eyeing her suspiciously.

"I didn't know," she answered, looking away.

"Margherita told me there's talk of the cobbler's widow having delivered a baby. They say it's Nastagio's child," Papa said, searching the room for signs of Trotula. "I wondered if you knew anything about it."

She considered how much she should tell him. She had no wish to worry him or to give herself or Trotula away, but it was not easy to feign ignorance of the events Papa described. Seeing him stand there with fatherly concern in his eyes only made matters worse.

When she did not reply at once, Papa commanded her, as though she was a child again. "You must tell me, Santina. Do you know anything about Nastagio's illegitimate child?"

Unable to answer him, she struggled to find words to explain what had happened.

"You must tell me, Santina."

It was impossible to lie to him. "We're only midwives, Papa," she began. "We deliver babies. What happens in people's lives is none of our concern."

He shook his head. "Ferondo Palmerini might not see it that way. He looks for people to blame."

"What reason could he have to blame me or Trotula?" Santina asked, trying to maintain her composure.

"Who knows? It might be enough reason that you helped his son's mistress. Men like him have either friends or enemies. If you're not a friend, then you're an enemy," he said. "Pray that Ferondo gets his son back. If he doesn't, he could be a difficult man to deal with."

"Ferondo nearly killed the woman," Santina blurted out. "He sent a doctor who had every intention of leaving her to die. We had to do something, or she would not have lived."

Papa pounded his fist on the wall. "*Dio Mio!* What have you done?"

"We had to help her. The baby was trapped."

She stopped herself from telling him more, since Papa would never understand the strange manner in which they had delivered Nastagio's son. Trotula had made it clear that she was to tell *no one* about the operation. The older midwife emerged from her room, having overheard Papa no doubt. Catching Santina's eye, she gave her a knowing nod.

To Papa, Trotula said, "I assure you that I am the one who bears full responsibility for the birth of Nastagio's child. Even so, it might be best if Santina returns home."

"It was best for her to return long ago."

"No, Papa," Santina protested. "I mean to stay."

"What do you think will happen if Nastagio gets away?" her father demanded. "You can well enough imagine Ferondo's response when he learns that his plans to dispose of the woman and child were foiled by you and Trotula."

"If Ferondo or anyone else inquires, they will be assured the work was mine," Trotula told him.

Papa still fumed. "As it should be," he muttered.

Knowing the two of them were united against her on this, Santina said nothing.

"I should take you home with me now, Santina. I should have prevented you from coming here in the first place. That was my mistake years ago."

Santina and Trotula kept silent. Calmer, Papa spoke again. "At least promise me this, Santina. If anyone questions you, say nothing. And send for me at once if anything happens. Perhaps I should have Giacomino stand watch."

"That would only serve to draw more attention to us," Trotula pointed out. "Besides, Santina is merely an apprentice. Ferondo has no reason to blame her."

Santina stood helplessly between the two of them, wishing they would stop treating her like a child. She was the one who ought to answer to Ferondo Palmerini.

Papa turned to leave, not at all appeased. "You should come home," he said once more.

"I am in God's hands," she replied.

He regarded his daughter sadly and kissed her cheek before walking out the door. After Papa departed, Santina turned to Trotula. "Do you think we should both leave San Gimignano?"

Trotula shook her head. "If Ferondo wants to find us, he will. There is no point in running away."

"What will we do if he comes to the cottage?" she asked.

"We'll worry about that when and if the time comes," Trotula replied, putting water on to boil.

Three days later Santina heard a loud rapping at the door. An unfamiliar voice was demanding admittance at once. Santina jumped at the sound, but Trotula calmly opened the door to the three men who stood at her doorstep. A burly young man in soldier's attire was followed by a refined, fair-haired man who resembled Nastagio. The two of them stood aside to make way for a portly gentleman with a long aquiline nose and thin, frowning lips. The man, who entered the cottage as if he were the Duke of Tuscany, was dressed in elegant finery and wore gold and jeweled rings on his fingers. With a sick feeling, Santina recognized him at once as Ferondo Palmerini.

The fair-haired man introduced himself as Christophano, Ferondo's nephew, before introducing the notorious banker. The guard, referred to as Benedetto, walked to the hearth and stood watch as though they were already on trial.

After apologizing for their unexpected visit, Christophano said, "My cousin, Nastagio, returned home yesterday, but he never awoke from his sleep."

Santina stifled a gasp, and Ferondo took Trotula's seat before the hearth. Trotula gripped the edge of the table.

"It is true, my beloved Nastagio is dead," Ferondo added, looking at the wall.

"I am so sorry, Messers," Trotula said quietly. "But why do you come to my cottage with this news?"

"This is merely an inquiry. You are accused of nothing," Christophano explained calmly.

Santina listened as Christophano explained that certain information had been obtained by the *podestà*. She wanted to ask how Nastagio's death had come to pass, but she was too scared to speak. The man reached into his purse and pulled out a small, green vial with a stopper made from a plug of wood wrapped in cloth. With a sinking heart Santina knew it was the vial that had contained the tincture of poppy.

"This was found in Nastagio's room. It's the poison that killed him," Christophano put forth.

Santina glanced over at Ferondo, who stared at the image of Christ and St. Peter, off in a world of his own.

"Did this come from you?" Christophano asked.

"That would be no poison if it came from my workshop." Trotula accepted the vial, sniffed the sticky syrup that remained around the lip. "It could be my work—perhaps comfrey root and birchbark, with honey to sweeten it. I often add nutmeg as well," she lied.

"Did you give it to Nastagio?"

"I had no cause to give Ferondo's son a remedy."

"I understand you delivered a baby born to a woman named Caterina."

They had forced Filippa to speak, Santina gathered as she moved close to Trotula. The older midwife paled, but did not flinch as she replied, "Her sister came to the cottage some days ago and begged me to help her."

Santina could see that Trotula was to be blamed for Nastagio's death. She tried to gather her thoughts, to say she was the one who had delivered the baby and given Nastagio the medicine intended for Caterina. It was her fault, but when she tried to speak, no words would come.

"It was—" she began weakly.

Trotula reached behind Santina and pinched her so hard the young midwife's eyes watered. "My apprentice and I can assure you that any remedy made in this cottage is mild and soothing in nature," Trotula said, revealing nothing. "Having not seen Nastagio, I cannot tell you what caused his death, but surely it was not the gentle cordial given to Caterina."

Santina understood she was to remain silent. Observing

Ferondo, she saw something dark and terrible in his eyes. He was a man who would not hesitate to use his power in cruel ways when he felt justified to do so. But what could he prove? Countless villagers would attest to Trotula's skill, and none had died from her remedies. Besides, these men would never know the vial contained the tincture of poppy.

"How fares Caterina?" Trotula asked, though Santina feared she knew the answer.

"There was an accident involving the carriage—a collision during the night," Christophano said, his voice flat as he avoided Trotula's gaze. "She did not survive."

Santina lowered her head to hide her tear-filled eyes. Caterina had been disposed of at last. Knowing she was being watched by the men, Santina willed herself to stifle her grief.

She heard Trotula ask, "What of the woman's child?"

"The child lives," he said quietly.

Somehow Trotula managed to appear unshaken. To Ferondo, who still appeared miles away, she said, "I am truly sorry for the loss of your son, Messer. May God bless him."

Santina could only assume that Nastagio had taken his own life after Caterina was killed in the accident. Ferondo surely knew this as well, though he would find someone to blame for the death of his son. Ferondo's own greed had driven Nastagio to despair, but no one would dare speak of it.

The richest man in San Gimignano sat in Trotula's cottage, and the poverty of his soul was all too apparent. Guilt weighed heavily upon him as he tried to make someone else accountable for his mistake. Santina felt no pity for the man.

After Christophano had finished his questioning, he and Benedetto went to the door, but Ferondo gave no indication of leaving. He remained unmoving in his seat, and Santina began to fear what he would do. The three of them were alone with no one to bear witness to his vengeance. Santina was not sure if he meant to harm them or merely to make known his authority.

Santina, following Trotula's example, sat at the table in silence. Finally, when the church bells rang in the distance, Ferondo deigned to rise.

"We will have no *streghe* in this town," he spewed before throwing open the front door and departing.

Wincing at his words, Santina finally grasped the full measure of the man's rage. He could use his power to mete out a depraved version of justice. Ferondo Palmerini—who had lost his son and heir—needed to make someone accountable for his unspeakable tragedy. Imagining what the man was capable of, the young midwife feared for her life.

The instant he was gone, Trotula went to pour three drops of olive oil into a plate of water. Santina did not have to look at the plate to know that *malocchio* was present.

The older midwife inserted the tip of a needle into the eye of another needle while chanting *eyes against eyes and the holes of eyes, envy cracks and eyes burst.* Then she dropped the needles into the water, sprinkled the water with salt, and recited her Paternosters.

Santina could only hope that prayers would spare them from the wrath of Ferondo Palmerini. As when Mama lay near death years ago, Santina wondered where to find the philosopher's stone that would save them.

Sister Anna

The washerwoman was expected the day after Ferondo Palmerini's visit to the cottage, but she did not come. Trotula said nothing of this. She only sat at the loom, weaving a green cloth with an intricate border of scarlet and gold.

"Why do you suppose she isn't here?" Santina wondered aloud, but there was no reply. Santina had an uneasy feeling that it was not illness keeping the woman away. She feared it had something to do with whatever murmurings were spreading throughout the village. People would have learned of Nastagio's and Caterina's deaths by now; the talk would be of nothing else.

The next day there was still no washerwoman. Santina tried to take her mind off her unknown fate by baking some sugared rolls. She would bring some to Papa, who was surely sick with worry. On the way to the house she would stop to visit the widow who was nearly blind and suffered headaches.

"I thought to see Madonna Francesca today," Santina announced as she prepared to leave.

Trotula looked up from her weaving. "Wait, just a moment." She reached around her neck and pulled out a necklace from beneath her gown. "This is yours now," she said, handing it to Santina. "Keep it about you at all times."

The embossed gold medallion had surely come from antiquity. At the center was an engraved image of the evil eye. Around the border were various creatures—a scorpion, a wasp, and a bird— all of which were attacking the eye. Attached to the bottom of the amulet were five tiny pendants—three pear-shaped amethysts and two pearls. Studying the precious piece, Santina said, "I can't take this, Trotula."

"Ninetta gave it to me, and now it's time for me to pass it on to you," she insisted. "I'll wear the *corno*. It's powerful enough."

Seeing that Trotula would not take no for an answer, Santina said, "I will cherish it always. *Grazie.*"

After all the trouble she had caused, she did not feel deserving of the heirloom. Still, she was grateful for the gift. In truth, when Santina left the cottage, she felt a measure of security wearing it beneath her gown. Riding along the road, she noticed a tall figure on horseback in the distance. As she continued on, the figure veered off into the woods. Santina quickened her pace. She kept turning around to look behind her, but the rider never appeared again.

She was relieved when she passed through the village gate and came to the glassblower's shop. The proprietor, who was an acquaintance of Papa's, stood outside. When Santina bid him *buon giorno*, the man only returned her greeting with a solemn nod. It might have been her imagination, but she felt there was something peculiar in the way he looked at her. Perhaps he was merely trying to place her face. Or perhaps he recognized her as the cloth merchant's daughter who had once left home against her father's wishes.

When she came to the cobbler's shop, Santina looked up at the second floor, to where she and Trotula had delivered Caterina's baby. She supposed the baby, Ioseph, now resided with a wet nurse. Standing alone on the street, she became aware of too much silence. Turning her gaze to the house next door, she caught a glimpse of a wrinkled face in a wimple staring down from an upstairs window. As soon as Santina spied her, the woman turned abruptly and moved from sight.

They know, she thought. *Somehow they know.* Had word spread so quickly about Caterina and Nastagio? Santina pressed on, riding at a canter to Papa's shop. He was not there when she arrived.

"Where is my father?" Santina demanded of Ruberto.

Papa's assistant looked to her in surprise. "I believe he's on his way to see you."

"Please tell him I've been here."

"Santina, you should not be traveling alone," Ruberto tried to tell her as she hurried out the door.

Santina suspected that Papa had gone to the cottage to insist upon her return home. Rushing outside without looking where she was going, Santina nearly ran over old Caravaggio, who stood near his cart full of sheep. "*Scusa.* Forgive me, Caravaggio."

The old man nodded, leaning forward on his cane. "Are you still with Trotula?"

"Of course, I am her apprentice. Why do you ask?"

"They're saying she's gone too far this time."

"Whatever do you mean?"

He glanced behind him before whispering to Santina. "Master Traverseri was asked to look at the body—Nastagio's lady. He discovered the cutting Trotula did to take the baby. They say the woman's accident is God's punishment for the *stregoneria,* the witchcraft."

Santina held the side of the cart to steady herself. The operation had been discovered. No one in the village would understand. *We will be tried,* she thought.

"No, Caravaggio. The mother and child would have died otherwise. It was not *stregoneria,* it was done to save them."

His cloudy gray eyes seemed not to see her. "They're saying things about the child."

"Such as what?"

"They think he has the curse of *malocchio* upon him."

Unable to listen any longer, Santina mumbled an excuse and hurried away. Riding back to the city gate, she had no thought of seeing Madonna Francesca. She could only think of the trial that she and Trotula surely faced. Perhaps Papa might intervene and speak with the *podestà* on their behalf, if only she could reach him before he left the cottage.

When she arrived she found Trotula still at the loom and no sign of Papa. The sight of her teacher lost in her own world, oblivious to the talk in the village, did nothing to ease Santina's fear. She knew she had to tell Trotula that the operation was no longer a secret, but she did not know how to begin.

"Your father was here," Trotula said, looking up from her work. "He left this for you," she said, reaching for a letter on the table.

Santina's hands shook as she unfolded the paper, though she could already guess what it would say.

"He's right, you should return home," Trotula said.

"This is my home," she said, opening Papa's note. *I command you to return home at once.*

Trotula smiled. "How did you find Francesca?"

"Ah, Madonna Francesca. She is so thin," Santina said, wondering how to explain that she had sped away from the village after Caravaggio accused Trotula of witchcraft. She was still gathering her courage to tell Trotula she never made it to Francesca's when Trotula announced her plan to visit Isabetta, the laywoman who helped with the cleaning at the Monastery of San Girolamo. The woman had been gravely ill with a respiratory condition for some time.

"I can go if you like," Santina offered, afraid of what Trotula would hear if she ventured from the cottage. "Just give me the remedies you would have her take."

"You might be needed elsewhere. Lisa is due any time now." Trotula regarded her with motherly tenderness. No doubt she sensed Santina's nervousness. "You cannot allow the Palmerini to make you forget who you are."

After all the mistakes she had made, Santina only wondered how Trotula could offer kind words. Nonetheless, she had delivered two of Lisa's babies, and she would do as she was told. There would be no dissuading Trotula. Santina would have to wait until the midwife returned to break the news about the talk flying through the village.

The following morning Trotula was still away. It was not unheard of for the midwife to spend the night as a guest of the Benedictines when cause arose, so Santina tried not to worry overmuch. She only wished Trotula had mentioned her plans to stay.

By *sext*, noon, Trotula had still not returned. Santina could neither eat nor drink. Deep inside she sensed something was amiss. Again and again she thought she would go to her father, but she was afraid she would miss Trotula's return. Finally, at *nones*, she put on her cloak and prepared to leave. It was then that she heard a knock at the door.

It must be Trotula, Santina thought. She would be holding a basket of meat or cheese, a gift from the monastery. Burdened with her load, she could not manage the key. Santina held onto her hope, but when she unlocked the door, the person she saw was a stranger, a uniformed guard.

Behind the guard stood two sisters from San Girolamo—Trotula's dear friend, Sister Anna, and another she recognized as Sister Maria. By the somber looks on their faces, she knew instantly that the news they brought would be grave.

"May we come in, Santina?" said Sister Anna.

"*Si*," she said, turning ashen. Feeling as though her legs would give way, she led them to the table.

"I must inform you of an offense that occurred not far from here," the man said, looking through her.

Santina fell to the bench as Sister Anna began to speak, her voice filled with anguish. "We were walking Trotula home. It was just after daybreak. She had been tending to Isabetta through the night."

"She was taken at knifepoint," the guard interrupted, as though impatient to complete his errand.

Santina simply stared, saying nothing. It was not possible he was speaking of Trotula. "Taken where?" she said finally.

"We don't know," he replied.

"Trotula would not be so easily carried off." The man was lying, trying to frighten her, she thought. Sister Anna sat down beside her on the bench. Sister Maria, who appeared in a state of shock herself, sat on Santina's other side. "Did you see it happen?"

"It was all so fast. A rider came up from behind. Trotula had a bad feeling about it, so we made for the woods," Sister Anna explained. "Only she lost her footing, and he gained on her. He jumped off his horse and grabbed her by the neck. It was clear that Trotula was the one he wanted. Sister Maria tried to stop him, but he pulled out a dagger. I screamed for help, and he kicked me almost senseless to the ground." The nun's hand went to her side, as though recalling her injury. "Sister Maria was very nearly run over by the horse. Whoever it was would not be stopped," she said tearfully.

Through eyes hazy with tears, Santina looked up. "Did you see who it was?"

"He hid beneath his hood. I saw little of his face," replied Sister Anna.

"Are you searching for him?" Santina demanded of the guard.

"Yes, but it was their own fault for walking about on their own. You women ought to know better."

"Ferondo Palmerini wanted her dead," Santina informed him. "He sent someone after her."

The guard looked at her as though she were of no more consequence than a mad woman on the street.

"I tell you, Ferondo Palmerini is to blame for this. He wanted revenge for his son's death. He'll be questioned, I expect."

"There is no reason to connect Messer Palmerini with what happened to Trotula," the guard replied.

"You would do nothing to stop this crime?" she spat. "I tell you, he came to the cottage and threatened Trotula. I heard him myself."

The nuns tried to calm her, but Santina would not be consoled. "Perhaps she will yet be found," Sister Maria said softly.

"We must pray for this," added Sister Anna.

"Pray? There has to be a search," Santina insisted.

The guard turned to leave. Before opening the door, he issued a warning. "You best return to your father's house. It would be unwise for you to remain here—unless you wish to be as unlucky as Trotula."

Blinded by tears, Santina wandered through the cottage. She came upon Trotula's book of Dante lying on the bench where she had left it the day before. Trotula had just been there. It was impossible that she would not return. She failed to understand how God had allowed this to happen, but she knew no one was more to blame for Trotula's disappearance than she was. It was Santina's own foolishness that started the trouble. She might just as well have handed Trotula over to Ferondo Palmerini herself.

She was vaguely aware of Sister Maria bringing her tea. "It's my fault," Santina said. "I brought this upon her."

"You must ask God to protect her," replied the nun.

"Something has to be done," Santina repeated. "We have to find her."

"Trotula is resourceful. Perhaps she will find a means of escape."

"Did you see nothing of her captor? Nothing at all?" Santina asked Sister Anna.

"He was taller than average and quite strong—and young to be so nimble," Sister Anna offered. "There seemed nothing irregular in his face from what little I could see. And he rode a quiet gray horse."

It could have been the guard who visited the cottage, Santina thought, *or any one of Ferondo's minions*. Most likely Ferondo could not be bothered with a trial and sought to exact his own form of punishment. Whether Trotula was dead or alive, Santina blamed herself for what had happened. In her mind she saw Trotula standing at Caterina's bedside, silently weighing the risks of performing the operation. She heard herself pushing Trotula. *We can't let her die, Trotula. We have to help her.*

From the beginning Trotula had foreseen the risk in helping Caterina. She had perceived the outcome of each action they had taken since the day Filippa came running to the cottage. Yet Trotula had gone ahead and performed the operation. *Why, Trotula? Why didn't you put a stop to it if you knew what would happen?*

But what choice had there been other than to help the mother and baby? Trotula had guessed what Ferondo would do, and she went ahead and guided Santina through the cutting anyway. They were midwives. They had only done their job.

The child, at least, still lived. Thank God Ioseph lived, though he would never know his parents. If she hadn't given Nastagio the poppy, perhaps he and Caterina would not have tried to leave San Gimignano, and Trotula would not have been abducted. Or would they?

Santina no longer knew what she should or should not have done. She only knew that Trotula must be found. The longer Trotula was missing, the more likely it was that she would never return. If she were dead, Santina would never be able to forgive herself.

18

The Nigredo

"We have to find Trotula. Please say you'll help." Accompanied by the nuns, Santina had returned to her father's house and made her desperate plea.

"The authorities are doing what they can," Papa replied, his solemn tone offering little hope. "There is nothing more to be done. You must accept this, Santina."

She doubted that the authorities were doing much of anything to find the woman who had crossed Ferondo Palmerini. "Very well," she replied, moving to the door. "Perhaps Giacomino will help me search the woods."

"You're going nowhere," her father said, blocking her path.

"What do you want with me here, Papa?"

"You're my daughter, Santina."

"After what I've done?"

He shook his head. "You are not responsible for what happened to her. This is most certainly the work of the Palmerini."

"You don't understand. Everything that happened is because

159

of me. I'm the one who encouraged Caterina and Nastagio to run away. Trotula was abducted because of what I did."

"You were merely her apprentice, Santina. It was her job to guide you. But it's over and done with. You're not going back there."

"What if she returns?"

Papa sighed. "You must realize it is not likely that she will."

Santina was made to remain inside the house, which was guarded by Papa's porter and stableman, Domenico. There would be no opportunity for her to escape. Regardless, she had little strength to try.

Removed from the cottage, a place she had come to regard as home, Santina wondered what would become of her. Was she no longer a midwife? If she was no longer a midwife, who was she?

That evening Margherita, whose fingers jumped to her *corno* at every unexpected sound, put Santina to bed as though she were a sick child again. The following day, as the maidservant carried tea, fritters, and thin slices of ham in and out of the room, Santina asked her to go to Giacomino for help. At the same time, she knew a search would offer little hope.

Margherita tried to console her, but Santina could think of nothing but Trotula's whereabouts. "Your Papa won't let anything bad happen to you. The house is safely guarded."

Santina was spared Trotula's fate, but she wished she was the one who had been taken by the horseman. Hour by hour, day by day, her sense of remorse grew. After four days had passed, she began to accept the fact that Trotula was mostly likely never coming back. One week after the midwife's disappearance, Papa visited Santina's room. She could tell by the look on his face that her worst fears were justified.

"Trotula's body was found," he announced with little ado.

She had been expecting the news, yet nothing could prepare her for the finality of Papa's words. "No," she uttered, the blood leaving her head. "It can't be."

"She was in the fountain. Dropped there after she was already dead, it seems. Her throat was slit. I'm sorry, Santina," he said. "The corpse was swollen, but the sisters identified the body. She had her charms about her."

Santina's hand went to her chest, where the gold medallion was hidden beneath her gown. She recalled the day Trotula had parted with her treasured medallion and taken the horn on a leather string. The amulet of bone had done little to protect Trotula in the end.

"Where is she now?"

"I expect the sisters will give her a proper burial."

"I want to see her."

"I know how you felt about her," Papa said, "but you had best keep your feelings to yourself. You have to at least appear as though you share the public opinion. You must condemn what she did. And you must understand this, Santina: it was *attaccatura* that misled you."

She stared at Papa blankly, trying to make sense of his advice. She was to lie about everything. She was to make a pretense of believing herself a victim of a spell by Trotula, a spell of attachment. She was to show disdain for the woman who had treated her like a daughter. In all truth, she did feel disdain, Santina realized, but it was aimed at those who betrayed Trotula.

In the stillness of the night, after Papa and the servants retired to bed, she wrote Calandrino of Trotula's death.

...You will think little of me now, Calandrino, and yet you must know that Trotula died for my mistakes. Her ways were misunderstood by the people of San Gimignano, who imagined she worshipped the goddess Diana and met

with other witches beneath the walnut trees and practiced the old religion.

While it is true that Trotula sometimes used magic, she was condemned for knowing too much science. She was, most of all, a good woman who strove with all her power to serve the Lord. Never would she have used her skills to bring harm. May God receive her soul in His glory.

No longer deserving the continuance of your honorable favor toward me, I pray Almighty Jesu have you in His blessed keeping

> *Santina, daughter of Iacopo*
> *Written at San Gimignano*
> *14 March 1347*

After sealing the letter, Santina knelt before Mama's bronze crucifix. Her prayers recalled those whose lives had been touched by Trotula's healing hands and the babies Trotula had brought into the world. She remembered how Trotula had welcomed her to the cottage when she was heartbroken over Calandrino. Trotula had believed in her and taught her well. Silently praising the life she had wanted to follow, Santina implored God to have mercy on Trotula's good soul. She prayed also for Caterina and Nastagio's son, Ioseph, who was to be raised by the brothers at San Damiano.

"Forgive me, Ioseph," she whispered. "Forgive me, Trotula. I am the one who should be dead. I ought to have spoken the truth."

Santina extinguished the candle. She was safe in her room, but it would be a long time before the horror was forgotten. She lived in a village where those who saved lives were murdered. Perhaps they would be rid of her next. If this was the case, there was no reason to offer assistance to anyone in San Gimignano ever again.

Accompanied by Papa, Giacomino, and Domenico, Santina was permitted to return to the cottage to retrieve her belongings. She could little bear the sight of the old leather shoes Trotula used to wear for gardening. Seeing the soapwort roots left to soak in the wooden tub, it seemed as though the midwife would return at any moment.

Urged to make haste by Papa, who found no comfort in the hilltop cottage, Santina quickly filled her *cassone*. She thought to take Trotula's medical books—Galen's *Opera Omnia* and the precious Islamic texts by Al-Biruni and Al-Zahrawi. Though she searched everywhere, the books were not to be found.

"Come, Santina, we've loaded the cart," Papa called as she looked once more through Trotula's room.

Who would have taken the books? Had the Palmerini sent someone to gather evidence against her as well as Trotula? Or had Trotula, anticipating a search, secreted the texts away? Reluctantly, Santina left the cottage for the last time and shut the door on her past as a midwife.

The following morning, Santina lay in bed in the home of her childhood. Half asleep, she became aware of a man calling out to her. It was not Papa or any of the servants.

"*Mi puoi aiutare*, please help me, Santina!" the now desperate voice called over Margherita's scolding.

She opened the shutters to see Adriano, the carpenter, standing in the courtyard below. As she gazed down at him from the second-story window, a glimmer of hope shone in his face.

"Santina, I beg you. Lisa's baby is too long in coming. Her sister and her aunt are trying to help her, but they don't know what to do."

Santina opened her mouth to say *I'll be right down*. In the next moment she recalled that she had no medicines, no instruments, no birthing chair. These were left behind at the cottage, as was her self-assurance, her belief that she had any worthwhile assistance to offer. The man's predicament troubled her, and yet Santina could only say *I am so sorry, Adriano* and close the shutters.

Let him seek the counsel of Ghita, the farmer's wife. Of course, Ghita is capable of delivering babies only when nothing goes wrong, she thought. Nevertheless, these matters were no longer Santina's concern. After uttering a brief prayer for Lisa and Ghita, Santina returned to bed. When she could stare at the cracks in the ceiling no longer, she thought to find the lute she had cast aside long ago. Santina had never played as well as Isabella or Lauretta, but she played on and on, gradually remembering the songs Mama had taught her.

In this manner she passed the days following Trotula's death. Papa seemed to accept her state of profound melancholia and left her alone. After a week, he came to her room. Although aware of Papa standing before her, Santina continued strumming her lute, saying nothing. Finally she looked up and saw that he was taking in her disheveled appearance, her descent into near madness.

"It's over and done with, Santina," he said. "There is no point in blaming yourself. It's time we talk about your future."

"My future?" she said, puzzled. "I believe Ferondo Palmerini made it clear that I should have none."

Papa admitted it was true that she could never resume her work as a midwife. He pointed out that she was completely unmarriageable as well. At length he told her, "I've spoken to the Mother Superior on your behalf."

"The Mother Superior?"

"Your choices are few now."

She set her lute to one side. "You want to send me to San Girolamo?"

"You will be safe there."

She remembered the hopes she once held for herself when she was a girl of fourteen or fifteen. The possibilities for her life were still vast and open then, but now the walls of the future were closing in, her choices were few. In some ways she was drawn to the religious life, to its simplicity and contemplative life of prayer. Joining the order would allow her a means of leaving the society of San Gimignano, for which she felt little warmth. Santina also knew that the monastery was not built to offer escape from one's problems. The community was meant to be a place where one's finest gifts were brought to serve God. After what she had done, she did not feel worthy of the Benedictine Sisters. Even if she wanted to, she could never become one of them.

Another possibility occurred to her. "Has Taddeo da Certaldo found a wife yet?" she asked.

Papa appeared to consider her question for a time. Finally, he replied, "I will speak to him."

The following day, Santina was allowed to attend Mass, accompanied by Margherita. On the way home, as they crossed the piazza, she came upon a blue peacock feather—perhaps from the hat of a nobleman. As she bent to pick it up, Margherita held her back.

"Don't touch it, Santina. Look away," she warned. "The peacock bears *malocchio*."

Thinking she was cursed already, Santina admired the feather with the iridescent circle of blue, green, and purple. She recalled Calandrino saying that the peacock, like its cousin the phoenix, spoke of the alchemist's journey. When the colors of the peacock tail appeared on the surface of the flask, the alchemist might falsely believe he had achieved his goal. The colors were fleeting in nature and served only as a clue that the alchemist was on the right path. She left the feather where it was.

Santina now clearly saw her mistake in believing she had achieved the philosopher's stone when she performed the Caesarean on Caterina. The operation might have saved a life, but it was clear she was a long way from having attained the wisdom of the alchemists. Thinking herself a fool, she wondered where to put her years with Trotula. Her skills as a midwife seemed like foreign money, worthless here, able to purchase nothing at all.

In a matter of days Papa set off for Certaldo. When he returned, he informed Santina that a marriage contract would be drawn up very soon. It was what she had wanted, and yet the news brought her little happiness. Gone were the fanciful notions she once held about marrying for love. Marriage, she was made to see, was matter of practicality or in her case, even worse, of desperation. Taddeo da Certaldo offered a solution to her current predicament, and still she felt entirely unprepared for the arrangement.

"Taddeo might change his mind if he gets wind of the gossip flying about," she said to Papa. Faced with the reality of her betrothal, she was filled with a growing sense of unease. Perhaps she ought to have taken the white veil and donned the black cowl after all.

Papa shook his head. "It's over and done with. We will not speak of it again. Taddeo need know nothing of your past difficulties. Besides, no one blames you for what happened, they blame Trotula."

She started to say that she ought to be truthful with the man who wished to marry her, but Papa's look silenced her. "He can provide well for you," Papa said. "It's your last chance, Santina."

When Taddeo came to visit the following week, Santina dressed in pale blue taffeta and took her seat next to him at the table. She found it difficult to feign the slightest interest in the man as he spoke of his brother and sister and his fine shop in Certaldo. It could not be denied that Taddeo da Certaldo was well dressed and displayed good manners. Even so, she found it difficult to overlook his unsettling tendency to stare at her as though inspecting one of his gems.

Santina's indifference to the man seemed to inspire in him a growing passion. His fixation upon her was puzzling, for she had done nothing at all to encourage him. Eventually she came to see that he interpreted her lack of interest in him as a sign of piety and devotion to higher matters.

"You are unstained," he said when Papa had excused himself from the table.

"I beg your pardon?"

"You are untouched by human affairs. It is written upon your countenance. It's as though you see through this world to the next one."

She tried to tell him the truth, to confess that she had made more than her share of human errors. Taddeo did not seem to hear her.

"You must believe me," she said firmly. "I have sinned grievously."

He shook his head and kissed her hand in devotion. Surely he would not have done so if he knew what had happened with the Palmerini. Should she not tell Taddeo that she had been a midwife's apprentice and nearly accused of *stregoneria*?

As the man she was to marry sat beside her, her attention wandered off to memories of Calandrino. The scholar knew her as no one else could, there were no secrets between them. Despite everything that had happened in the years since they were parted, Calandrino still inhabited her heart. Love him though she might, he would not return to save her from the unfortunate situation in which she now found herself. She could not help but wish it was otherwise. She glanced at Taddeo as he ate his *torta* without a crumb falling from his lips or a worry in his head. *How could it be that she was to become this man's wife?*

Certaldo

antina weighed, in one hand, a loveless marriage to
Taddeo da Certaldo and, in the other, a cloistered life
with the sisters of San Girolamo. Papa, for his part, urged
Santina to marry with haste, before Taddeo could learn
of her shameful past as a midwife. Taddeo had a fair amount to
recommend him, including a profitable shop and a fine home in
Certaldo. The jeweler's singular and enduring interest in Santina,
although somewhat overwhelming, was not exactly a flaw.

"It will be a useful alliance," Papa said. In fact, Iacopo was
already making arrangements to open a new store in Certaldo. The
shop, which would offer Taddeo's gems as well as her father's
luxury items, would be overseen by Ruberto. Giacomino, now
twenty-four years of age and no longer the indolent youth he once
was, would assume Ruberto's former position. "Consider yourself
fortunate, Santina. He is a gentleman."

Santina doubted she would ever feel about Taddeo the way
her sister, Isabella, felt about Bruno or the way Lauretta felt about
Sandro. The arrangement was sorely lacking, but she felt more

inclined to marry than to live out her days as an outcast or a nun. Despite everything that had happened, there remained a part of her that still yearned to see something more of the world. Surely life with Taddeo da Certaldo, who traveled frequently, would at least afford her a measure of freedom and the chance to escape from San Gimignano.

The *sponsalia,* the details of the negotiation, proceeded quickly between the two men. Recognizing the future marriage to come, Papa agreed to a handsome dowry of four hundred gold florins, to be paid at the time of the *nozze,* the ceremony. Papa would also fill Santina's wedding *cassone* with his finest cloth—silk, damask, camlet, and taffeta. Besides this, Papa provided Santina with another three hundred florins; these she was to keep to herself. *Just in case you should need it. You will not, of course. But just in case.*

Well provided for, Santina prepared to depart for Certaldo, where she was to reside with Isabella and Bruno until her wedding the following year. In removing Santina from San Gimignano, Papa thought to diminish the chances of Taddeo overhearing unpleasant talk. While the jeweler was heartened to know that his fiancé would soon be living nearby, he bristled at the notion of a year-long engagement, which Papa had arranged in order to placate Santina and was hardly unusual. *You must be patient with her,* she heard Papa tell him. *She has given up her intentions to enter the religious life, and she must adjust to the notion of marriage. And of course there are preparations to be made.*

In July of 1347 Santina began the brief journey to Isabella's home in Certaldo. Sitting beside Papa in the open carriage, she passed the Piazza della Cisterna and heard the church bells ring out. As she bid farewell to San Gimignano, Santina wondered if she was committing an unfair deception. She would try, at least, not to disappoint Taddeo and to become the person he imagined her to be. Perhaps she would even grow to love him eventually. For the time being, she would try to atone for her past mistakes, to be a good and faithful wife.

Unfortunately, the mere thought of kissing the man left her cold. She remembered how she had once felt about kissing the scholar, how her days and nights were consumed with thoughts of him. Although she wanted to believe she might eventually feel more for Taddeo, she was beyond the point of seeking perfection in her life; her sins were too great. She was determined to be content with what she had been given. Perhaps, in time, even the darkness of the Palmerini and the sorrow of Trotula's death would pass, and the alchemist's painful *nigredo* would lead to the dawning light of the *albedo*.

It was not to be, however, that Santina might so easily leave her past behind in San Gimignano. Just as they were about to pass beneath the arched city gate, she saw a tall young man approaching on horseback from the opposite direction, from beyond the wall. *It cannot be,* she thought. But as the rider neared, the man's tall, graceful bearing seemed all too familiar.

"Stop!" she implored Papa. When her father only urged the horse ahead, Santina grabbed his arm. "*Per favore.* It's Calandrino."

"Santina Pietra!" the scholar called out, nearly upon them now.

When her father still refused to slow down, she went to stand but toppled back to her seat. "For heaven's sake, Santina, you'll get yourself killed," Papa said, forced to a halt at last.

"*Buon giorno,* Messer Iacopo, I bid you peace," Calandrino said.

"Calandrino." Papa said nothing more to the man who was once his trusted friend.

"I have just returned to San Gimignano. I had hoped, in fact, to speak with you. Will you be long outside the gate?" Despite the pleasantry he spoke, Santina detected a change in his voice. He did not seem the lighthearted scholar she had once known.

"The duration of my travel is none of your concern."

"Yes," he acknowledged as his eyes drifted to Santina. "And yet I dared to hope, after the passing of time, that you might have forgiven my past transgressions and count me once again as friend."

"I bear you no ill will, Calandrino," Papa said wearily. "Only my daughter and I are obliged to continue on our way."

"Might I dare ask for the favor of speaking with you upon your return?"

"Santina is to be married," Papa said, without mincing words. "She will not be returning to San Gimignano anytime soon."

Calandrino's face went blank. He said nothing at first but looked to Santina as though to ascertain if this were the truth. As though a strangler had his throat, he uttered, "You are to be married?"

"*Si,* she is to be married," Papa answered for her. "Did you imagine one so beautiful would not?"

In that instant it was clear that Calandrino, despite his prolonged absence, had not forgotten her. She wanted to explain to him that it was a marriage of necessity, that Papa had arranged the betrothal in order to remove her from San Gimignano and the scandal of the Palmerini. At the same time, several travelers coming up from behind had grown impatient and were shouting, urging them to move to the side of the road.

Papa continued on through the gate, and Santina turned around to look back at Calandrino. He was still watching her. He remained unmoving on his horse, oblivious to the commotion around him. He grew smaller and smaller as Papa took Santina farther and farther away from San Gimignano.

"I need to speak to him. Please turn back," she begged her father.

"No good can come of it, Santina. You must remember you are betrothed to Taddeo." Though Papa's response was firm, Santina could not help but wonder if he, too, now regretted the hastiness of her engagement.

"But he has returned to see me."

"He has returned too late."

It was difficult for Santina to argue this point. If Calandrino cared all that much about her, he might have spoken to her father years ago. And while he had finally returned, it was not likely that he had come to ask for her hand in marriage. If he had serious intentions at all, Santina reasoned, he would have dropped everything and hurried to San Gimignano after she had written him about her trouble with the Palmerini. As usual, Calandrino came and went according to his own desires. Regardless, the scholar might not find her quite so appealing after catching wind of her state of disgrace, she thought. He would learn what people thought of her and Trotula soon enough. Tongues wagged freely in the village.

Santina turned around to face the direction in which they traveled. There was a time when she would have jumped out of the cart and chased after Calandrino. She wanted to do so now, but she knew well enough there was no avoiding Taddeo da Certaldo, who eagerly awaited her arrival.

***

"Though it is not a love match, you will be happy enough with Taddeo," Isabella insisted as she led Santina from the ground floor entryway to the guestroom on the second floor of the narrow brick home. She had a splendid view of the hilltop village, dotted with many cypresses, and a glimpse of *Palazzo del Vicario*, the governor's palace. The palace, with its arched windows, crenellated façade and tower, was the home of the governor from Florence and the place where justice was administered. Just down the road from Isabella's was the ancestral home of the poet, Giovanni Boccaccio, who now resided in Florence.

"If he returns, we'll invite him to dinner and he'll read us his poetry," Isabella imagined.

Despite her sister's cheerful welcome, Santina could not match Isabella's light mood. Her nephew Alessandro, a toddler, gave her reason to smile once again. As if to comfort his aunt, the little boy presented her with his favorite coverlet. When she picked up the child and held him in her arms, she almost thought she might find a measure of contentment in Certaldo.

Although Santina sorely missed Trotula's cottage and life in San Gimignano before all the trouble began, she soon found solace in tending the kitchen garden behind the house. She took it upon herself to ensure that the little plot would produce vegetables nearly year round and a wide variety of herbs. When Isabella's maidservant, Bandecca, came down with a cough, Santina discovered the impoverished state of her sister's pantry. She wasted no time in brewing Trotula's cough syrup with mullein, coltsfoot, and licorice, as well as an assortment of remedies for common ailments.

When she worked with her herbs or tended the garden, Santina could forget about Taddeo, who came to call all too frequently. Free from his watchful eyes and ears, she did not have to tread so carefully, remember to speak softly, and appear sufficiently grateful. She was down on her knees, happily digging in the dirt, when Salvestra, who helped Isabella mostly with the cooking, announced that Messer Taddeo wished to speak with her. She looked up from her weeding to see her fiancé, who had arrived unannounced.

"Why has your sister set you to such a task?" he asked, taking in the sight of her hands covered in mud.

"I offered to tend the garden, Taddeo," she replied as she stood and wiped her hands on her apron.

"Does not your brother-in-law employ servants to do such work?"

"Yes, but the garden was a bed of weeds when I arrived," she explained. "Surely cultivation of the kitchen garden is expected of housewives here in Certaldo."

"You will have no cause to concern yourself with such menial duties when you come to live in my house, Santina," he said. "My wife need not be a gardener."

Santina wanted to say that she had every intention of tending the garden after they were married. However, she merely excused herself to wash and change her dress. She felt little inclined to sit and converse with the man after he had spoken to her thus. Although she had not yet been two months in Certaldo, she was beginning to see that Taddeo might place more demands upon her than she had initially envisioned. She truly might have been better off with the Benedictine sisters.

Santina's commitment to Taddeo weighed heavily upon her. More than this, she grieved for Trotula, she yearned to see Calandrino, and she began to think more and more of her long departed mother as well. In the quiet of her room, while Taddeo still waited, she heard Mama's voice.

Do not allow yourself to be overcome by his limitations, Santina. Taddeo understands you little. Consider it a blessing there are places within you he will never be able to reach. Seek refuge in your alchemist's workshop and find your own peace.

Wearing a clean dress of pale rose brocade and the amethyst pendant once forced upon her by Taddeo, Santina joined him in the salon. Dutifully, she smiled when he spoke of the conveniences in his fine house and the servants she would have at her disposal.

When he presented her with a gold and pearl bodkin, she tried to appear sufficiently pleased. After he departed at last, she visited her garden and picked a handful of nettle. Inhaling the scent, she was reminded of Trotula and her first visit to the midwife's cottage. *Give me strength, Madre de Dio.*

As though making a point of catching her unawares, Taddeo visited Santina at odd hours, sometimes early in the morning, other times at midday, and on certain occasions he came upon her unexpectedly when she was out in the village with Isabella. While her sister interpreted Taddeo's behavior as a sign of devotion, Santina felt as though she was constantly being watched. Nevertheless, she sought to appear courteous and attentive to his every word. When he was away she retreated to her inner *bottega,* a place unrevealed to him, impenetrable to his touch. Santina was content to spend as little time as possible with her fiancé, but Isabella was convinced that Santina only needed to become better acquainted with the man. In mid September her sister took it upon herself to plan a banquet in celebration of the autumn equinox and to invite Taddeo and his brother as well as Ruberto.

In preparation of the fall feast, Santina and Isabella searched the market for the freshest fowl and finest spices. After returning home with overflowing baskets, Isabella disappeared to arrange her hair in braids and ornaments while Santina assisted Salvestra with roasting the chickens and baking the *erbolata,* cheese pies with herbs, while Alessandro played underfoot. When this was accomplished she covered the table with a white cloth and set out the fine silver goblets.

Santina might have continued along with her ordinary life in

Certaldo if only an unexpected visitor had not appeared that afternoon. She was festooning the room with broom blossom when Luigi, Bruno's manservant who seemed to spend much of his time in the cellar, came to tell her that a young friar was at the front door seeking alms and asking for Santina Pietra.

"I tried to be rid of him, but he refuses to leave," Luigi grumbled before walking away.

The gray-robed, red-haired friar appeared dusty from his ride but bore a sunny disposition. "You are Santina of San Gimignano?" he asked. "Daughter of Iacopo?"

She was hesitant to answer. Too many troubles from San Gimignano might have followed her here. Wondering if her guilt been discovered at last, she spoke in a near whisper. "Why do you wish to know?"

"I have a gift. From your friend, the scholar. Do you know him?"

"Calandrino Donati?" Did he think of her still, even though he knew she was to be married?

"It is truly you, then," he ascertained.

He reached into his saddlebag to bring forth a package wrapped in parchment, sealed with wax, and tied with string. Reverently, he presented the gift to Santina. Too stunned to speak, she held it in her hands, guessing from the weight and feel that the scholar had sent her a book. By the time she opened her mouth to inquire more about the contents, the messenger was already darting toward the road.

"*Aspetto*, wait!" she called after him, but it was no use. She watched the young friar disappear into the distance. She wanted to tear open the package at once, but she did not dare while the servants were near. *Whatever have you sent me, Calandrino?*

Destino

Clutching the mysterious package sent by Calandrino, Santina hurried up to her room and closed the door behind her. Her hands shook as she broke the wax seal and tore through the paper wrapping. Years later, when she would remember receiving the book, she would think of it as the day when *destino*, her fate, found her again.

The book, little bigger than the palm of her hand, had a reddish-brown leather cover, which was hand-tooled with a geometric pattern of intertwining roses and gold lettering. There was a quality of ancient holiness about it, much like the book with the copper binding that Calandrino had brought to Papa's store years before. Flipping through the pages, she saw Calandrino's carefully rendered illustrations along with passages from Plato and Hermes Trismegistus, the Egyptian sage and father of alchemy. Tucked inside the middle of the book was a folded letter.

To most well beloved Santina, Calandrino sends greetings in the Lord and prays you will receive this letter in good will.

179

Too much time has come between us. Through your gracious sister Lauretta, who urged me against this correspondence, I learned that you are to be married to Taddeo da Certaldo next spring. I confess this news brings me no happiness. Since the day your father entrusted me as your tutor, you have held a most especial place in my heart. While duty called me to foreign cities, I have never ceased to pray for your well being and eternal happiness.

Concerning the matter of the Palmerini, please believe me when I say that your safety is and always will be of the greatest concern to me. As promised in my last letter, I began the journey to San Gimignano just as soon as I was able to take leave. I regret the terrible ordeal you have suffered, Santina. I regret, more than I can express, that I did not have the opportunity to speak to you before you became betrothed to Taddeo. It is, of course, not my place to question the arrangement, and yet is seems as though much happened in haste following the great tragedy.

I will tell you little of myself, except to say that I was blessed with kind companionship from the good citizens of Carpentras. It was in this Provençal city where the manuscript purchased from a peddler in San Gimignano has been translated at long last. This was an endeavor that began, in a way, at your father's house. While the experiments undertaken in the workshop may seem to have been in vain, the processes described within the manual may prove quite illuminating. If you will study these pages, Santina, you will surely discover a light along the path to the eternal.

A copy of the manuscript is herewith sent to you, who have surely long wondered about the contents. I am greatly indebted to Maestro Samuel Abroz, a Spanish Jew who I met in Carpentras. He came to me as a miracle from God when I had given up all hope. At long last the translation of this most rare text is complete.

There are few who can be trusted, Santina. While you will find nothing offensive to our Lord within the book, pearls must not be cast before swine. I implore you to keep the writings close.

Having once known your heart, I believe I can count you among my closest of confidants. Here in Milan your old friend asks your forgiveness for past sins and remembers you with the greatest affection. May Jesu have you always in his blessed keeping and bring you great happiness and perfect peace.

> *Calandrino*
> *Written in Milan on 22 August 1347*

Santina held in her hands the manuscript that had compelled Calandrino to wander across Europe in search of a learned Jew. After the passing of years she had ceased to believe a translator would ever be found. In truth, she doubted if the wisdom contained within the manuscript was worth the sacrifice of the life they might have shared, but Calandrino obviously thought otherwise.

She wondered what would have happened if he had not discovered the book in the first place. Perhaps he would have found another reason to leave her. In a way Santina wished the scholar had not written, for his tender words only added to her misgivings about Taddeo. She folded the letter and replaced it to the book. *I began the journey to San Gimignano just as soon as I was able to take leave.* She had written him of her trouble back in February, and yet he did not reach San Gimignano until July. He alluded to another letter, one that she never received. Perhaps he had offered some sort of explanation, but she was quite certain it was the translation of the alchemical text that delayed his return.

Calandrino was and always would be a scholar first and foremost. Clearly, he had not made haste to come to her aid even given the long journey from France. His ancient manuscript mattered above all. Now he was off in Milan, embarked upon yet another quest of some kind, so it would seem. He loved her in his way, but he had waited until calamity struck to return to her. And although he had returned, she was far from sure that he intended to offer a marriage proposal. Regardless, she was already betrothed. *I wish it were otherwise, Calandrino. But there is nothing to be done.*

Burdened with regrets over what might have been, Santina was nonetheless drawn to the mysterious text. She wanted to do nothing more than remain hidden in her room and delve into *A Manual to the Science of Alchemy*, but Isabella was calling out to her from the hallway. "It's almost time, Santina. Have you done something about your hair?"

With a wistful sigh Santina tucked the precious book away in her *cassone* and put on her blue damask gown. Hastily, she twisted her long hair into a knot and tucked in Taddeo's gold and pearl bodkin. Her thoughts were all of Calandrino, his letter, and alchemy, but when Luigi wandered into the kitchen reeking of wine, she complained convincingly of the friars who were forever seeking alms.

When the guests arrived, Santina greeted them as though she had long awaited their arrival. Taddeo's brother, Giorgio, showed her every kindness and Giorgio's wife, Niccolosa, offered to assist with preparations for the upcoming wedding. Ruberto, however, looked at her as though recalling all her secrets. Even as he greeted her politely, she could not help but think of the day he had

96

36

discovered her and Calandrino alone in Papa's shop. He had borne witness, as well, to the disgrace brought to her by the Palmerini.

Not to be undone by Ruberto, Santina stifled her longing to weep and took her seat at the table as the *erbolata* was served. She made every attempt to follow the men's conversation of politics, the jewel trade, and the latest writings of Giovanni Boccaccio. Nevertheless, her thoughts kept veering off in the direction of the manual and Calandrino, who still remembered her well.

After the scholar had broken her heart and departed for Bologna, her interest in the *Great Work* had waned. Yet the *matter of Egypt*, as Calandrino had once described alchemy, never entirely left. Indeed, the scholar's letter served to remind her of the knowledge for which her soul still hungered.

"I see why Bruno is gaining weight." Giorgio's remark brought Santina's thoughts back to the table as Salvestra carried in the final course of the banquet. "Well done, Salvestra," he said. The layered *torta*, towered high on the silver tray, would have been fit to serve the Pope.

"Salvestra is a most excellent cook," Bruno said. "But Isabella has a hand in everything prepared in the kitchen."

Santina knew the truth was that Isabella spent as little time over the stove as possible, but Bruno's devotion to her was unfailing. As the couple exchanged glances, Santina felt the heat of Taddeo's gaze. Uncomfortable, she turned away and caught sight of Ruberto, who bore the appearance of having witnessed some indiscretion. She had the sense that Papa's worthy employee perceived exactly the way things stood between her and Taddeo.

Santina's aversion to her fiancé was not, as Isabella imagined, that he was still a stranger to her. The problem was much deeper, for she could never love Taddeo while she loved another. Her wedding, planned for the following June, was not far enough away.

But that evening, at least, Taddeo and the other guests would return home. She would be able to read *A Manual to the Science of Alchemy* in peace and she might forget, for a short time, that she was engaged to a man she could not love.

It was as if she had returned to the secret laboratory of her girlhood. With Calandrino's book in her hands, she felt as though something astonishing was about to happen. She was no longer in exile in Certaldo, but in a world of possibilities. On the second page she read the warning to anyone who was not a priest or an adept. Santina was not a priest, and she was not sure what it meant to be an adept. But since Calandrino had seen fit to send her the book, she continued on, ignoring the admonition.

Thumbing through the pages, she noted a complex and detailed procedure for the production of gold, as well as numerous warnings regarding the necessity of maintaining strict secrecy. Interspersed throughout the text written by Isaac the Jew—priest, adept in Cabala, master of the elixir of life and the philosopher's stone—were rare writings by ancient philosophers as well as beautifully colored illustrations. She saw images of the *Sun King* and *Moon Queen* in various states of separation and union. She read that each image would require careful contemplation to know its full meaning. Drawings of Egyptian gods and goddesses and the sage, Hermes Trismegistus, were also scattered throughout the text.

Returning again to the beginning of the book, she read the preface, as translated by Maestro Abroz. Before embarking on the experiments, the author wrote, it was necessary for the adept to complete a series of preparatory lessons. One could not begin the Great Work, it was said, until the heart was pure.

Lesson I

The initial preparation for this work is this: Release all base thoughts—all darkness and depravity of mind. Let all thy interactions with men be honest and straightforward. Avoid the company of the vainglorious. Hate hypocrisy and deceit.

The lessons, which continued on for several pages, were followed by a section devoted to the discernment of those activities that sought to satisfy vain and earthly desires from those that sought to fulfill a good and holy purpose. Isaac the Jew put forth that the alchemist worked not only with metals, but with his will and determination to create what he most truly desired.

Know this, thou art not born to suffer an unalterable fate and wicked destiny. Rather, thou art born to dominate the world and create! Yet this God-given right is oft forgotten. Children who come to this earth believing in the promise of life grow up to limit their imaginations and accept defeat. Corrupted to see themselves as weak and powerless, hopelessness, fear, and poverty prevail.

Yet this is not what God, in His infinite wisdom, has ordained. Rather, achieving the desires of the heart and mastering of the physical world by persistent efforts are the noblest of endeavors....

For sufficient reason, the methods employed by the masters have been shrouded in secrecy.

Santina looked up from the page. Was she was dreaming when she saw a hazy form against the open window—a young woman resembling Mama? *Is that you?*

The woman smiled as she stretched out her hand to Santina.

Bene, the manual has returned to you, Santina. Use it well, and it will guide you.

The apparition faded into the light, disappearing as fast as it had come. It was a strange and glorious wonder. Mama had returned to her. So had Calandrino's book. She was no longer alone in Certaldo but joined by otherworldly spirits. She was startled by the screeching of an owl outside her window. As Santina closed the book, she dared to hope her life could be more than it was. If there was any truth to alchemy, perhaps she would not have to marry Taddeo.

⚜

Santina was careful to read the alchemical manual when she was well alone. It was not that Isabella or Bruno would have condemned her for reading an ancient alchemical text, it was that she was reluctant to confess she had received a precious gift from Calandrino. One golden fall day she slipped the book into her apron pocket and disappeared to her garden retreat. While she was supposedly picking apples, she sat beneath the fruit tree and lost herself in the secret world of alchemy inhabited by dragons and magicians with steaming potions. She never heard Taddeo's footsteps coming down the garden path.

"Santina?"

She continued reading, eventually becoming aware of his voice. She looked up to see Taddeo looking over her shoulder at an image of three naked figures frolicking in the fountain of youth—the alchemist's elixir of life—surrounded by magical symbols of the Great Work.

"Whatever are you reading, Santina?" Taddeo spoke as though she were in mortal danger.

Snapping the book shut at once, she wondered how in the world she would explain herself to her fiancé.

The Revelation

Santina stood before Taddeo, who waited for an explanation of the fearsome book. "It's just an old text, something to help me practice my Latin," she said. Before she could slip the book into her apron pocket, he snatched it from her hand.

"*A Manual to the Science of Alchemy*?" Taddeo leafed through the pages, and Santina hoped he would dismiss the manual as archaic writing of little relevance.

"*Dio mio,* this speaks of black magic." Clearly not about to drop the subject, he held open the manual to a page with an illustration of a crowned serpent eating its own tail. It was the *ouroboros*—the alchemist's symbol of death and rebirth. Letting the book fall to the ground, Taddeo made the sign of the cross.

"It's only writings from the ancients," Santina said, bending to pick up the text.

"To put such ideas in your delicate mind," he said. "Where in God's name did you find such filth?"

Santina wondered where to begin. She could not easily tell

him about Papa's *bottega,* but she had to explain the book somehow and she was growing weary of lies.

"You might very well be angry with me if I tell you the truth,
Taddeo," she said. "Are you sure you wish to hear it?"

"You are to be my wife, Santina. Whatever this is about, you
have to tell me. It's harmful to your soul to keep secrets from me."

While she doubted this was the case, she told herself that
Taddeo should know the real woman he was to marry. At the same
time, she was well aware that the truth might prove too much for
the pious jeweler.

"The book was given to me by a scholar from the University
of Bologna, someone I've known since I was a girl," she began. "I
assure you there's nothing evil in it."

"Would you have Pope Clement investigate us, Santina?"

"I have committed no heresy, Taddeo. The book is a rare text,
translated from ancient Hebrew."

When Taddeo remained silent, she dared to tell him more. She
spoke of the dabbling that had taken place in her father's workshop,
the mixing of chemicals, the efforts to make gold. "But this is not
just a recipe book, and making gold is not what is essential. What
the alchemist seeks more than anything is the philosopher's stone."

"Just what is the stone, Santina, if not an instrument of
stregoneria?"

She fell silent for a moment and then continued. "I used to
think the philosopher's stone was the alchemists' word for an elixir that would heal all sickness. But I have come to understand it as
a means of change—as the key to transforming the soul as much
as the metal."

"Transforming the soul? Just what are you saying, Santina?"

"The alchemist seeks the deepest meaning of the Gospel," she
said, trying to find words Calandrino might have used to explain

the matter. "He seeks to live as a true disciple. Surely this is not displeasing to the Lord."

When Taddeo nodded, she thought she had somehow managed to make sense to him. Then he spoke to her as though she were a mere child. "You have put your mind where you ought not to have, Santina. These are dangerous thoughts."

"How is it dangerous to seek the divine?"

"It's blasphemy to imagine you have the power to transform your own soul. How could your father have allowed it? These are unfit thoughts for a fragile young woman."

"Do you mean I'm entirely unworthy because I'm a woman?" she said, growing impatient. "I've worked harder in my life than you imagine, Taddeo."

Taddeo tossed back his head and laughed heartily. "You have been cared for since you were a child, Santina. You know nothing of the world."

She could little hide her disdain. In the heat of her anger she did not consider how Taddeo might react to the unveiling of her past. She only sought to make him understand that she was not the pampered young lady he imagined her to be. Forgetting any semblance of feminine humility, she spoke to him entirely as herself.

"In San Gimignano I worked as a midwife's apprentice. I delivered babies. Sometimes I took care of sick children, and I sewed up bloody wounds and set broken bones."

He looked at her as though she had gone mad. "Has the devil got hold of you, Santina?"

"It's true, Taddeo. All of it." There was no taking back her words after she had spoken.

He regarded her as though she had committed a grave sin. There was no point in going any further with her story. If she told him the part she had played in the birth of Ferondo Palmerini's grandson, Taddeo would no doubt send the authorities after her.

"Why did you never tell me this before?"

"I wanted to," she said. "I tried to several times. Papa thought it best not to."

"He thought it was best to deceive me?"

"He thought not to vex you. And for good reason he feared the revelation might cause you to think differently of me," she replied, avoiding his disapproving eyes. "Truly, Taddeo, I never meant to lie to you."

Taddeo's silence told her there would be consequences for misleading him. She had known all along that her fiancé would never accept her past or the merits of Calandrino's book. The jeweler had not bargained for such a wife. Neither was he a man who would easily forget the commitment he had made, the contract he had signed, or her generous dowry, although she might wish otherwise.

At length she asked, "What will you do with me now?"

"I confess this is a great shock to me, Santina. To have committed such a cruel deception." Reaching for the text he said, "The book must be destroyed."

"You can't," she replied, holding fiercely to the manual. When she saw the fury in Taddeo's eyes, she did her best to compose herself and appeal to him as a man of business. "It is a precious text, Taddeo. It might be worth a tidy sum." Upon coming to Certaldo, Santina had set aside her own desires for the most part. She would draw the line when it came to this treasured manual.

"You have much to learn about the sacrament of marriage, Santina," he said. "I will speak to your father of this matter." He turned away abruptly and left her alone beneath the apple tree that was laden with unpicked fruit.

After the scandal in San Gimignano, Santina had determined

to become a good and obedient wife. For several months she had done her best to keep peace with Taddeo. To do so now would require a painful sacrifice. But how could she give up the book entrusted to her by Calandrino?

Santina tried, in a halfhearted way, to atone for withholding the truth of her former life, but Taddeo remained cool, maintaining his distance. No doubt he was waiting for her to hand over the manual, which was hidden safely inside her *cassone*.

Santina had no intention of giving Taddeo the alchemical text, and in truth she would have been enormously relieved if he thought to dissolve the marriage contract. At the same time, she loathed the thought of bringing more sorrow to Papa, who had suffered enough on her account. After all the trouble she had caused, Santina felt disinclined to further disgrace her family or go crawling back to San Gimignano. Feeling at a loss for what to do, she wrote Calandrino.

To my dear friend Calandrino, Santina sends her most kind greeting in the Lord.

That you thought to send me the alchemical text pleased me very well. I only regret having missed the opportunity to discuss the book with you before my departure from San Gimignano last summer. Nevertheless, I am grateful to Lauretta for having informed you of my new residence here in Certaldo.

Although I am not a scholar, it seems to me that the manual is a wondrous book. There is something otherworldly in the voice that speaks through these pages. The text comes from another time and place, and yet the wisdom gleaned from the writings may prove quite useful. Who does not wish to take command of his own destiny? Until now the way has never been clear.

Do you believe what is written, Calandrino? Do we truly have a hand in the design of our own futures? If this is the case, then I wonder why it is I still reside here in Certaldo, biding my time until I must marry a man for whom I am ill suited.

Rest assured the manual is in safekeeping. I remember well the day I first saw the original text. You brought it to my father's shop, and we were later discovered by Ruberto. After this you were compelled to leave San Gimignano.

While there is little use in lamenting what has passed, I am sorry that you learned of my betrothal in the manner in which you did, during our chance encounter at the gate.

I am still desiring to hear of your welfare. May Almighty God have you in safe keeping always.

> *Santina*
> *Written at Certaldo*
> *9 October 1347*

After sealing the letter with wax, Santina wished she had the courage to pose a question. *Why did you really return to San Gimignano? What would you have said to me, given the chance?* Even if he had returned for her, there was little she could do to avoid her forthcoming wedding. She would be married to Taddeo before long, and it was her own doing. After Trotula's death, she had refused to envision any other future before her. She had not followed the way of the alchemist, and now it was too late to change her mind.

It is not too late; you are not yet married. You must consider, very prayerfully, what it is you desire, she heard Mama say. *Then you must do what you can and allow God to do the rest.*

In the quiet of her room Santina paused, at long last, to consider her heart's desire. She recalled *The Emerald Tablet*—the words attributed to the sage Hermes Trismegistus as translated in the manual. *That which is below is like that which is above, and that which is above is like that which is below. Through this are performed miracles of the one thing...*

Within the enigma was an answer. She considered the realms of Heaven and Earth, separate to the casual observer, united to the adept. If the mysterious workings of the world above could be deciphered, might one create miracles here below in the Tuscan hillside?

It was perhaps a flight of fancy to think Calandrino might be returned to her by the power of alchemy. Three years and enormous tragedy had come between them, but warm memories of him still clung to her skin. While she could not yet bring herself to ask for him back, she was determined in her intention to safeguard his treasured text. If she did nothing, Taddeo might summon her father, who would surely force her to relinquish the book. In order to keep the manual safe and honor her promise to Calandrino, an act of cunning was required. And so the following day she composed a note, scented with oil, to Taddeo. Conveying due humility, she requested the opportunity to apologize for her former selfishness.

When he arrived she was sitting alone in the corner of the central salon, knitting socks on four needles. Santina wasted no time in saying what she had to say. "It was a mistake to conceal my past, Taddeo. I am deeply sorry," she said from her place in the late afternoon shadows. "I only kept silent because I sought not to vex you."

Setting the knitting aside, Santina picked up the book with the beautiful reddish-brown leather cover. She held it out so he could see the dreaded thing once again. Head bowed, she walked to the hearth and knelt before the fire. The book opened, she dropped it onto the burning log and watched as the pages were engulfed in flames.

Her heart pounded, not because she feared Taddeo would uncover her deception, but because she had succeeded in this victory over him. Her fiancé might think otherwise, but he could never force her into obedience, much less break her will.

Santina picked up the tongs to push the smoldering pages deeper into the flames. Streams of gray smoke swept through the room as she remained kneeling before her sacrifice until every page turned to ash. Taddeo would have to see that she would disobey him no more on the matter.

"It's gone, Taddeo. I will never speak of it again." This was not a lie.

Finally hearing what he wanted to hear, Taddeo walked across the dimly lit room and deigned to speak with her for the first time in weeks. Holding her chin in his hand, he allowed her to look into his eyes. "Very well then, Santina. I forgive you. The mistakes of your past were not only yours, but also your father's. He failed to guide you. From now I will protect you from all evil."

Santina suppressed the urge to smile, for she recalled that Papa had struggled endlessly to make her behave the way daughters were expected to behave. Perhaps, after having tried for so long to acquire her, Taddeo was reluctant to acknowledge she was not the impressionable young woman he imagined her to be. To do so would be like admitting one of his precious gems was made of paste.

She had managed to deceive the jeweler in more than this way. Taddeo had left her with little choice, for he refused to move beyond his limited philosophy. Clearly, he had no desire to ponder the thoughts of ancient sages or to know the young woman he had chosen to marry. The ruse cost her little, for the treasured text, with the exception of its decorative cover, remained securely hidden, deep inside her *cassone*. She had burned instead the pages of a marriage handbook—a parting gift from Lauretta. The book stressed modesty of dress and demeanor for merchants' wives among other things. She would never dare to read *A Manual to the Science of Alchemy* again unless she was safely hidden away from Taddeo.

Shortly after Santina sent her last letter to Calandrino, startling news reached the quiet village of Certaldo. Genoese trading ships had returned to Messina in Sicily from the Black Sea with all dead or dying sailors. Upon being refused to land, several of the ships continued on to Genoa. The Genoese tried to drive away the sick with flaming arrows, but the pestilence made its way inland nonetheless.

"What does it mean for us?" Isabella asked, clearly troubled by talk in the village.

"It is still far enough away," Bruno said, trying to calm her.

Santina said nothing, but she could not shake the uneasy feeling that fell over her. In light of the sickness that threatened to encroach upon them all, the matter of her unhappy engagement abruptly diminished in importance. She thought at once of Trotula, for she would have known what to do to prepare for the contagion.

As though in answer to Santina's fears, a letter from Calandrino arrived. The scholar did not write to offer further comment regarding the alchemical manuscript. Rather, the letter was entirely practical in nature.

> *To beloved Santina be this letter taken. I, Calandrino send greetings in the Lord.*
>
> *Having no wish to trouble you, I must yet send warning of that which may soon be upon us. You have no doubt heard that the pestilence has visited Genoa and threatens to spread quickly through Tuscany. Knowing you are well versed in the brewing of various remedies, I now urge you to make haste in your preparations to combat the disease.*
>
> *There is no use fretting over that which might or might not be, and yet it may behoove those who are adept in the treatment of the sick to prepare for the arrival of the contagion. It is wise to prepare a number of infusions— butterbur and blessed thistle might be effective, as well as angelica root, coriander, and cloves. If you go anywhere near the afflicted, you must cover yourself with oil infused with sage, rosemary, thyme, lemon balm, hyssop, mint, rosemary, and cloves. For washing and cleaning, prepare several barrels of strong vinegar steeped in the same herbs, along with quantities of garlic. You should sip the remedy as well.*
>
> *I offer this advice humbly, knowing well the limitations of our human hands. Nonetheless, perhaps my warning will prove useful against the deadly enemy. I pray you will take heed and begin at once to plan for the possibility of calamity. You will need vast quantities of medicines and dressings if the contagion should arrive.*
>
> *I confess my wish is to be with you now, Santina, and to*

see you safe. While I must respect the commitment you have made to another, your welfare remains of the utmost concern to me during these uncertain times. If you should find yourself in need during the days ahead, you must go to Fra Bernardo, the brother herbalist at the Convent of San Francesco in San Miniato al Tedesco. Listen to me well Santina: he can be trusted, and he will give you shelter.

I pray this letter reaches you. May Almighty God preserve you and keep you in good health.

> *Calandrino*
> *Written at Milan*
> *28 November, 1347*

Holding the letter in her hand, Santina was not at all reassured by his words. Calandrino hinted of darkness to come. Although she prayed it would not be, she thought it made good sense to prepare the suggested remedies, which were reminiscent of those Trotula had relied upon. She pictured Calandrino steeping his herbs in Milan, in between poring over his texts. She wished he was not so far away, but of course he could not come to her, a betrothed woman.

During the days ahead she set herself to the task of preparing specifics for whatever evil influences were making their way to Certaldo. She filled countless barrels and ceramic jars with Trotula's cure-alls. For fevers, as well as protection from *stregoneria,* she prepared angelica roots. She made rubbing oils of comfrey and coriander and cordials of butterbur and blessed thistle. She pounded poultices of yarrow, marigold, and ground ivy, rolled pills of ginger and cloves, and filled linen sacks with all of what remained for later use in sachets, bathwater, and infusions. Around her neck, hidden beneath her bodice, she wore Trotula's gold amulet.

She did not accept that the pestilence had been cast by *maloc-chio* as some believed. (Neither would she blame the Jews, as some unfairly did.) Nonetheless, Santina went about making *brevi*, in the way that Trotula had taught her. The charm bags filled with herbs offered a little comfort to those who wore them, if not a cure.

Santina's preparations were complete when Taddeo, bearing a gift of songbirds for roasting, came to call one afternoon. Admitted to the kitchen by Luigi, her fiancé came upon her just as she was arranging her assortment of herbal remedies in Isabella's pantry. Taking in the array of jars, he asked, "What's all this about, Santina?"

"The cold weather is coming upon us," she replied. "It would behoove us to be well prepared."

Taddeo gave her a curious look but said nothing more. Although he had made it clear she was expected to put her past as a midwife's apprentice behind her, he thought not to question the remedies she had made. Perhaps he feared the disease that had come from the trading ships more than he feared the power of women who meddled with medicinals.

In late January, when it became known that the pestilence had arrived in nearby Pisa, Santina was as ready as one could be to face utter disaster.

The Pestilence

T he pestilence ravaged Pisa in January of 1348 before cutting a cruel swathe inland and moving northeast to Bologna and south to Siena. Throughout the Italian peninsula that winter, people wondered what city would fall next. In Certaldo it was soon discovered that Messer Pizzini, who sold armor, was struck by a mysterious illness. Two days later he lay dead.

"Master Serpolta came and bled him and tried to do what he could for him," Taddeo came to tell Bruno. "The *podestà* summoned the doctor for questioning, but the cause of death has not yet been confirmed," he continued as Santina listened in on the conversation.

"It could be anything," said Bruno, persuading no one.

Before departing, Taddeo issued a warning. "The women should stay indoors. They must be protected."

Telling herself that Messer Pizzini's death might have been caused by any number of illnesses, Santina withheld comment. Yet she had to admit this was most likely a result of the disaster brought by the trading ships.

Her speculation was confirmed when Messer Pizzini's wife, daughter, and three of his servants died within days of each other. She could only pray that the illness contracted by the merchant might somehow be contained within his household. The *podestà*, taking swift action to control the spread of the disease, appointed officials to burn the refuse of the sick. Additional preventative instructions soon followed. The importation of cloth was strictly forbidden and those afflicted were to be isolated. When someone died, the corpse was to be placed outside the front door of the house and the funeral briers were to be summoned.

A preternatural quiet settled over the town, and the safety measures offered little reassurance to the citizens of Certaldo. The usual sounds of labor, human voices, laughter, quarreling, and the rattling of carts were replaced by a silence interrupted only by the grim melody of a funeral dirge. Santina, who ventured out-of-doors only to take respite in the winter garden, offered Taddeo a pomander of cloves to mask the stench in the streets. As the pestilence wore on, he complained bitterly of the cost to his business, for few thought to purchase gems during the dark days of the pestilence.

Most people did what they could to avoid exposure and, like Santina, limited their activities to the bare necessities. Some left the city and departed to the surrounding countryside. Regardless of the efforts made to contain the sickness, the disease spread like wildfire. Master Serpolta wore the physician's beaked mask stuffed with straw, but he succumbed to the contagion shortly after the outbreak. His unfortunate death made others pause before treating the afflicted. Santina held hope that Isabella's household would be spared, but the morning came when Bandecca, the maid-servant, called out from the street.

"I cannot come to you today, Madonna," she said to Isabella.

Santina braced to hear the reason. "My mother and father both are sick with it. I confess I don't know how to help them."

"May Almighty God have you in keeping, Bandecca," Isabella replied, "but you must stay away until the pest has passed."

As Santina stood listening, her first instinct was to go and help the girl. One glance at her young nephew reminded Santina she could not risk bringing the seeds of illness back home.

"They're burning up with fever," Bandecca continued. "And the sores are so painful."

Santina could well appreciate Bandecca's fear. The contagion was fully upon them now, but no one knew of an effective treatment. For several years Santina had helped Trotula dispense advice and remedies to mothers who sought their counsel, but treating victims of the pestilence was another matter.

Santina knew that the dreadful disease could kill within a matter of days and was known to spread simply by coming into contact with the food or clothing of a sick person. The ugly black swellings—the *gavoccioli*—that became painful ulcers and eventually burst were an affliction she had never seen before. Still, she might offer Bandecca a little hope by sharing a few of the remedies she had prepared.

Stepping beside Isabella at the window, she called out to Bandecca. "I'll give you something to take to them." A strong infusion and a good rub would at least offer some relief.

"What should I do for the sores? They are so terrible."

"You must apply a poultice, Bandecca. I'll tell you how to do it."

Speaking through the open window, Santina explained how to make a plaster of yarrow and honey and how to administer the infusions and wash the linens in boiling vinegar. She told the maidservant that she would set the remedies and a few *brevi* outside the door and remember the girl's parents in her prayers.

From the window Santina watched as Bandecca, a solitary figure carrying a basket filled with brews and herb-filled charms, walked down the road. She was not sure she would ever see the girl alive again.

During the pestilence of 1348 there were those who ran from their family members, even their own children, and others who hid inside locked rooms in an attempt to avoid contamination. A number of varied and contradictory strategies for coping with the disaster developed over time. Some people took purging enemas while others visited public latrines, thinking that the foul odors were somehow efficacious. There were those who prayed day after day without sleeping, and there were those, such as Bruno's brother Stagio, who insisted it was best to enjoy life to its fullest, since one might soon be dead anyway. Stagio consumed large quantities of wine and food, went to parties, laughed, sang, and opened his house to everyone.

On the other hand, some heard it said that avoiding human contact and restricting the amount of food and drink one consumed would be most preventative against the disease. Ruberto ascribed somewhat to this philosophy and ate sparingly, though he readily accepted the tonics Santina offered. As she sent Luigi off to the shop with another basket of herbed vinegar and infused oil, she could not help but recall the times Ruberto had advised her against working with Trotula.

Several neighbors, having learned of Santina's healing remedies, began to make their way to Isabella's house. Although Isabella refused to open her door to anyone but family, it was not in Santina's heart to refuse those who sought assistance. From the upstairs window, she listened to the woeful tales of many desperate souls. After the visitors moved away from the house, Luigi would drop the prescribed herbs and remedies outside the door while complaining that Santina was inviting the sickness to come too close. She ignored Luigi's remarks but continued to mop the floors with Trotula's vinegar.

The dance of death, the burning of corpses, and the ringing of bells seemed endless that winter. Homes were abandoned, businesses closed, and countless merchants, lawyers, doctors, and city officials were now dead. Communication with Rome as well as with neighboring cities was lost. She knew nothing of Papa, Lauretta, or Calandrino. Meanwhile, a third *podestà* took office. The intolerable grew still more unbearable when Taddeo's brother was stricken.

"We cannot stay here any longer," Taddeo announced after breaking the news about Giorgio. "We'll go to the countryside—to my sister's farmhouse in Empoli."

"You would leave your brother?" she replied.

"I'm a jeweler, not a doctor. I can't stop the pestilence. Neither can you," he said. "Anyway, I've summoned a physician to his house."

"Is there a physician left in Certaldo?"

"He's from Florence—Master Malatesta. He claims to have an effective treatment," Taddeo insisted. "I've paid him generously. He'll do what he can."

Santina recalled the so-called physician sent to Caterina by Ferondo Palmerini. She could not help but wonder if this Master Malatesta was of the same ilk. It was likely that Taddeo had purchased an excuse to abandon his brother rather than a qualified physician. She would not pretend she did not see this possibility.

"What do you know of the man?" she said. "It seems unwise to leave your brother in the hands of a stranger."

"He was recommended by the apothecary," he said impatiently. "What more can I do?"

There was, in fact, nothing more *Taddeo* could do. But Santina knew it was within *her* power to offer assistance. "I can bring Niccolosa some herbs that might give Giorgio some relief," she said at last. "After Giorgio is well, I can join you at your sister's."

"*Dio mio*! How can you think of it?" he cried. "If you enter my brother's house, you may never leave."

The truth was that Santina, although concerned for Giorgio, had no wish to be parted from her sister during these uncertain times. If she left Certaldo with Taddeo, she might never see Isabella again. Yet Taddeo would no doubt deem this a poor excuse for staying behind. She thought for a moment before saying, "But of course, we are not yet married. We cannot travel together."

"Father Albertus has agreed to marry us before we leave. The banns have been read, there's no need to delay any longer. You'll have to set aside your ideas of a grand nuptial banquet—we haven't the time," he announced, and Santina envisioned a macabre wedding amidst the dead and dying. Before heading to the door, he looked her square in the eye. "I will come for you two days from now, at *terce*. Be prepared to travel, Santina."

Married, in two days time?

After Taddeo left, Santina stood motionless. After the initial shock subsided, she considered her choices. If she refused to accompany Taddeo, he would either go on without her or take her with him by force. She could not countenance the thought of marrying him, and yet the wedding was inevitable, provided they both survived the plague. She could not deny that leaving the village might prove wise, for the sick numbered more each day. On the other hand, she might be just as likely to survive hidden inside Isabella's house. If Taddeo traveled to Empoli without her, he might very well sue Papa for breach of contract, demand payment of her dowry, and bring further disgrace to her family name. After all the mistakes she had made, Santina could not bring herself to dishonor her father again.

Reluctantly, she told Isabella of her fiancé's demands. Upon hearing that Santina was obliged to marry at once and travel to Empoli, Isabella wept uncontrollably. "I'm afraid I won't ever see you again."

"Believe me, I have no wish to accompany Taddeo. But what choice do I have?"

After sending Luigi off with a basket of remedies for Niccolosa and Giorgio, Santina began packing food, medicines, and warm clothes for her trip. As she touched her gown of crimson silk and surcoat of rich damask—her wedding attire—she could not help but cry bitter tears at the thought of the fate awaiting her.

That night as she fell asleep, she imagined lying in a meadow with Calandrino. It was a warm summer day, the air was sweet with the scent of grass and wildflowers, and the scholar held her in his arms. For a brief moment, the pestilence was but a bad dream.

Although Santina had reconciled herself to Taddeo's horrid demands, an unanticipated obstacle appeared the day she was to marry him and depart for Empoli. She awoke in the early morning hours to the sound of Isabella's voice. *"Santina, wake up. Something's wrong."* Within the darkness, her sister's form gradually took shape. In her arms Isabella held little Alessandro. The child lay limp as though asleep, but he whimpered softly. *Dio Mio, not Alessandro.*

"Is he feverish?"

"*Sì*. Bruno is sick as well," Isabella said tearfully. "Alessandro was cranky when I put him to bed, but I didn't want to believe it had come."

Santina bolted out of bed and made her way to the kitchen. Opening the pantry, she stood before her assortment of remedies. *Madre di Dio, what am I to do? Trotula's vinegar and oil. Calandrino said to apply the oil before going near the sick.* Reaching for the brews, she said to Isabella, "Wash yourself with the vinegar immediately and rub the oil into your skin."

Hands covered in the aromatic oil, Santina entered Bruno's room. Immediately, she was hit with the putrid, sweet scent of sickness, like rotting apples in the air. An intruder in the night, the pest had come upon them. *God help us.* "We must burn rosemary. And wash the floors. The air is full of poison."

Bruno, face mottled with fever, uttered a moan in greeting. Isabella laid Alessandro down on the bed beside his father. Lifting up his tunic, Santina looked in horror at the purple rings that had already erupted under his arm.

She knew at once that the boy's battle to live would be painful and difficult. Looking from Alessandro to Bruno, Santina wondered how she could leave them. Setting aside her dilemma with Taddeo for the moment, she went about preparing a hot infusion to bring down their fevers and ease their discomfort.

After administering the healing draught, Santina prepared a poultice of yarrow and honey for the skin, as Trotula had done for wounds, thinking this would be just as effective as costly Venetian theriac sold by the apothecary. While Santina had no use for the apothecary's concoction—which was made of sixty-five ingredients and the dried flesh of roasted serpents—she wished she could offer stronger herbs for the relief of pain. But poppy, henbane, and mandrake did not grow in Isabella's kitchen garden. Santina made do with what she had, and as she worked she found herself speaking silently to Trotula, asking for guidance. *Keep constant vigil, Santina. Bid them drink all through the night.*

Having tended to Bruno and Alessandro till sunrise, Santina left the sickroom. When she entered the kitchen again, she found both Salvestra and Luigi dressed in traveling clothes, bags packed, preparing to slip unnoticed out the back door.

"I'm sorry, Madonna," Luigi said. "But we cannot remain in the house."

"I cannot blame you for this. But Bruno would have you paid what you are due," she replied.

After consulting with Isabella and settling with the servants, Santina stepped outside to the garden. Standing before the pink sky, she wondered if Taddeo would still insist that she accompany him to Empoli. The calamity would be over one day, but Isabella would never forget if Santina left her in her time of greatest need. She wanted to help her sister, and there was also a part of her that wondered if the healing art she learned from Trotula was strong enough to vanquish the pestilence.

Bending to pick a dry sprig of rosemary, Santina noticed a shiny rock on the ground. She saw it had a reddish-brown hue and shiny flecks of copper. Feeling the cold weight of it in her hand, Santina thought of the red stone, the *rubedo*, which was attained during the last phase of the alchemical experiment.

This final act was illustrated in the text by the wedding of a Red King to a White Queen. The Red King bore the likeness of the sun and the White Queen bore the likeness of the moon. The *rubedo* occurred when the impure soul—called the volatile sulfur—had been thoroughly cleansed of imperfections and coalesced into the sulfur of the philosophers, or the salt of magnificence. The soul, or White Queen, made new and pristine in this way, was then reunited with the body, or Red King. The event signaled a time when the newly transformed alchemist could accomplish great feats. Santina began to sense what this meant for her.

For months she had done her best to accept her betrothal to Taddeo and atone for her past mistakes. At the same time she had largely ignored the skills she had acquired during her years with Trotula. Santina could not deny that she was now being called to put those skills to good use. Slipping the stone into her apron pocket, she knew what she would tell Taddeo when he came for her. What Taddeo would do with her was another matter.

Alessandro

Trueto his word, the bridegroom arrived in two day's time and rapped on the front door promptly at *terce*. When Santina did not respond at once, he shouted out to announce himself. "It's Taddeo. Open the door!"

"I must bid you stay away," she called from the window. Santina was not dressed in traveling clothes, but a plain woolen work dress. "Both Bruno and Alessandro have fallen ill." She stood motionless, nervously awaiting his response.

For the occasion of his wedding day Taddeo wore a velvet tunic with luxurious braid trim, a cloak lined in green silk, and a puffed plumed hat. Stepping back from the door, he gazed up at Santina. "Are you quite sure it's the pestilence?"

"There is no doubt," she replied. "I cannot go with you, Taddeo. I have to stay and help Isabella."

She could sense his indignation all the way up in the second floor room. "I must wonder if you say this in order to avoid the trip," he said.

"You're welcome to come in and look for yourself, Taddeo," she offered. "But it's not a pleasant sight."

At length Taddeo commanded, "Open the door."

She led him up the narrow staircase and down the hall of polished brick to the sickroom. When Santina opened the bedroom door, Isabella looked up but said nothing in greeting. Upon the curtained bed, father and son lay side by side. Bruno, drawn beneath his overgrown beard, dozed quietly, while poor Alessandro stirred restlessly. Despite the frequent burning of rosemary and juniper, the sickly scent of illness floated faintly through the air. Santina went to Alessandro and lifted his tunic. Taking in the sight of the unsightly purple lumps, Taddeo turned about and sped down the hall.

"I forbid you to remain," he called out to her. "Gather your things and come along."

"I can't leave them," she replied. "Unless you would have me chained and carried away with you."

Taddeo cursed violently. "What manner of woman would abandon her fiancé?"

"What manner of woman would abandon her own sister?" she countered, following him down the stairs.

Taddeo threw open the heavy oak door and stood at the threshold. "To think of what I have endured with you." The look of devotion she had once seen in his eyes had turned to something far more hateful.

She froze, wondering what he would do next. The house and street beyond were eerily silent, not a soul seemed to stir, and Bruno was not there to protect her.

"You continue to flout God's will, Santina Pietra. You and your blasphemous ways."

"If it's blasphemous to try to save lives, then you will have to condemn me," she said, keeping her distance.

"I should have brought you to the priest when I caught you reading that book of *streghe*," he said. "You are too willful, Santina. You disobey me, you disobey God."

He regarded her silently, as though expecting a retraction on her part. When Santina did not speak, Taddeo issued his final threat. "If you do not come with me, you will no longer be my fiancé."

Even if she wanted to marry Taddeo, even if Calandrino was begging her to come away with him, she could not leave Certaldo. Not now. "If I don't stay and do what I can for Bruno and Alessandro, I'll never be able to forgive myself. You'd be married to a woman as good as a corpse, Taddeo."

When he met her gaze she saw that his heart had turned to bitterness. She could only hope that his foul mood would be tempered after the pestilence had run its course.

Santina watched him disappear down the road. She should have been relieved, and yet she was not. Closing the door behind her, she had an uneasy sense that she had not seen the last of Taddeo. In the kitchen she boiled water for tea. God's will for her in the days ahead was clear. How or when Taddeo would punish her for disobeying him remained uncertain.

Alessandro cried out in agony as Santina changed the poultice that covered the pus-filled buboes. When he vomited, Isabella began to weep again. Santina sopped up the mess and sent her sister out of the room. "If you will, put more water on to boil, Isabella. Then see to Bruno's bath and your own. Remember to add the vinegar."

When the poultices were in place, Santina went about steeping the herbs. She sat with Bruno and Alessandro for hours, forcing them to drink a brew of angelica root, coriander, cloves, and ginger sweetened with honey and then another of butterbur and blessed thistle. Later, as she applied a soothing comfrey rub to Alessandro, Santina stopped to wonder why the innocent were made to suffer such torment. Clearly, the pestilence did not discriminate between the young and old or the good and bad. *You must look beyond this world to the next for fairness* she recalled her mother saying years ago.

Eventually, Bruno and Alessandro appeared to be resting more easily. At the very least, she had brought relief from the fever. The herbs had worked their magic; the rest was up to God. When Isabella returned wearing a fresh gown, she was heartened to see her husband and child resting peacefully.

"They look much better," she observed. "How did you manage it?"

"It's only the herbs," Santina replied. "It doesn't mean they're cured, Isabella," she cautioned, knowing full well the battle was far from over. "Their fevers have come down, that's all. They still require close watching."

That evening, Bruno's and Alessandro's fevers rose again, and she knew the night ahead would be a long and difficult struggle. After Alessandro was settled, Santina suggested Isabella try to sleep. "I promise to awaken you if anything happens," Santina assured her.

Shrugging off her own sleepiness as Isabella walked wearily to bed, Santina prepared for the nighttime vigil. In the dark silence she could feel the angel of death hovering, waiting to sweep down and take Bruno and Alessandro at any moment.

Many in Certaldo viewed the pestilence as God's punishment. Santina found little cause to believe that her brother-in-law or nephew had done deeds worthy of provoking God's wrath. Bruno was a good man, and Alessandro was an innocent child. As she witnessed their suffering, she could find no explanation for the tragedy. She could only do her best to help them through their pain.

Even as she filled Bruno and Alessandro with her brews, Santina feared her best efforts would not be enough to save them.

Perhaps Taddeo was right in thinking any attempt to fight the pestilence was futile. It was likely that Bruno and Alessandro would die, regardless of her ministrations. Perhaps she would die as well. *Have I flouted Taddeo's will only to perish?*

The next night seemed an eternity. Exhausted, she tried to keep Bruno and Alessandro from slipping away. Sitting alone by candlelight, boiling yet more water over the fire, Santina was filled with doubt as she drifted near sleep. She saw Taddeo taunting her; she heard Papa scolding her for causing trouble again; she saw Calandrino growing smaller and smaller as she left San Gimignano through the city gate.

Enough, she heard from a voice in the distance. Was it Mama? *It is well you heeded the call, Santina.* In the darkness she saw both Madonna Adalieta and Trotula, two images from memory or from Heaven. *We are with you,* they said before fading away.

The second night blurred into the third day. By that evening, Alessandro became delirious with fever. Screaming, he pulled at his poultices. "Something is biting me," he cried. "Help me, Mama."

The egg-sized *gavoccioli* under his arm burst, spewing a putrid yellow cream over the bed. Santina was barely able to stop herself from gagging but managed to clean the mess and staunch the seeping wound. She removed the soiled bedding for burning later. In the meantime she forced Alessandro to sip a calming cordial.

"Hush," Santina said, stroking his head. "Listen well to the angels. They are with you now, Alessandro."

The cordial taken, he soon fell into another fitful sleep. Bruno, it seemed, was resting more comfortably. When the first light began to appear in the sky, he was sleeping soundly and his fever had broken.

"You might still live, Bruno," Santina said softly as she watched him. "Perhaps it's not your time after all."

When Isabella, still half-asleep, peeked in on them, Santina spoke the truth. Quietly, she explained that Alessandro showed no sign of improvement and had perhaps taken a turn for the worse. Shaken, Isabella went to her son and knelt at the bedside.

"*Dio mio,* spare my son," she wailed. Santina knew too well the loss would be more than Isabella could bear.

As the day wore on, Bruno grew steadily stronger while Alessandro slipped further and further away. Santina and Isabella took turns caring for the boy through the fourth night. She continued to pray that he would rally like his father, but the child only grew weaker. Toward evening Santina saw ominous, red spots rising under Alessandro's lips and nose. When Isabella noticed the spots, they had already grown dark purple in color. She gasped at the sight of them.

"What's happening to his skin?" Isabella demanded as though someone were to blame for this latest affliction.

Santina knew Alessandro was lost. "It's time to summon the priest," she gently told Isabella.

"No. It can't be. Alessandro cannot leave me."

Bruno spoke, his voice a raspy whisper, "Santina has done everything she can." He held his son as Isabella wept. They all watched helplessly as Alessandro's fingers, lips, and nose turned to black. Soon his breathing grew labored, and his soul was finally loosed from his body.

Alone in the kitchen Santina considered the meaning of Alessandro's death and Bruno's survival. Many in Certaldo had come to question God's love during this time of torment, and many had come to deny Him altogether. For Santina, there was grace even as one life was spared. It was enough to convince Santina she had been right to remain in Certaldo. Taddeo would perhaps see that now—as long as she did not succumb to the pestilence herself.

The Cemetery

The calamity of the time was such that there were too few left to mourn the dead, and those who survived had grown weary of burials. The priests, too, could not easily keep up with the daily losses of life. Even the loss of a child was cause for little notice. Following Alessandro's death, friends, relatives, and neighbors did not gather. Nevertheless, Santina ensured there was a dignified procession, led by four clerics who carried candles and performed the solemn funeral rites.

She stood at Isabella's side as Alessandro's body was lowered into the ground. In the days that followed, Bruno still lay in bed, weak but recovering. Having done all she could for Isabella's husband, Santina felt obliged to check in on Taddeo's brother and Niccolosa and to explain the way things stood between her and Taddeo. Carrying a basket of jellied meat, chestnuts, and medicinals, she traveled along the main road and up the hill toward the *palazzo*. As she walked, she saw several bodies left on the front steps of respectable homes. The corpses had been carried outside to await the arrival of the funeral briers and burial in mass graves. A corpse now commanded as much respect as a dead goat.

When Santina arrived at the house, she knocked on the door, but no one answered. Fearing that the couple had succumbed to the disease, she turned to leave. Just then, Taddeo's sister-in-law came to the door.

"Does Giorgio live?" Santina asked at once.

Niccolosa, appearing as though she was seeing a ghost, eyed Santina warily. "*Si,* your brews kept him alive. But he is still weak and lies in bed."

"*Grazie a Dio.*" Santina perceived that the pestilence had taken a toll on the woman, for she seemed badly shaken. "I'm sorry I could not come sooner. Only three days ago we buried Alessandro."

Niccolosa made the sign of the cross. "May God grant that we follow Alessandro to Heaven when we leave this life." After a brief silence, she looked down the street either way as though to ascertain they were not being watched. Then she pulled Santina inside the house. "You ought not to be here, Santina. I fear for you," she whispered.

"There is no escaping the pestilence, Niccolosa. It's everywhere."

"It's not that," she replied. "It's that Taddeo was just here."

"He has already returned from Empoli?"

"I must tell you the truth, Santina. He will not marry you." Niccolosa stared at the floor. "He says that you deceived him and that you are not who you appear to be. I tried to tell him he should be grateful to you for curing Giorgio and for keeping me well, but he said you practice *stregoneria.* He said it's not for you to decide who should live and who should die." This confessed, Niccolosa finally dared to look Santina in the eye.

"*Witchcraft?*" Santina shook her head. Taddeo knew well enough that she worked with herbs, not evil spells. Was he so blinded by rage that he would bring false charges against her? She supposed it was possible that some might misconstrue her efforts. As she had learned in San Gimignano, women who were skilled in the healing arts were suspect in the minds of many. Perhaps it should have come as no surprise that she would be persecuted for assisting victims of the pestilence.

"You are quite sure you heard correctly?" she asked.

Niccolosa nodded. "One of the guards from the palace was with him—a friend of Taddeo's who will gladly do his bidding. They would have you imprisoned in the *palazzo*."

The room seemed to sway as Santina imagined the outcome of Taddeo's witchhunt. The magistrates would accuse her, just as Trotula had been accused after Ferondo Palmerini vilified her name. Taddeo would appear justified in turning against a woman who was said to practice alchemy and work spells. Grasping the danger she faced, Santina knew she had to act at once.

"I have to leave Certaldo. He cannot find me."

"Where will you go?" Niccolosa asked, her eyes welling with tears.

"I'm not sure," she said, still unsure of her plans. "Do you think I'm a witch, Niccolosa?"

Taddeo's sister-in-law fingered the cross she wore on her neck. "No, of course not. Only one who is skilled."

Santina understood that others who felt less affection for her would be more easily convinced by Taddeo's lies. With Niccolosa's assistance she would remain hidden a while longer. When darkness fell and the residents of Certaldo retired for the evening, she would make her way across town.

Wrapped in Niccolosa's dark woolen cape, the hood pulled low over her head, Santina stepped out into the night. Upon her return to Isabella's—provided she could evade Taddeo—she would pack what supplies she could gather and flee from Certaldo. A half moon lit the way as she wound her way through desolate streets. Wondering if Taddeo lurked somewhere in the darkness, Santina felt what it was to be hunted.

It was the madness of the time as much as an unyielding mind that inspired him to accuse her. She supposed Taddeo, like many others, felt forsaken by God as the death toll wore on. The devastation wrought by the disease led to the belief that virtuous behavior went unrewarded. Fear of the afterlife was forgotten by those who were already living in hell. Amid the chaos Taddeo was free to turn against her and break the promise he had made. Knowing this, Santina walked in fear for her life.

As she turned the corner near the town square, the *Piazza dell'Annunziata*, she gasped at the sight of a figure standing directly before her. Like a phantasm of the night, the haggard old beggar woman, who was often seen outside the church, emerged from the shadows. Clad in filthy tatters, she carried a basket in which a mangy calico cat nestled.

"*Per favore*, Madonna, will you help me?"

Her hands trembled but Santina searched her purse for a coin. It somehow felt as if the old woman had been waiting for her. Surely it was not the case?

"God bless you," croaked the woman.

"Please, tell no one you have seen me."

The woman's toothless smile was eerily knowing. "No need to go home just yet, Madonna."

"Pardon me?"

"The night has only begun."

Holding her cloak close at the neck, she hurried away, leaving the crone cackling to herself. Whether the woman was mad or a seer, Santina thought to heed her remark and delay her return to Isabella's. If Taddeo was indeed lying in wait, she would do her best to avoid his trap.

Ave Maria, gratia plena, Hail Mary, full of grace. Santina turned away from the piazza and headed back in the direction of the governor's palace knowing Taddeo or his minions could be around the next corner. She prayed for invisibility, for safe shelter somewhere in the ghostly town.

The village gates were still closed, preventing her immediate escape. When daylight came she would flee, God willing. She did not know what would become of her, but the injustice of being hunted gave her the will to continue.

When she neared the Church of Saints Tommaso and Prospero and heard horses in the distance, her courage waned. The hoofbeats moved closer, and her only thought was to hide herself. Racing down the road, she spotted an abandoned cart outside a home where a fetid corpse lay near the front door. Turning to look behind her, she saw no one. She jumped into the cart and covered herself with hay. Unmoving, she waited, straining to hear voices.

Two, perhaps three men were talking and moving in her direction. The voices were muffled, deep. She could not make out the words. Daring to lift her head, Santina observed the men from a distance. There were three of them, all wearing the familiar beaked masks stuffed with straw for protection from the contagion. Then she noticed the spotted white horse. If she was not mistaken, it was the horse that Ruberto rode.

It would be a blow if Ruberto had joined Taddeo against her. She was well aware that Ruberto had borne witness to her recklessness throughout the years. Perhaps he decided she should finally pay for her transgressions. She imagined Ruberto would abhor being out in the foul night air, unless his aversion toward her was greater than his fear of the contagion.

When the three of them moved off, Santina climbed down from the cart and hurried along in the direction of the church. Not knowing where the men were headed, she thought to seek protection within the grim darkness of the graveyard. She hoped that even if they circled back this way again, they would not pause long in their search. Surely none of them could countenance the place where the newly dead were stacked, one upon the other, within shallow graves. Those who hunted her would find this place too repulsive, too ridden with the pestilence.

Sick from the scent of death that oozed from the damp earth, she slipped warily between tombstones. In this fearful setting she did not know if the company of the recent dead tormented her more than the fear of being discovered. Unable to return home, unable to leave Certaldo, she was like a ghost herself, trapped between worlds.

Looking out to the street, she spied the silhouette of an old woman, basket in hand. It was the beggar she had seen by the piazza. Had the woman followed her here? Ducking behind a tomb, Santina watched the crone looking in on the cemetery, almost as if searching for her. Finally, the woman moved off, leaving Santina alone with the dead.

Overhead, bare tree branches creaked as an icy breeze skittered across the graveyard. Santina shuddered, afraid to think that some of those buried here haunted the grounds. In this macabre place each minute stretched like an hour. Perhaps these were her last moments of freedom before she would be tossed into prison. On that dark night, Santina found herself wishing Taddeo was buried beneath the ground where she walked. To the world he was a successful merchant, a good citizen. The real man was a fiend concealed in fine clothes.

She was lost in these black thoughts when she heard the sound of hoofbeats coming from the west, from the direction of Isabella's house. Santina felt her legs give way. Surely the riders were not midnight revelers or thieves. Whoever it was—perhaps Ruberto and Taddeo among them—intended to find her. In a moment of weakness, she thought to give herself up. There was no place to hide or take refuge. *Che Dio mi salvi. Help me God. Show me the way to safety. Don't let them find me.*

If she could not leave the graveyard, she would have to disappear within it. The moonlight cast a glow over the white marble of a sarcophagus. Inside the tomb were the dried remains of one long gone, not a victim of the pestilence. She would be well concealed within one such burial vault.

It was a struggle to try to open a weathered marble sarcophagus. Santina pushed with all her strength but could not budge the lid. In despair she listened to the approaching horses; there was little time. If she did not find a place to hide soon, she would be discovered.

Madre de Dio, guide me, she prayed. The moon clouded over again, as if to conceal her from those who gave chase. Again the hoofbeats moved off and went silent. Perhaps there was time. Where could she hide? *Help me. Mama, Trotula, help me.* She saw the light of a lantern in the distance. *Madre di Dio. They are too close now.* Horses were circling the piazza. She could do nothing but crouch behind the tomb and pray she would be concealed. *Ave Maria, gratia plena. Ave Maria, gratia plena.*

She bent low to the ground, shuddering as low menacing voices moved closer and closer to the tomb where she hid. Was this to be her death? Peering around the corner of the sarcophagus, she saw the men had split up and were marching through the grave-yard. One of them was nearly upon her now. She would surely be discovered. To her left was a mound of dirt beside a yet unoccupied grave—unless a corpse had been dropped within. She thought she would be well concealed if she lowered herself into the pit, but would it be impossible for her to climb out again? Would she be trapped, just the same, whether by searchers or walls of earth?

Get thee into the grave, Santina. It was Mama's voice calling out to her. There was no time to think. Not knowing how she would free herself, Santina crouched at the edge of the pit. Looking down into the hole, she saw only blackness. Perhaps she would lay herself in her own grave on this unholy night. She could only hope a cadaver had not been laid to rest below. Low voices drifted nearer. Closing her eyes, Santina jumped and dropped to the hard cold earth with a soft thud. Surrounded by narrow walls of dirt, she was a prisoner. With little room to move about, she felt what it was to be Osiris, trapped by his brother within the funeral coffin. She recalled the Egyptian myth written in the manual.

> *Out of this union the divine Horus, or the new Osiris, was born. There can be no rebirth until there is death. And so until one has experienced the blackness of the funeral coffin, one cannot begin the Great Work nor experience the resurrection.*

She fully felt the blackness of the funeral coffin, but she did not know if she would experience the resurrection. From cold or fear, Santina began to shake uncontrollably. Her pursuers were so close; she could do nothing. If they discovered her in the grave, she would be imprisoned in the palazzo. Perhaps she would be killed without a trial and share Trotula's fate.

She pulled out Trotula's gold amulet from beneath her gown and held it tightly. *Pater Noster, qui es in caelis, Our Father who art in Heaven,* she prayed silently. *Don't let them find me. I am not ready to die.*

"It is not the place to find her." It was Ruberto's voice.

She heard the third man. "The crone is mad. She cannot be believed."

The crone? Had the old woman given her away? Perhaps Taddeo had purchased her as well as the others who assisted him in his hunt.

"You forget," said the cruelest voice, Taddeo now among them. "The woman is afraid of nothing, not even the pestilence."

From within her death chamber, Santina heard the sound of movement above. The sound of stone scraping against stone.

"It is a criminal offense, Taddeo," Ruberto reminded him.

"Search the tomb."

"You cannot think your fiancé has hidden herself in with a corpse."

Taddeo and Ruberto went on disagreeing until their voices edged further and further away. Santina heard nothing for a time, but then again there was movement, the hideous sound of stone scraping against stone. He would violate the tombs in order to find her.

"You're as mad as the crone," said the third man.

Taddeo let out a sinister laugh. "I am not the one who works spells."

He had made her the enemy, as vicious as the plague itself. In Taddeo's mind she was the woman who had betrayed him. Clearly, he would do anything in his power to extract vengeance for the suffering he believed she had inflicted upon him, for the suffering caused by the pestilence itself.

Something heavy, perhaps a rock, struck stone. Then there was silence.

Heart racing, Santina flattened herself against the bottom of the pit. She froze, sensing movement above her. Something tickled her cheek, but she dare not stir. If Taddeo detected a sound, he would shine a light over the grave and discover his prey.

"The damn witch must be somewhere." It was as if he knew her scent. The hound would not leave.

"We might check your brother's house again." It was Ruberto's voice this time. "Other than her sister, Niccolosa is the one most likely to give her shelter."

The voices trailed off in the direction of the church. Eventually, Santina heard the horses take flight. She believed the men were gone now. Their departure gave her little relief, for she was now trapped inside a pit with no means of escape. Standing, she saw the grave was as deep as she was tall. She could easily reach her hands over the edge of the pit but could not pull herself up, for she had not the strength.

There was no way out. Seeing that Taddeo would have his wish, she could only weep. She listened to the sound of the wind in the trees and tried to tell herself that she was safe for the time being. Perhaps a gravedigger would take pity upon her in the morning. She imagined herself invisible, like Osiris, who could move freely between life and death and appear in any shape and any form. She looked to the sky and saw the moon emerging from behind the clouds, bright in the sky again. Then it was not the moon, but the cruel light of a lantern shining down on her.

She was discovered. The chase was over. She braced herself for the punishment Taddeo would surely inflict upon her.

Bruno

"*Per favore! I have done nothing wrong.*" Trembling within the dirt grave where she hid from Taddeo, Santina pleaded with her captor.

"Shhh." In the dark she could make out a figure standing above her. "Say nothing, Santina."

She knew the voice. "Ruberto?"

"Grab hold of me." He knelt at the edge of the pit and extended his arms. Unsure if she could trust him, she hesitated. "It's all right. Taddeo is gone," he said.

Having little choice but to believe Ruberto, she reached up to him. She prayed there was no witness as he struggled to pull her up.

"*Grazie,* Ruberto," she said when she was finally free.

"It will not be easy to avoid him. I'll do what I can to keep him at Giorgio's for a time, but I suspect he'll come looking for you at your sister's house next."

"Why are you helping me?" She searched his unsmiling face, remembering the times in San Gimignano when he had warned her of the danger in working beyond the wall with Trotula. She

225

had always imagined him to be a man who found fault with others, who followed the rules but knew nothing of life. Once again Santina's judgment had proven incorrect. She only hoped that Taddeo would not discover Ruberto's duplicity.

"Your father charged me with your safety. After what happened to Trotula, he wanted to make sure no harm would come to you in Certaldo," he replied. "I'll do what I can to honor my promise." With that, Ruberto disappeared into the night.

She could scarcely take in what he had said, but Papa's hidden reason for opening a shop in Certaldo began to appear and his love for her shone through the darkness that night. Later, she would also come to wonder over Ruberto's enduring loyalty. He was a man of honor, and he had granted her reprieve.

Santina stood motionless amid the dead after Ruberto hurried off. She would give the men time before making her way back to Isabella's house. She prayed that they, who were shrouded in darkness, would not find her.

Concealed in the shadow of Boccaccio's house, Santina considered how to make her escape from Certaldo. Although she had come to the village resigned to becoming Taddeo's wife, her future lay elsewhere. If she was to avoid imprisonment, her only choice was to flee when the village gates opened at daybreak. Until then, she hoped to remain hidden in the home of her sister.

Although the hour was late and the house shuttered, Santina imagined that Isabella was still awake, sick with worry. Santina would have rushed in at once if the possibility did not remain that the madman had returned ahead of her. For all she knew, Isabella might have been forced to admit Taddeo and offer him a seat before the hearth. Santina could only hope that Ruberto had succeeded in luring him back to Giorgio's house. As she moved cautiously ahead, she sensed the devil's work in the air.

Seeking shelter in the shadowed doorway across the street from her sister's home, Santina deliberated how to signal her arrival while still remaining unseen. She stared up at the corner window of the room where she had nursed Bruno back to health. Hopefully, Isabella was within.

She scoured the road for a few pebbles then took aim at the faded blue shutters. It took several tries before she hit her mark. Eventually, the shutters began to open. Santina flattened herself against the side of the house. When she finally dared to look up, she saw Isabella's silhouette in the window, *grazie a Dio*.

Santina could not call out and alert those who might be listening in the shadows, but she could softly whistle a song they both knew. Isabella would remember Francesco Landini, *Behold the springtime, which makes the heart rejoice....*

Echo la primavera, che 'l cor fa rallegrare.

Isabella nodded to the darkness, as though signally her understanding. Santina remained hidden until the front door began to open and her sister peered out.

"Taddeo isn't here, I take it," Santina whispered when she reached the door.

"He was here earlier," Isabella said, ushering her quickly inside. "Wherever have you been, Santina? Taddeo will not forget his grievance against you. He would bring you before the *podestá*. And it is not that you refused to marry him and accompany him to Empoli," she rattled on.

"I know," Santina interrupted. She explained what had occurred at Niccolosa's house and how she had been abetted by Ruberto and narrowly avoided Taddeo in the cemetery.

"That you escaped him is a sign from God."

"I hope you're right, but I cannot remain here, Isabella. Taddeo will most certainly return, and I would not put you in danger. There is no telling what he will do."

"We'll hide you somehow," Isabella countered. "Where else would you go?"

She had thought, initially, to return to Papa's house, and yet it seemed probable that Taddeo would seek her out in San Gimignano if he failed to find her in Certaldo. Santina recalled Calandrino's letter, now strangely prophetic. *If you should find yourself in need during the days ahead, you must go to Fra Bernardo at the convent of San Francesco in San Miniato al Tedesco. He is my friend, and he will give you shelter.*

"I'm going to San Miniato," she announced.

"San Miniato? But why?"

"To see Fra Bernardo. When Calandrino last wrote, he said I should go to a friar named Bernardo if I needed help."

"Fra Bernardo? What do you know of him? Besides, you can't travel alone, and Bruno isn't well enough to accompany you."

"If I'm not to be thrown into prison, I have no other choice."

She began to gather her belongings for the daylong walk to San Miniato along the Via Francigena. In her room she came upon the red rock—*the red lapis of the philosophers*—which she had found in the garden on the day Bruno and Alessandro were struck with the pestilence. With the red stone, the adept would be guided by the eternal wisdom of the heavens rather than changeable, earthly desires. It then became possible to move through all manner of calamities and emerge unharmed. With the red lapis, mastery of the physical world was achieved.

That the red stone might be mine as well, she thought. She put the rock and the alchemical manual into her leather bag while silently vowing that Taddeo would not break her. She had managed to fool him more than once before, she could outwit him again. The key was to avoid being guided by fear and instead to follow the way of the alchemist.

In her *cassone* she found the sack of gold florins given to her by her father, *just in case* he had said. *Bless you, Papa.* She added the coins as well as her gown of crimson silk and damask surcoat, headdress, leather slippers, and a small bottle of Trotula's infused oil to the satchel she would carry concealed beneath her cape. She had no need of her fine clothes just yet. For now, she would travel as a man.

While Bruno, still weak, slumbered unaware, Santina and Isabella crept into the bedroom. Shoved in the back of his wardrobe, Isabella found his old pilgrim's attire—a dun-colored garment and cape with hood. Leather boots, toes stuffed with kerchiefs, would have to do for footwear. At her waist she carried a dagger. Over the cape she fastened her water gourd and pilgrim's scrip, or wallet, filled with a bit of food and a few coins. Finally, she tied up her hair and donned Bruno's low-crowned, wide-brimmed pilgrim's hat.

"Would you know me now?" she asked Isabella, who stood watch at the window.

"There is one more thing to be done." For the effect of pallor, Isabella applied a whitening of chalk and flour to Santina's face. With soot from the hearth, Santina's nose and fingers were blackened so that she appeared to be a ravaged victim. "Though it was done by my own hand, it unsettles me to look at you," Isabella said when she was through.

Soon the first faint light of day broke through the sky. The gates would open shortly, and Santina prepared to leave. It was then that a loud knocking sounded at the door.

"*Dio mio*, it's surely Taddeo," Isabella said, gripping Santina's arm.

"Calm yourself," said Bruno. Still groggy from sleep, he had been apprised of Santina's plan. Walking unsteadily, he led the way downstairs. In the entryway he set about emptying the carved *cassone*.

"Hide in here, Santina," he said as the heavy knocking continued. "I'll take repose on the chest when Isabella admits our guest. If it's Taddeo, he knows I've been ill and won't want to come near me. Isabella will take him upstairs, then you must hurry. We'll detain him for as long as we can."

The door shook as the pounding grew more impatient and accusing voices sounded from outside. Santina was sure the door would burst open at any moment. As she climbed into the chest and Bruno closed the lid, she uttered a swift, "God help us."

Inside the darkness of the *cassone,* she listened to Isabella scurrying about. Confined to the small space, she willed herself to be still even as there seemed no air to breathe. When she heard the door open she prayed, *let him pass, just let him pass.*

"What business have you here?" demanded Isabella.

"Santina is under arrest," said a voice she recognized from the cemetery. "She is to be brought to the *palazzo.*"

As though with great effort, Bruno responded. "And yet the *strega* has still not returned home. She may have turned herself into a cat, or perhaps a horse."

"How dare you speak that way about my sister," spat Isabella. "Do you forget she saved you from the pestilence?"

"Perhaps I am saved, perhaps not," he replied slowly. "Santina would decide who lives and who dies."

Santina winced, thinking of Alessandro. Bruno's condemnation was all too convincing. The front door slammed shut.

"You will not mind if we look about." It was Taddeo's voice.

"You're no longer welcome here, Taddeo. My sister has done nothing wrong."

Would he find her inside, trembling, knees to chin? Lightheaded in the confined space, Santina drew quiet breaths. The scent of Taddeo's poison permeated the *cassone*. He was a man who no longer knew the cause of his anger but was fixed upon a path of vengeance.

The footsteps receded into the distance and moved up the stairs to the main room and all the while, Isabella, in a deafening voice, berated Taddeo nonstop. The lid of the *cassone* rose slowly and Bruno stood over her. "Hurry," he whispered.

Defying her fears, she moved soundlessly out the door. The street was empty save for two horses. She started to pass them very quietly, but then a thought occurred to her. The horses were saddled and ready to depart in an instant. *Do I dare?* Cautiously, she approached Taddeo's palfrey. Slipping her hand inside her scrip, she searched for the dried apples she had packed. The horse eagerly took the sweet fruit from her hand and allowed her to stroke his neck. He still made no sound as she untied him and guided him slowly down the road. Only after she had covered a goodly distance did she mount him. Collapsed over the saddle, her blackened fingers at the horse's neck, she ambled unquestioned through the city gate in the dim morning light.

Left behind, Taddeo was free to search all of Certaldo for his fiancé, the woman who was perhaps a witch.

Santina eventually came to rest in an abandoned pear orchard where the first tender buds would soon open, promising a harvest of sweet ripe fruit. The sun had risen bright and unclouded, warming the earth, evoking scents of spring. It was almost as though winter had receded in the night.

Traveling along the Via Francigena, the pilgrims' road leading from France to Rome, Santina had encountered a few weary souls along the way and several fetid corpses with telltale blackened skin. When she had come upon the occasional pilgrim or peddler, she passed at a canter. There seemed little chance of being identified, but for all she knew Taddeo could be following her trail.

While she did not yet know where her future lay, she felt the hardest part of her journey was behind her. It was as though she was coming to the end of the Great Work, to the green lion stage, when a power far greater than the alchemist's own was imparted to the practitioner. Santina had a sense that she had not escaped Taddeo by her wits alone. Unseen forces, she believed, had also played a part in her victory.

She felt warm light from the late winter sun washing over her, absolving her of her debts to Taddeo da Certaldo. Closing her eyes, she saw an illustration from the manual—the alchemist receiving a crown. The crown was bestowed when the alchemist recognized he was not the source of his own achievements. In the picture the alchemist was on his knees, his head bowed humbly while light poured down from overhead in this moment of glory.

Riding on, Santina remembered something Trotula once said. Standing before her stained glass window in the cottage, the midwife had explained it was not the glass that created its own brilliance—it was the sun that made the window sparkle like jewels.

At the time, Santina had argued Trotula's point. She had put faith in her own human actions and greedily sought the elixir of life, the secret to reversing the course of death. Now she could only laugh at the girl who held herself in such high esteem. Finally she knew Trotula's meaning, and the destiny she sought emerged on the horizon.

According to the manual, when all was given up and lost the alchemist would be resurrected, his new life standing before him. After descending into the mysterious depths of his soul, he would return renewed and altogether changed. It was called the *coniunctio*, the mystical union of the sun and moon—the body and soul—mingled with divine Spirit. It was then that the kingdom was entered.

By the time the Tuscan sun was low in the sky, Santina neared San Miniato. She stopped to eat some salty Parmigiano and gaze up at the *convento* on the hill. In the expanse of shimmering green, the friary appeared haloed in light. The pestilence had taken countless victims, but at that moment the world seemed full of hope once again.

As Santina searched her bag for a cloth to clean the chalk and coal from her face, she caught site of Calandrino's letter poking out of the alchemical manual. It was almost as though she heard his voice. *If you will study these pages, Santina, you will surely discover a light along the path to the eternal*, he had written. Calandrino seemed so close, and yet he remained unreachable. She could only wonder if the pestilence had ravaged Milan and if she would ever see the scholar again.

26

Fra Bernardo

The Convent of San Francesco stood just beyond the city of San Minato, higher up on the hill. As Santina neared her destination, the terraced gardens and budding trees of the friary grounds came into view. When she stood at last before the exterior doors of the *convento*, Santina's hair hung long and loose beneath her pilgrim's hat. She was, once again, Santina of San Gimignano.

As a groom led the palfrey away, the guestmaster welcomed Santina as he would any pilgrim. He seemed to overlook, during the madness of the pestilence, the peculiarity of a solitary young woman taking the treacherous journey alone. Even so, Santina was aware her arrival would not go unnoticed. She dared to offer the friar two gold florins and ask that he refrain from mentioning her arrival to anyone who might come asking.

It was the amount of Santina's offering that seemed to give the guestmaster pause to study her carefully. As though trying to discern what manner of pilgrim had come to his door, he asked, "Who gives you chase, Madonna?"

"One who seeks vengeance."

"Do you have need of a confessor?"

"It is not my misdeed but another's—the one who gives chase."

He seemed inclined to believe her. Quietly, he led the way to her cell. The room was simple but clean with soft blankets and a pallet filled with straw. It was also well away, the friar reassured her, from the unfortunate victims of the pestilence who were being treated by the brothers. As the guestmaster turned to leave, she posed the question that could not wait till morning.

"Is there an herbalist named Fra Bernardo among you here at San Francesco?"

"*Sì.* Do you know him?"

"No, but he is known by a friend of mine."

"You will likely find him out in the barn tomorrow morning after *lauds*, milking the sheep."

Santina was grateful for the kindnesses shown to her, as well as the knowledge that Calandrino's friend was near. She had a sense that all would be well and that she would be offered refuge at the *convento* until which time she could find permanent lodging. Unaware of the sharp turn her journey would take in the days ahead, she feasted upon crusty bread, pecorino, olives, and figs before vespers.

The next day Santina awoke with hopeful anticipation. Covering her hair in a wimple and dressing in her crimson gown, she attended Morning Prayer. Afterwards, she made her way through the gardens and past several outbuildings. She found the barn easily enough and was greeted by a cow out in the pen. Inside the barn, smelling of hay and dung, she came upon a gray-robed friar who was milking his sheep. He was old, well past fifty, and had a refined, nearly saintly countenance. She thought not to interrupt him in his task, but to wait until she was noticed.

When the friar set aside the pail of fresh milk, he saw her at last and smiled. "*Buon giorno*," he said.

"Fra Bernardo?"

"I am Fra Bernardo." He rose and spoke warmly to the unexpected visitor. "What brings you to the barn, Madonna?"

"It is a long tale, but I am sent by my friend, Calandrino of San Gimignano."

He nodded. "You are Santina Pietra."

"Were you expecting me?"

"Calandrino sent a letter some months ago. He hoped you would come."

Santina was puzzled by this, for Calandrino must have known she would not have been compelled to leave Certaldo unless trouble had arisen. "I'm not sure why Calandrino hoped I would seek you out. I'm afraid it's desperation that brings me to San Francesco."

"Calandrino wished you no harm. It's only he hoped you would come if the need arose. That, and he desires to see you."

She could not help but smile at this. "I confess I'd like to see him as well. But as you may be aware, he now resides in Milan."

"Do you know why Calandrino advised you to come to San Francesco?"

"Because he suspected, quite rightly, the toll the pestilence would take," she replied. "He thought to help me if I should find myself alone."

Fra Bernardo nodded then suggested they take a walk through the grounds. The sun was concealed by a thin veil of clouds, and the hills were a soft, muted green. The friar led her out along the terraced gardens that already held the promise of early spring crops. Looking to the distance Santina could see the orange-tiled rooftops in the village below. The peaceful view belied the fact that much of Tuscany lay in mourning.

As they walked on, Fra Bernardo asked Santina what she knew of Calandrino's past. She replied that she knew him to be an orphan who was raised and educated by the brothers of San Damiano. She knew, as well, that he had gone off to serve as a page to a Sicilian knight before attending the University of Bologna.

"The friars were quite devoted to him when he was a boy," Fra Bernardo observed.

Santina considered his comment. "My father seemed to think Calandrino displayed a great deal of ability. The brothers thought to nurture his gifts, I suppose."

"Indeed Calandrino was a gifted child. Yet this was not the reason the boy was groomed in this manner." After hesitating, the friar added, "It was because I was a member of the order, and Calandrino is my son."

Santina thought she could not have understood him correctly. "You mean as his priest?"

"I am an old man now, but I was once young and uncertain," he replied, "and in love with his mother."

Santina was stunned by the friar's admission. She would have liked to ask who Calandrino's mother was, but it was not her place. "It must have been hard for you to give her up," she remarked.

As though recollecting his nearly forgotten past, the friar gazed out at the rolling hillside. "Trotula was unlike any other woman I had known."

"Trotula? You don't mean Trotula the midwife?"

"You were her apprentice, were you not?"

Trotula was also young once. But Santina had never thought to consider that the midwife had made her own share of mistakes. She had loved the wrong man and borne a child. She struggled to collect her thoughts. *Calandrino is Trotula's son?* "She never spoke of it," Santina said quietly.

"Trotula gave him up on the condition that he would be given an education—and that he would not be made to take vows. She suffered the loss greatly, but she wanted the boy to have every opportunity."

"Does Calandrino know his mother?"

"He was told when he came of age," Fra Bernardo explained. "He already knew Trotula, for he spent his youth wandering the hills. My son became quite fond of her, more so when he learned the truth, of course. He took to looking in on her."

The truth of Trotula's past began to sink in. She had earned her wisdom through trials and sorrow. Having paid the penalty for her choices, she had sought to keep Santina from making similar mistakes. Santina only wished Trotula would have confided in her. It seemed the midwife might have told her about Calandrino after all that had passed between them. "I believe what you say, Fra Bernardo, and yet I can little understand why neither one of them spoke the truth to me before," she said.

"They both kept their silence in order to protect me," he replied. "And it would not have been an easy thing for Trotula to share with her apprentice."

Santina nodded. "If Calandrino was brought to be raised by the friars at San Damiano, why did you leave San Gimignano?"

"The Father Superior thought it best to keep me at a distance. I had no choice in the matter."

Santina gradually absorbed the tale, and the mysteries surrounding Trotula began to unravel. The midwife's collection of rare Arab texts had been gifts from Calandrino, no doubt. The unexplained familiarity between the two of them, the sharing of recipes and medical knowledge, was in actuality a conversation between mother and son. Even Trotula's frustration with Nastagio now appeared in a different light. She was a woman who had faced the consequences of forbidden love and been forced to accept the limits of what that love could bear. She had spoken from experience when she begged Nastagio to obey his father.

Santina recalled the first day she visited Trotula at the cottage. She had lamented the loss of Calandrino, but Trotula challenged her to become useful rather than pine away for a wandering scholar. Perhaps Trotula had been a little heartbroken at that time as well. She was a mother who had been forced to say goodbye to her son over and over again.

"*Grazie,* Fra Bernardo," she said, still stunned. "I only wonder why you tell me all of this now."

"There seems little reason to keep secrets anymore. The pestilence has taught me that, among other things," he said. "I will let Calandrino explain the rest."

Bewildered, she said, "I confess, it is not easy for me to make sense of what you've said this morning."

"Several of the brothers will soon be departing for Santiago. They'll take the way of St. James and pray for an end to the pestilence. Milan is not far off the pilgrim's tour."

Santina's mouth fell open. "You would offer me safe passage to Milan?"

"If it is your wish."

She had loved Calandrino since she was a girl. Throughout her years with Trotula and her ill-fated betrothal to Taddeo, she had never ceased to think of him. It was a secret she had tried to conceal, but in the end there was no denying what was written in her heart. "You have no idea for how long I have wished for this exactly," she replied.

Still marveling over Fra Bernardo's story, Santina set aside her unanswered question and whatever it was Calandrino had yet to tell her. She would see him again. She would travel to Milan, where Taddeo would not find her.

Via Francigena

fter bidding Fra Bernardo a grateful farewell, Santina departed from San Francesco and resumed her journey along the pilgrim's route. Having left Taddeo's palfrey with the Franciscans, she went on foot, accompanied by six friars. Traveling north toward Canterbury, the pilgrims paused to venerate the local saints at the shrines they passed and took shelter at night in the *conventos* along the way. Santina was grateful for the simple hospitality of the brothers who did their best to provide comfortable accommodations despite the ongoing burden of caring for victims of the pestilence.

The party made stops at the city of Lucca and then St. Peter Abbey in Camaiore, where two of the confreres were struck with the pestilence and died one week later. As their bodies were lowered into the ground at the overcrowded cemetery, Santina wondered how many of them would reach Santiago in Spain. Having survived thus far, Santina hoped she could continue to rely upon Trotula's potent remedy. She urged the remaining four to be diligent in applying the herbs that had been given to them by Fra

241

Bernardo. With heavy hearts and well-oiled skin, the party continued to the town of Pietrasanta.

As they walked along the route, the friars spoke of Fra
Bernardo's generous ministrations to the afflicted. They went on
to tell Santina news of Pope Clement VI, who was the fourth pope
to reside in Avignon rather than Rome. It was said that Clement
was kept isolated inside his austere stone palace, which was surrounded by battlements where hot oil could be poured down on
attackers, if need be. *There is little need for vats of hot oil*, Santina
thought, *for the current enemy can sneak in through walls of stone.*
She had dared to hope the outbreak was drawing to a close, but Fra
Bernardo and the brothers at San Francesco had suggested otherwise. The stream of victims who coughed up blood and suffered a
more virulent and contagious form of the disease persisted, apparently. The other form—the type that caused the painful swellings,
or buboes—was still seen as well.

The contagion continued to ravage Europe, and no one could
argue with the physician who advised the Pope to remain in a
room kept warm by two roaring fires, despite the balmy weather in
southern France. From his secluded spot, Clement showed mercy
on those who died too quickly to receive last rights by issuing
a decree stating that those who died from the pestilence would
receive remission of their sins. Clement thought, as well, to conse-
crate the Rhone River so that bodies might be tossed into the water
when the cemeteries could offer no more space.

Putting aside thoughts of those who were buried in the Rhone,
Santina passed through the city gate of the next stop along the Via
Francigena. Sarzana was a market town that offered hats, scrips,
water gourds, food, and other such supplies to the few pilgrims
who still passed through en route to Rome. After trading Bruno's
sturdy old boots for new leather shoes, she and her group rested

overnight with the Franciscans. In the morning they continued on to Pontremoli, where they walked through beech and chestnut groves and crossed old stone bridges before making the steep and difficult crossing over the Appenine Mountains at *Passo della Cisa*, the Cisa Pass.

Next was Fornovo di Taro, a commune in the province of Parma, followed by Fidenza, where they paid homage to San Donnino, who was beheaded many years before. The saint, after picking up his severed head, was said to have placed it on the spot where the Cathedral of St. Donnino would rise. From Fidenza, Santina went on to Piacenza and then to Pavia, her last stop on the Via Francigena.

At the Augustinian *convento* in Pavia, sleep evaded her. Santina thought she heard the moans of the dying, though perhaps it was just the woman sleeping on the other side of the room. She tossed and turned while wondering how she would manage to find Calandrino once she reached Milan. *Calma,* she heard Mama say. *All will be well, Santina.* She tried to trust, as Fra Bernardo had said, that a priest named Father Marco at the Basilica of Saint Ambrose knew Calandrino's whereabouts and could be counted on to serve as guide. *May Father Marco yet live.*

While Santina felt sure Calandrino was eager to see her, she had no idea what to expect of him once she arrived in Milan. His last letter said only that she should seek out Fra Bernardo should she require assistance. Santina recalled what Papa once said, that it was foolish to think the scholar would marry. Whatever the future had in store, Santina told herself that she would be near Calandrino and this would be enough.

Santina was no longer the naïve young girl he had known years ago. Undoubtedly, he was a different man as well. They had both traveled far and wide since the days they once shared in San

Gimignano. Her affection for him was not the self-indulgent love of the past, but rather a bond forged from a shared beginning and a commitment to the untrodden path. It had to do with the book she carried with her from Certaldo and fought to keep from Taddeo's grasp. The knowledge she gleaned from those pages had given her the strength to endure Taddeo and to run from him when he would have her imprisoned as a witch.

While Calandrino was surely near, Santina could survive well enough on her own, for she held the philosopher's stone in hand. Whoever found the stone would also know the secret of how to transform lead into gold, to turn even hardship into a thing of beauty.

Somewhere in Milan, the lively city at the foot of the Alps, was Calandrino. But as Santina stood at the *Porta Ticinese*, the city gate, the Milanese guard thought to turn her worn and ragged group away.

"The *podestà* has given strict orders. No travelers are to be admitted," the guard announced from the watchtower.

Devastated, Santina retreated with the friars, thinking the long, difficult journey had been for naught. As she stood beside a tall spruce tree, Santina wondered that Calandrino and Fra Bernardo had overlooked the matter of Milan's policy to bar admittance to travelers. Perhaps the measure had only been instituted after Calandrino wrote to her from Milan in November. *Surely I would be dead by now if I harbored seeds of the pestilence*, she thought as she looked to the gate that kept her from Calandrino. She briefly considered the friars' kind offer to continue the tour to Santiago with them. She could return to San Miniato afterward, and perhaps Calandrino might eventually make his way to her. But she had not hidden in a grave, fled from Taddeo, and traveled all this way to be turned away so easily.

A peddler with a cart of knives, belts, hats, and other assorted items paused hopefully before her. Santina examined his wares and fingered a well-made cap with silver braid and a white gauze veil. When she purchased the cap as well as a dainty basket, she began to devise a plan.

That evening Santina and the friars would stay the night at an inn just outside the gate. After a meal of bean and vegetable soup and passable wine, Santina retired to her room. She burned leaves of sage and set the twig on the bed as protection from the evil eye. Next she used stones, which she had heated in the hearth, to press her fine gown of crimson silk. This accomplished, she asked for a tub of hot water for bathing. While the innkeeper's wife was clearly put off by this request, she was appeased when Santina offered her a handful of silver coins for her trouble.

The next morning, she dressed carefully in her silk gown and stylish surcoat of rich brocade interwoven with threads of gold and silver—cloth too ornate for a cloth merchant's daughter, Lauretta had warned. She braided and twisted her freshly washed hair, donned her new hat, and left her grimy pilgrims clothing behind in her room.

Santina gathered her courage as she and the friars made their way back to the *Porta Ticinese.* Holding a basket brimming with freshly picked dandelion greens, which concealed the alchemical manual and her sack of gold underneath, she held herself tall and straight as she came before the gate while the friars stayed back to watch from a distance. In a loud clear voice she demanded admittance at once.

"What is your business in Milan, *per favore?*" replied the guard.

"Open the gate before I have you arrested, fool. I am Sibilia Ambrogio, niece of *il duca.*"

There was only silence as the sentry, no doubt, took in the refined appearance of the lady who would be admitted that spring morning. Santina took deep breaths and stood her ground until the gate began to creak open and the young man in uniform eyed her with apprehension.

"I am sorry, *Donna* Sibilia, but you must know the gates have been ordered closed."

"Closed to travelers, *idiota.* Not to ladies picking dandelions. Would you have me walk all the way around to the north gate?" Before he could answer she dropped a gold florin into his hand.

Whisking past the guard, Santina entered her new city. Everything would be different in Milan, she thought as she listened to the sounds of commerce and a driver shouting at his obstinate mule. Peering inside doorways open to the warm spring air, Santina spied craftsmen at work. In the distance she heard the laughter of children. There was solace in the steady rhythm of life running through the veins of the Lombard town. As though waking from a dream, Santina became aware of something most peculiar. There were no signs of the pestilence here. It hardly seemed possible, and yet there was no stench, no playing of the funeral dirge, no look of death on the faces of those she passed.

She caught the eye of a boy pushing a cart filled with rounds of cheese. "It is a beautiful day in *Milano,* is it not?"

The boy smiled at her and bowed. "It is a fine day, Madonna."

"And there is no sign of the pestilence. Why is that, young man?" she asked.

The boy seemed to give careful thought to the lady's question. "It must be the Lord's will," he replied.

Santina smiled, handed the boy a silver coin, and asked the way to *Sant'Ambrogio*, St. Ambrose.

Making her way to the west, away from the town center,

she found the basilica with two bell towers easily enough. When Santina walked inside the long low church of red brick, her eyes went at once to the high altar, a masterpiece of glittering gold. As though a moth drawn to light, Santina approached the work of art. The front elevation of the altar depicted scenes of the life of Christ and Ambrose. Tracing the gold relief made by the hand of a master, she recalled the world of art and beauty that had been forgotten during the time of the Great Mortality.

Moving from the altar to beneath the circular apse, Santina admired the mosaic of Christ overhead. As she gazed upon the image of the enthroned *Cristo*, she had a sense that all would be well. Eventually, Father Marco or someone who knew him would arrive. She would be led to Calandrino. Quietly, patiently, she waited.

She had been there nearly two hours when the door opened. Someone coming to pray, she guessed. The figure, a tall man wearing a finely embroidered tunic, was walking up the center aisle. He strode with intent, as though on some form of mission at *Sant'Ambrogio*. As he came closer, she caught a brief glimpse of the face beneath the floppy cap. Surely, it could not be. But it was.

"Calandrino?"

"Santina?" he said, nearly inaudibly.

"*Si*," she whispered, hardly daring to believe her eyes.

"*Deo Gratias,* thanks be to God." Calandrino dropped to his knees and kissed the floor. When he stood again he looked into her eyes and spoke tearfully. "I have come here to pray to the blessed Saint every day since I arrived from San Gimignano. My prayer was for you to return to me." He approached her cautiously, as though afraid she was a chimera, about to disappear into the stone walls of the basilica. "It is a holy miracle."

Santina nodded, speechless, taking in the sight of him. Although he might have missed her, he looked the picture of health, strong and fully alive. "Perhaps it is a miracle," she replied at last. "It was also quite a long walk, Calandrino."

He broke into laughter as he reached for her hand. Santina began to laugh as well, and Calandrino embraced her. "*Cara,*" he said. "You are here, and I will never let you go again."

When he kissed her in welcome and held her close and tight, she wanted to believe he meant every word. His touch felt much as she remembered yet somehow it was different. There was a steadiness about him, as though he was no longer halfway to his next destination. Wrapped in his arms, Santina's doubts and fears about what would happen next were almost forgotten. *Somehow I am certain we will see one another again*, he had said when he left her in San Gimignano. He had spoken the truth back then. And yet, there were still unanswered questions.

When they left the sanctuary, Calandrino led Santina outside to the expansive portico with elegant arches supported by columns and pilasters. In the quiet of the loggia, Calandrino took her hand. Santina told him of Bruno and Alessandro's battle with the pestilence, the accusations made by Taddeo, and her narrow escape from Certaldo. "I hope you will not condemn me for what I've done," she said when she was through.

Calandrino's smile was gentle as he replied, "It is hardly a sin to help those who are suffering. You were unjustly accused, Santina. You had little choice but to flee."

"I thought I would die in that grave. It was the darkest hour," she said recalling the horror in the cemetery.

"You are not the girl I knew. You have changed."

Neither was he the man she had known years ago. Back in San

Gimignano, Calandrino had been preoccupied with his ancient texts, determined to prove his worth and discover the alchemist's secret. Now there was a quality about him that suggested he was no longer driven solely by matters of the mind or the demands of his patron.

"It seems to me that you have changed as well, Calandrino," she remarked. "Perhaps you have found whatever it was you were looking for," she observed.

He laughed at the notion. "I will never stop seeking, not until God calls me home."

There was something she wanted to ask regarding the alchemical manual, though she felt hesitant to do so. Hoping not to sound foolish, she said, "After your translated the text, were you able to make any gold?"

Calandrino laughed once more. "Did you read the book, Santina?"

"Over and over again. It was the wisdom of the book that sustained me through my greatest trials. Though I confess there are passages beyond my comprehension."

"There are passages of the book beyond all human comprehension," he said, much to her surprise.

"Have you given up on alchemy, then?"

"We are never through with the process of perfecting ourselves," he replied. "This is the essential task of the alchemist. Yet the most precious gold is found within the soul, not the alembic. True riches cannot be touched, but only felt within the heart."

She smiled at this veracity. "I believe this to be true, Calandrino. And yet you once put forth great effort in Papa's workshop."

"The efforts were not in vain. Each of our struggles serves to bring us to the next challenge."

Silencing the voice of the young girl within her who still believed it was possible to make gold, Santina turned the conversation to more recent events. "There is something I must ask you," she began. "Back in San Miniato, before I left, Fra Bernardo spoke to me of certain matters."

The smile vanished from Calandrino's face. "How much did Fra Bernardo tell you?"

"Rest assured I know he is your father."

Calandrino nodded. "Did he also tell you about my mother?"

"*Si*, I know Trotula was your mother," she replied. "I was stunned, of course. But looking back, I might have guessed as much."

"Why would you have?"

"The medical texts she owned, for one. Those were a scholar's books, not what a midwife might easily acquire. And the conversations that passed between the two of you, and the resemblance in your eyes. I only wished she had told me herself." When Santina looked at Calandrino now, she could see Trotula in his noble features. "Fra Bernardo said there was something more you would tell me."

Calandrino was silent for a moment. "Do you remember when you wrote to me of the Palmerini?"

"Yes, you never replied," she said, recalling the frightening time in San Gimignano when she had dared to hope that Calandrino might come to her and Trotula's aid. "I didn't hear a word from you until I saw you at the gate in San Gimignano after—after it was too late."

"But I wrote back to you at once."

"I never received such a letter. It might have arrived after I returned to my father's house," she guessed. "Regardless, you never came."

"But I did," he put forth. "I left Carpentras almost immediately. I pushed my horse near death."

Befuddled, she said, "But you didn't arrive until July."

Calandrino drew a breath before beginning his tale. "The

Palmerini planned to kill my mother. She knew this, and so she asked me to come but to conceal my presence from you. She and the sisters had devised a plan."

As Calandrino spoke, Santina recalled the horror of those dark days. Once again, she blamed herself for Trotula's suffering.

"My mother was not abducted, Santina. It was only made to appear this way. In truth, she escaped with me to Milan."

"But her body was found in the fountain," Santina protested, thoroughly confused by Calandrino's story. It was hardly possible to refute the existence of the corpse.

Calandrino shook his head. "If you recall, Trotula was caring for a woman named Isabetta, who had been ill for some time. She died, in fact, several days before Trotula went to see her at the convent."

Santina slowly absorbed what Calandrino meant by this. "Do you mean to say it was Isabetta's body that was discovered in the bath?" She tried to imagine Sister Anna and Sister Maria hauling a decomposing corpse through the village and dropping it into the fountain under the cloak of darkness.

"Not easily recognizable when it was finally discovered, I imagine. But wearing Trotula's clothing and charms."

Santina held the column to steady herself. "Do you mean to suggest that Trotula is alive?"

"I'm sorry we had to deceive you, Santina. But Trotula insisted on protecting you. She didn't want you to be put in a position of lying for her."

Trotula is not dead. She is alive. Santina recalled the last time she saw Trotula. She had been sitting calmly at her loom, as though unaware of the growing danger. All the while, she had seen how the story would unfold. And so she had done what was necessary. She outwitted the Palmerini. Knowing that Trotula had survived, Santina wept.

Calandrino was looking at her, full of apology. The deception had caused Santina enormous suffering, but she understood he had acted to save his mother. More than this, she understood how wrong she had been about Calandrino. He had not remained hidden in France, preoccupied with his books, when she and Trotula had called upon him. He had come at once, he had risked everything to help them. "I'm sorry," she said.

"For what?"

"For doubting you."

"You had every reason to doubt me," he said. "I wanted to tell you the truth when I came to San Gimignano the next time, but you were already on your way to Certaldo. I might have told you in a letter, but Trotula feared it would end up in the wrong hands."

"Where is she now?" Santina asked, wiping away her tears. The thought of Trotula alive and well, brewing remedies and birthing babies, filled her with indescribable happiness.

Calandrino smiled. "Trotula is here, in Milan."

It seemed a stroke of luck that Trotula and Calandrino had ended up in Milan, where the pestilence had not taken hold. "How was it you came here, of all places?" she asked.

He shrugged. "It was the place where Trotula thought to conceal herself."

Milan was a large city, a place where one accused of witchcraft might hide, Santina thought. However Trotula had managed to find her way to the north of Italy, Santina gave thanks for her good fortune.

Milano

Calandrino guided Santina past the town center toward the east end of the wall. Shortly before they came to Trotula's house, a long plume of blue-gray smoke jutted diagonally across the mid afternoon sky. Following a woodsy, cedar-like scent, they came to a gate that opened to a small courtyard and a frame house with a green door, bordered by a climbing rose. After walking up the three flights of stairs to Trotula's rented room above a tailor, they found no one at home. They circled around the back of the building, where Santina saw juniper boughs burning steadily in a large pit surrounded by stones. Beside the fire was a garden plot where Trotula was working the soil, sowing seeds that would yield early spring plants, leeks and onions, perhaps.

The midwife appeared much the same as she did a year earlier in San Gimignano, despite all she had endured. As Santina stood watching, she wondered if Trotula would welcome her again, as when she ran from Papa's house and had nowhere else to turn. Or perhaps Trotula would be sorry to see the young woman whose poor judgment brought about the Palmerini's witch hunt.

"*Buon giorno,*" Calandrino called out. "You have visitors."

Trotula's eyes alit when she caught site of Santina. Belying any signs of aging, she rose easily from her knees, "Santina? Is it really you?"

Santina could not manage a reply but slowly made her way to Trotula.

"*Ave Maria,* you're here," the midwife exclaimed. "*Dio mio,* how I prayed for this day."

Santina fell into her open arms and held her thin, fragile frame. "*Mia figlia,* my daughter, all is well now. Nothing can harm you again," Trotula said as she stepped back to gaze at her apprentice. The two of them laughed and cried as Calandrio looked on, knowing only a little of what the two women meant to one another. In that moment Santina understood the past had been forgiven and the long hard struggle to recover what Ferondo Palmerini had taken was over.

As when Santina, a heartbroken young girl, arrived at the hilltop cottage years ago, the midwife brought her inside, made her tea, and commanded her to tell everything that had happened, from start to finish. Santina shared the grief she had suffered when she imagined Trotula dead, and she spoke of her unfortunate betrothal of necessity to Taddeo, and her fierce battle with the pestilence. Trotula was heartened to know that Santina had heeded Calandrino's advice to prepare vast quantities of medicines and that the brews had proven effective in some cases. Hearing of Taddeo's cruel accusations and his relentless pursuit of Santina through Certaldo, the midwife was horrified.

"If you had not run, you would likely have been burned alive," Trotula remarked.

Shuddering at the mere thought, Santina's hand went to her chest, where Trotula's amulet was hidden beneath her gown. If it was not magic, the amulet had been a reminder of Trotula and the woman's indomitable strength in the face of adversity. "I am only glad I knew where to run. If Calandrino had not directed me to Fra Bernardo at San Miniato, Taddeo might have caught up with me."

Trotula appeared wistful at mention of the friar. "Bernardo is a good man, a skilled herbalist." As though pushing aside the memory, she stood to pour more tea.

Santina looked up to the bundles of herbs hanging from the ceiling. The room, with its sweet woodsy scent and the broom at the door, reminded her of the cottage. It was not likely she would ever return to that place of her memories,

"Why did you decide upon Milan?" Santina had to ask. "Did you have a sense you would be safe here?"

"How would I have known?" she replied. "It seemed far enough from the Palmerini, but I asked *Santa Maria* to guide me. I believe she did."

Santina considered the strict measures that the *podestà* in Milan had taken in order to keep the pestilence from spreading from house to house as it had in other cities. No one was permitted to enter or leave the home of a victim, food had to be dropped at the door. Perhaps it would have behooved them in Pisa to do the same, Santina thought as she took another sip of Trotula's potent brew.

Santina was only too glad to take up residence with Trotula, though the space consisted of nothing more than a main room with a fireplace and an adjoining kitchen area with a bucket and spigot over the sink. Calandrino, who resided in the guesthouse at Saint Ambrose for the time being, was a frequent visitor. With no patron to fund his scholarly pursuits at this time, he took what work Father Marco could offer a layman. He worked in the monastery kitchen, carried water from the well, and helped with the laundry. In the evening, by candlelight, he still pored over his Arab texts. Meanwhile, Santina set herself to the mundane tasks she had always done at the cottage. When Trotula was called to attend a birth, Santina accompanied her. Already word had spread in Milan of *Agnesa*, the skilled midwife.

Even as Santina settled into her life in Milan, she did not forget those she left behind. She had written Isabella upon her arrival, but she could only guess if the letter was delivered. While she intended to write her father as well, it would not have been easy to explain that she had run from Taddeo, now lived in Milan with Trotula, and hoped to marry Calandrino. Perhaps Papa might eventually come to understand, but Santina first needed to know what had become of him and the rest of her family, to know who lived. Calandrino, understanding that matters were still unsettled, waited patiently.

The pestilence marched on, moving across Europe through the spring of 1348. By June, the disease had reached everywhere in Italy, though Milan was still spared for the most part. It was not until the cooler weather approached that the contagion seemed to abate. After All Souls' Day, when Trotula suggested the worst had passed to the north, a blessed letter from Isabella finally arrived.

To my beloved sister, Santina, Isabella sends greetings in the Lord.

You can little imagine my joy in receiving your letter dated 26 April of this year. For months I feared the worst, as several letters sent to you at San Miniato went unanswered. I am comforted to know that you, Calandrino, and Trotula are in safekeeping, though living in distant

Milan. I must say, Santina, I am surprised that you have taken up as a midwife once again, especially after all the trouble in San Gimignano. However, I know it is not an easy thing for a woman to sustain herself and that you have to rely upon whatever little means you can acquire during these difficult times.

I must now share with you, my dearest sister, sad news.

Our Lord God was pleased to call to himself the soul of our beloved father, Iacopo Pietra, on 3 April 1348. Lauretta wrote that Margherita would not be moved from his bedside throughout his suffering, which was brief. The next day he was buried at Collegiatis. May God bless him and grant that he pray for us.

On 20 May 1348, the Lord was pleased to take to Himself the soul of Lauretta's husband, Sandro Torello. Lauretta's stepson, Manuele, was taken on 24 May. May God receive their souls in His glory and protect Lauretta's surviving children.

The Lord has seen fit to give us a sign of hope during these darkest of days. Bruno and I are expecting a child in February of next year. May God bless this child eternally.

I am reluctant to mention your former fiancé, but you must know that Taddeo died the week after he tormented us so cruelly. Niccolosa informed me that he suffered greatly at the end and that she did what little she could for him.

Recommend me to Calandrino and Trotula. May God bless you and keep you and send you eternal happiness.

Written at Certaldo the 9th day of October 1348

Papa was gone. She could think of little else Isabella had written in her note. While Santina had somehow sensed that his soul had departed, she had held hope that she would be proven wrong. Folding the letter, she tucked it inside her alchemical manual. She cried, finally knowing with certainty that she would not see her father again in this mortal life. She was grieved as well to know how Lauretta suffered. In truth her grief was lessened by the knowledge that Taddeo would never find her. Despite the cruelty he once inflicted, she prayed for his soul. In the end he had been a weak man who, having exerted his own will rather than having trusted in God, brought about his own demise. Although he was gone, Santina felt little desire to return to Certaldo, or to San Gimignano for that matter. Her home, for the time being, was in Milan with Calandrino and Trotula.

One sunny morning in mid November, Trotula left to check on a new mother while Santina stayed home and prepared a salve of Lady's Mantle for bartering at the market. Calandrino, rabbit in hand, came knocking at the door. While he thought to offer the rabbit for stew, he also intended to settle a matter with Santina at long last.

As she ground the herb with a mortar and pestle, Calandrino looked at her admiringly. "To think I nearly lost you," he said. "I love you dearly, Santina. I have waited too long to make you my wife."

Santina took in the words she had longed to hear since she was a girl of seventeen. Back then when she was living with Papa in San Gimignano, she had wondered why Calandrino would not speak of marriage. She had long since ceased asking this question.

If he had never run off to Bologna, Spain, and France, *A Manual to the Science of Alchemy* would have remained lost to antiquity. She would never have lived with Trotula, learned the art of midwifery, and discovered the philosopher's stone for herself. She would not have become the woman who Calandrino now loved. What's more, if Calandrino had not gone on his crusade, he might never have come to appreciate the simple pleasures of an ordinary life, a home, and family.

"You waited just long enough," Santina said in response to his proposal. Calandrino lifted her off her feet and swung her around, her wine-colored dress whirling like a top.

As it is below, so it is above, Hermes Trismegistus had written in the Emerald Tablet. In order to achieve miracles, the alchemist is required to employ the principles of the heavens here on Earth. *If one follows the recipe exactly*, Santina thought, *it is entirely possible.*

Glossary

Most of the Italian words used in this book are translated when they first appear in the text. Some of the words are particular to the period and have no modern usage.

Time of day is indicated by canonical hours, or the time when prescribed prayers were recited by religious orders. These times changed depending on the season and the time of sunrise and sunset. *Lauds* was before daybreak. *Prime,* the first hour, was around six a.m. *Terse*, the third hour, was around nine a.m. *Sext* was noon or the hour of the midday meal. *Nones* was around three in the afternoon. *Vespers* was at sunset and the time of evening prayer.

In chapter one of *Alchemy's Daughter*, Santina's sister refers to a book of prayers called the *Book of Hours*. Popular during the Middle Ages, these types of devotional books were often made especially for women. The books encouraged spiritual practice and offered specific prayers to be read at various times of day, similar to the daily prayers recited in monasteries.

Below is a list of Italian (or medieval) words used in the book.

Aspetto	Wait
Attaccatura	Spell of attachment
Ave Maria gratia plena	Hail Mary full of grace
Bene	Good
Bottega	Workshop
Buon giorno	Good day
Brevi	Tiny charm bags containing herbs and sacred images
Calma	Be calm
Cassone	Storage chest
Cara	Darling
Che Dio me salvi	God help me
Come sta?	How are you?
Confessione	Confession
Convento	Convent, monastery, or friary
Corno	Animal horn amulet, worn for protection
Destino	Destiny
Deo Gratias	Thanks be to God
Dio lo benedica	May God bless it
Dio mio	My God
Donna	Honoric title for esteemed women
Duomo	Cathedral
Erbolata	Cheese pie with herbs
Fattura	Witch's spell
Famiglia	Family
Figlia mia	My daughter

Finito	Finished
Florin	Gold coin
Fra	Brother, title of a friar
Gavo-ccioli	Swollen lymph nodes affecting victims of the plague
Gioiellere	Jeweler
Grazie	Thank you
L'Annunciazione	The Annuciation
La Religione Vecchia	The Old Religion, or the beliefs of pre-Christian witches
Madonna	How a married or unmarried woman was addressed
Madre de Dio	Mother of God
Malocchio	The evil eye
Messer	Mister or sir
Mia cara	My darling
Molto bella	Very beautiful
Monna	A familiar form of address to a woman
Nessuno	No one
Nonna	Grandmother
Nozze	Wedding ceremony
Palazzo	Palace
Palazzo del Popolo	People's palace or Town hall
Palazzo Pretorio	Governor's palace
Pazienza	Patience
Per favore	Please
Podestà	Mayor or chief magistrate

Santa Maria	Saint Mary
Scusa	Sorry
Soldi	A former Italian coin
Sponsalia	Negotiations concerning a bride's dowery
Sto meglio	I'm better
Strega/ Streghe	Witch/witches
Stregoneria	Witchcraft
Ti amo	I love you (boyfriend or girlfriend)
Torta	Cake
Un momento	One moment
Via	Road

Bibliography

During the decade spent writing and rewriting *Alchemy's Daughter*, then forgetting about the novel altogether for years at a time, I read and referred to numerous books that served as sources of inspiration and Medieval Period detail. In particular, the books listed in this brief bibliography helped to further my understanding of the Middle Ages, midwifery, herbal medicine, and alchemy.

Boccaccio, Giovanni, and G. H. McWilliam. *Ten Tales from the Decameron*. London: Penguin, 1995.

Bohjalian, Christopher A. *Midwives*. New York: Vintage, 1998. Print.

Bremness, Lesley. *The Complete Book of Herbs*. New York: Viking Studio, 1990.

Brooks, Geraldine. *Year of Wonders*. New York: Viking Penguin, 2001.

Cantor, Norman F., *The Civilization of the Middle Ages: A Completely Revised and Expanded Edition of Medieval History, the Life and Death of a Civilization*. New York: HarperCollins, 1993.

Dersin, Denise. *What Life Was like in the Age of Chivalry: Medieval Europe, AD 800-1500*. Richmond, VA: Time-Life, 1997.

Franz, Marie-Louise Von. *Alchemy: an Introduction to the Symbolism and the Psychology*. Toronto: Inner City Books, 1980.

Gaskin, Ina May. *Ina May's Guide to Childbirth*. New York: Bantam, 2003

Gies, Frances, and Joseph Gies. *Women in the Middle Ages*. New York: HarperPerennial, 1992. .

Goddard, David. *The Tower of Alchemy An Advanced Guide to the Great Work*. New York: Weiser Books, 1999.

Helmond, Johannes. *Alchemy Unveiled*. Salt Lake City: Merkur Pub Co, 1997. Print.

Jung, C.G. *Psychology and Alchemy*. Trans. R.F.C. Hull. 2nd ed. Princeton: Princeton/Bollingen, 1968.

Manchester, William. *A World Lit Only by Fire: The Medieval Mind and the Renaissance Portrait of an Age*. New York: Little Brown and Company, 1993.

Rose, Jeanne. *Jeanne Rose's Modern Herbal*. New York, NY: Perigee, 1987

Schrader, C. G. *Mother and Child Were Saved: The Memoirs (1693-1740) of the Frisian Midwife Catharina Schrader.* Trans. Hilary Marland. Amsterdam: Rodopi, 1987.

Tuchman, Barbara W. *A Distant Mirror The Calamitous 14th Century*. New York: Ballantine Books, 1987.

The Way of Hermes New Translations of The Corpus Hermeticum and The Definitions of Hermes Trismegistus to Asclepius. Rochester: Inner Traditions, 2000.

About the Author

Mary A. Osborne is the award-winning author of *Alchemy's Daughter* and *Nonna's Book of Mysteries*. Her stories were inspired by travels to Tuscany and the walled village of Certaldo—home of medieval author Giovanni Boccaccio—where Ms. Osborne envisioned her young heroines slipping through the narrow, cobbled streets and ancient piazzas. Reading about alchemy, including work by C.G. Jung, gave her the idea for *A Manual to the Science of Alchemy,* a fictitious book from which excerpts appear in both *Alchemy's Daughter* and *Nonna's Book of Mysteries.* An enchanting blend of history, alchemy, adventure, and romance, her writing appeals to adults as well as teens.

Ms. Osborne's first novel, *Nonna's Book of Mysteries,* was a *Foreword Reviews* 2010 Book of the Year winner and an American Library Association 2011 Amelia Bloomer nominee. Her second novel, *Alchemy's Daughter*, received the gold award for both young adult fiction and young adult historical fiction in the 2014 Literary Classics Youth Media Competition. Her third book, *The Last of the Magicians*, is slated for release in 2018.

A graduate of Rush University and Knox College, where she was mentored in the Creative Writing Program, Ms. Osborne is a registered nurse and holds degrees in chemistry and nursing. Her freelance work has appeared in publications including *Hektoen International, NewCity*, and *Examiner.com.* She is a Chicago native.

Learn more about the author at MaryAOsborne.com. Learn more about the subject of alchemy at the author's alchemy website, MysticFiction.com